the
bulletproof

ISBN-13: 978-1539885702
ISBN-10: 1539885704
Copyright © 2016 Loretta Lost
Cover design by Damonza

Table of Contents

I survived
because the fire inside me
burned brighter
than the fire around me.

- Fallout

Chapter One

Cole Hunter, 2016
Before I got shot

My tie is strangling me.

Reaching up to grab the silk fabric roughly, I fumble to loosen it as I take several shuddering deep breaths. My neck is sticky with sweat, and I just want to rip off my collared shirt and lie down somewhere dark and quiet. It's early in the day and I shouldn't feel so tired. If my assistant walked in and heard me panting like this, he would think I'd just run a marathon instead of leisurely taking the elevator up to my office.

What the fuck is wrong with me?

The doctors all say that it's just a combination of stress and anxiety. They say I have to sleep more, work less, and talk to a therapist. After years of ignoring them, I finally began seeing a shrink. I enjoyed our sessions so much that I began making the drive to her clinic multiple times per week. I even have her on speed dial. I thought Dr. Nelson was helping me sort out the mess in my head, but somehow, I'm only getting worse. I am sleeping less. My thoughts are more scattered than ever before. I am completely drained, my lungs feel raw, and my whole body aches from head to toe.

I think I'm dying.

Sometimes you just know that sort of thing.

I used to feel peaceful here, sitting at my desk, soaking up panoramic views from the crystal-clear glass windows. Anyone would feel humbled and blessed to be sitting where I am. Every day, I try to steal a moment to pause and gaze out at the city from this office, nestled in one of the tallest buildings in Los Angeles. In the past decade that I've been on the architectural scene, the skyline has been sculpted and improved—often by my own hands. Many of the newer structures near the waterfront, including the one I'm in, began as mere scribbles in my notebooks. It still blows my mind every day, to bear witness to the way that ideas and dreams can take shape in concrete and steel.

But lately, I don't feel much. The accomplishments that brought me such joy feel like distant memories, and I am detached as if someone else did them. Maybe I've grown disillusioned with it all. These buildings, so hypnotizing in their beauty, don't seem to mean anything to me anymore. The drawings in my notebook, on my computer, are just black lines on white space.

Nothing seems to matter.

Coughing violently, my chest floods with pain. It's a familiar pain, and reminds me of an injury I sustained years ago. I wonder if all those injuries are catching up to me now. I just want to quit. Sometime in the past few weeks or months, I hit rock bottom. I've been trying my best to hide it and keep going, but I can't maintain this charade much longer. Everything I've done, everything I've tried to do—it's not enough.

And I can't do this anymore. I'm done. It's over.

Looking out at the skyscrapers, I smile sadly, imagining that I am a weary king presiding over his kingdom. Who will take over when I'm gone? There is always my good friend Miranda Walters, and Levi Bishop... Frowning, I reach for my phone to check my appointments. I have to prepare for a conference call with Levi and my construction team in Karachi in about an hour. But I have some time before then, and I feel like there's something I need to do.

I need to prepare for my death. I need to decide who takes over when I'm no longer able. And there's only one face that fills my mind. Only one person capable enough, only one person I would entrust with my legacy and my life's work. Only one person on this planet, out of all the people I've met, who I consider my partner, my family— my other half.

She is gone. She has been gone for a really

long time. I thought I was dealing with it, but in my long sessions with Dr. Annabelle Nelson, I've only come to realize what a gaping hole there is in my world, without her. Maybe talking about it and forcing myself to face it every day hasn't been as healthy as all the doctors think it should be.

It was easier when I just kept pretending that I was going to see her again tomorrow. But now, I am fairly convinced that I am never going to see her again. It's a crushing defeat that I was never prepared to handle. In recent weeks, my health has declined, and I know I'm running out of time.

Sliding my hand out, I retrieve an unfinished letter. I was not even able to complete the first sentence. Reaching for my pen, I slowly add one final word, and a period.

Dear Sophie,
By the time you read this, I might be dead.

As I finish writing the word, the reality sinks in and my throat goes very dry. It's different when you put your worst fears down in writing. It makes them feel undeniably urgent. The pain in my chest increases tenfold, and causes me to grunt and double over slightly. I rise to my feet, placing both of my palms flat on the mahogany desk, on either side of the letter. A bead of sweat rolls down my nose and falls onto the paper, dotting the letter 'i' in her name.

When the pain subsides a little, I am struck by an idea. My hand rips the letter off my desk, crumpling and tossing it into my wastebasket. I reach for my cell phone and quickly dial my most trusted colleague before pressing the speaker button. While the phone rings, I reach for another blank sheet, and sit to begin my letter anew.

The slender fountain pen clutched in my hand was a graduation gift from Sophie, almost ten years ago. She told me she was getting me a Porsche, but it turns out she meant a pen designed by Porsche. I remember being very grateful that she hadn't stolen a sports car for me. Again.

To this day, it's still my favorite pen.

Now, my hand is clenched so tightly around the titanium writing instrument that I fear that it might snap into pieces.

Dear Scarlett,
If you're reading this, it means that something has happened to me.

I curse softly, realizing that I addressed the letter to the wrong name. My head hurts. What would she prefer to be called? Is there a chance anyone will see this? I don't even care anymore.

The ringing of the phone finally stops as a female voice answers. "Sorry about that, Cole. I was on the phone with the senator, and he was very upset about the towers."

"You can tell Senator Powell that I don't give

a shit about—" An explosive cough racks my chest, rendering me unable to respond. It feels like my lungs are being shredded with razor blades. When I finish wheezing, I stare at the white paper, startled to find it showered with droplets of blood. I look at my hand, and my eyes widen at the sight of blood dripping down my skin. What the actual fuck? I knew I was sick, but...

"Cole? Are you there?" The older woman's voice is filled with concern. "Jesus, Cole! Are you okay?"

"Miranda," I say hoarsely as I lean back in my chair. "Please get my lawyer to come to my office. I need to make some adjustments to my will."

"Stop. Stop it. You're overreacting," she says, but her voice has grown shaky.

"Please. Get Mr. Bishop."

"Cole," Miranda says with warning. "You've got to get to the hospital. I've been telling you for days..."

"No, no hospitals. I have tried, but the doctors aren't helping."

"I'm a mother of three, Cole. Trust me when I say you can't tough it out and take chances when it comes to your health. You know I love you like you're my own damn son. So if you don't get your ass to a hospital right now, I will come up there and drag you out of that office myself!"

The kindness in her voice makes me smile, and I can't help feeling a bit of nostalgia for my own mother. My tie is beginning to feel tight again, even though I have loosened it many times this morning. I reach up to pull it off, and I curse under my breath when I realize that I have gotten blood all over the expensive fabric. Luckily, it wasn't a favorite.

I toss my ruined tie into the wastebasket and breathe deeply, rising to my feet and looking down at the letter. I don't even care anymore. Wiping my hands off on my pants, I reach for a fresh sheet of paper.

"Cole, promise me you will go to the hospital?" Miranda demands.

"I just need a breath of fresh air," I tell her. "Maybe a few minutes on the rooftop will do me some good. Mr. Bishop can meet me up there." I curse, remembering my conference call. "Miranda, if I'm not feeling better in half an hour, can you reschedule the conference call with Levi? Tell him I'm in a meeting with his father."

"That meeting is important, Cole. We can't reschedule it. We could lose Karachi if the team doesn't meet this deadline."

My stomach turns at that word. That word makes me sick.

"I could talk to them for you—" Miranda is suggesting.

"No way," I tell her firmly. "Those men need to be threatened and scared out of their minds if they're going to complete the task on time. You couldn't scare a teddy bear. It needs to be me. Just give me five minutes on the roof, and have my assistant bring me some tea. After I discuss my will with Mr. Bishop, I will make it to that conference call to chat with his son."

"You need to get better, Cole. I need you. This whole company needs you."

"I know. Depending on how this meeting goes, you and I might have to get on a plane and head to Pakistan this evening."

"Whatever it takes, honey. I'm beside you every step of the way."

"Thank you," I tell her softly.

Jamming my finger on the end button, I move to the glass doors on the north end of my office that lead up to the garden. It's one of the signatures of my designs—injecting the tranquility of nature into urban settings. My steps are sluggish, and I need to grasp the walls to support me as I stumble through the doors and up the stairs. The stunning Zen garden is complete with a koi pond and relaxing waterfall. It hurts to breathe, but I inhale raggedly. As I reach the scenic garden, I exhale and allow the cool ocean breeze to waft through my shaggy brown hair, healing me. Since I became successful, I stopped cutting my hair constantly in an effort to present the image of a well-groomed professional.

I'm not just a mathematician or an engineer. I'm an artist.

When clients come to my office, I often entertain them up here in the garden. I don't like talking about my work very much, but I figure that sitting up on this rooftop, way above the city, relaxing and watching the fish while being served tea by my assistant, is an excellent demonstration of what I can accomplish.

Now, if only the tranquility of this garden could help to clear my head so that I could write this damned letter. I slap the white paper down on a black granite slab and stare at it angrily, hoping for inspiration.

Dear Sophie,

I begin writing again, with the Porsche pen, until a sharp pain in my skull causes my eyes to shut tightly. Reaching up to grasp my head, I stagger backward, groaning in pain. What is wrong with me? Is this a migraine? It doesn't matter. My lawyer should be here any minute now. I need to get this letter written.

Hearing a noise, I turn sharply to look at the doors leading down to my office. This is a bad idea, because my head explodes in blinding pain. Why is my body betraying me like this? I move to the edge of the rooftop, grasping the railing as I stare down at the tiny cars below, deadlocked in a traffic jam. Tiny multicolored lights dance in my field of vision, obscuring the street below.

Focus, Cole, I inwardly chant. *You need to focus.*

I don't expect my knees to buckle beneath me. Somehow, my arms feel like jelly, and when my hands lose the strength to grip the railing, the pen slips out of my hand and tumbles to the street below. I can't even make an effort to catch it as I crumple to the floor of the rooftop. Squinting at the bright blue sky with determination, I try to resume my task.

"Dear Scar," I mumble, attempting to write the letter out loud. That will make it easier once I am able to concentrate and put the words down on paper. I just need to get my pen—but it is so far away.

The vast expanse of blue begins fading to black quite quickly, and my eyelids are refusing to stay open. As the world disappears, I feel like shit for not finishing my task, even though I can no longer remember exactly what it was…

I just have the nagging feeling that something important is unfinished.

"Cole!" shouts a man's voice from nearby.

It is comforting to hear another human voice. I am grateful to know that I am not entirely alone in this moment, but it still feels that way. I think I've felt alone for years.

Chapter Two

Cole Hunter, 2016
Still not shot yet

When I pry my eyes open, I am greeted with the unmistakable fluorescent lights of a hospital. There is an oxygen mask over my face, and I groan in disgust as I remove it, feeling embarrassment creep up around my neck. I can't believe I collapsed at work. What's wrong with me? I had that conference call, and… Miranda's going to kill me.

I feel around frantically for my phone, knowing I need to reach her and tell her to cover for me in the meeting, although I'm sure she already is. The conference was supposed to be at midnight in Karachi. The team is working around the clock, and it's the only time they had available. If we don't get a handle of the situation in Karachi, we could end up losing the project entirely.

We could stand to lose millions.

But as I search for my phone, I am frustrated to find nothing near me. There are only the clean white sheets of this very small bed, and an empty bedside table. My eyes quickly scan the shape of the room and the position of the window, and I recognize the work. It's a hospital I designed, and it's not particularly close to my office. I did not choose the location, and I never had any intention of becoming one of this hospital's occupants.

"Fuck," I mutter to myself, reaching for the bed's railing and pulling myself up. I am immediately hit by a wave of dizziness, and I begin coughing so much that it hurts all my internal organs.

Reaching for the oxygen mask I pushed aside, I bring it to my mouth and inhale desperately in defeat.

"Mr. Hunter, you're awake," says a male nurse rushing into the room, carrying a pouch filled with yellow fluid. He places a hand on my shoulder and gently pushes me back down onto the bed. "I am sorry, but I have to recommend you don't get up or overexert yourself. I need to administer this medicine to you intravenously."

"What is that?" I ask him as he prepares my arm for a needle. "What are you giving me? Is this chemotherapy? Do I have cancer?"

"I am not at liberty to discuss that. The doctor will come in to explain your condition soon. For now, this isn't chemotherapy. It's chelation therapy. They do look similar. I am sorry for the lack of explanation, but we have to move quickly on this."

"Chelation?" I ask, wincing as he shoves the needle into my arm. "Why?"

"We did some tests and discovered that there's an unusually high presence of certain heavy metals in your blood. We still have more tests to do, but this should help cleanse your blood. In the meantime, I've been instructed to ask you a few questions so we can better determine how to treat you. Do you have any history of substance abuse?"

"No!" I reply in disbelief.

"Tobacco, alcohol, any recreational—"

"No. What the hell is wrong with me? Am I dying?"

He hesitates. "I am sorry. I am not authorized to discuss the details of your condition. The doctor will have a chance to see you shortly. Have you been exposed to any construction sites lately?"

"Of course. I'm an architect and developer, I am always visiting construction sites."

"Has anyone else been coughing or complaining of respiratory distress at those sites?"

"No," I say with annoyance. "I don't run a fucking coal mine. All my projects are done with extremely high safety standards."

"I apologize, sir, these are just standard questions to determine exposure. Have you had any painful urination lately?"

"No."

"Any back pain or decrease in urinary output?"

"No, look—I don't have time for this. Do you know where my phone is? I have an important meeting to attend."

"Your mother has your phone. She's waiting outside."

I stare at him in utter confusion for a few seconds. "My mother is dead."

"Oh—my apologies. Well, there's a nice older woman who has been fussing over you since we brought you in."

Miranda. Coughing, I grasp the railing again. That means she's not going to be back at the office in time for the meeting. "Can you ask her to come talk to me and bring my phone? She has to cover the meeting for me."

"Sir, I'm going to have to ask that you avoid any stress right now. Until we figure out what's wrong—"

"You don't understand. My company—I just can't get sick now. If I was dead, then I'd have an excuse to miss work, but as long as I'm conscious and breathing, I need to be in the office."

"But you weren't conscious," the nurse points out, "and you need assistance breathing."

"No," I say, pushing aside the oxygen mask. "I'm fine. Call the doctor and tell him I have to go back to work, and I'll schedule another time for this chelation treatment."

"This isn't a spa, it's a hospital. I'm afraid that if you don't sit here for at least three hours and allow this medicine to drip into your bloodstream, your kidneys are going to fail and you're going to die. You've been exposed to extremely high levels of a toxin. Most likely within the last twenty-four hours. Have you been anywhere unusual?"

I try to remember my activities of the last twenty-four hours. Reaching up to rub my forehead, I exhale in exasperation. "I don't think so. I need my phone to check my appointments. I have so many meetings in a day—can you go get Miranda?"

"Sure," the nurse says, but he turns back to me with an odd look. "I'm not supposed to tell you this, but the doctor thinks you've been poisoned. We've informed the police and they're sending someone over to ask you some questions."

I pause. I try to respond, but another fit of coughing interrupts me, and splatters the front of my hospital gown with blood. When that settles down, I stare at the blood with a deep frown before looking back up at the nurse.

"Rodriguez," I tell the nurse. "Get me Detective Rodriguez. And my cell phone. And my lawyer."

Chapter Three

Cole Hunter, 2016
Getting shot

"Cadmium poisoning?" Miranda says as she sits at my bedside and looks up information on her phone. "Are you sure they said it was cadmium? There are three possible worksites where you could have been exposed. But it looks like we've had regular safety inspections and the levels are all way lower than they need to be to meet health standards. Besides, you've been mostly in the office. Other men would have gotten way sicker, way faster."

"Have employees been calling in sick?" I ask her as I hunt for statistics on my own phone. "Are there an unusual amount of absent workers?"

"No, not at all. In fact, all the construction projects around the city are ahead of schedule. They have been taking fewer sick days than usual."

My eyebrows crease as my brain tries to

process everything that's happening. "Miranda... the doctors think that it's possible someone specifically poisoned *me.*"

"What? That's ridiculous." She looks up at me with narrowed eyes. "Or... do you think it could be a jealous competitor? You have stolen clients from quite a few firms, and you've put some completely out of business."

"Their lack of talent put them out of business," I inform her.

She sighs, turning to play with the vase of flowers she bought me in the hospital gift shop. She then turns to look at me suddenly. "There's another possibility," she says. "It could be Benjamin. He's really angry about that trick you pulled with the Justice Towers."

"He's a sick bastard," I say, sitting up with a groan. Clutching my chest, I remember the first time I met Senator Benjamin Powell. I was fifteen years old, in a hospital bed similar to this one, and more injured than I am now. He loved seeing me vulnerable like that, and groggy from morphine. He thought he could intimidate me into becoming one of his pawns. He thought he'd succeeded.

"Would he do something like this?" Miranda asks softly.

I remember the way that Benjamin took pleasure in causing more harm to my already wounded body. "Definitely."

"Have you shared any food or drink with him in business meetings about the towers?"

17

"No—although there was champagne at the ribbon cutting ceremony."

"That was our champagne. It would have been safe."

"I don't know what to tell you, Miranda." Coughing quietly, I cover my mouth with my hand, trying to conceal the bleeding from her so that she doesn't worry. "My calendar looks normal—I haven't done anything unusual. I think the doctors might be wrong about the cadmium. Or maybe I was exposed a long time ago. They said the cadmium exposure could cause cancer, and they're scheduling me for an MRI after the chelation."

"God, I hope not, Cole. I had to watch my dad wither away after he was diagnosed. I will never forgive you if you make me go through that again."

"I won't," I promise her, reaching out with my non-bloody hand to touch hers. "Thank you for being here for me."

She squeezes my hand and looks at me with concern. "Do you know—is there some way I can get ahold of Scarlett?"

Her words hit me like a stab in the gut, and I look away, trying not to wince. "I can only reach her by letter, and she isn't responding. However, I do have the phone number of her… fiancé."

Miranda's eyebrows jump slightly. "No. Fiancé? You're joking."

I shake my head and shrug, trying to appear noncommittal. "Apparently, she's getting married."

Loosening her grip on my hand, Miranda

looks at me in shock. "Cole…"

"It's fine. Remember, she's not our Scarlett anymore. She's Sophie, now."

"She will always be our Scarlett. *Your* Scarlett. Give me that damned phone number. I refuse to believe she's marrying some other guy."

"Who's getting married?" asks a voice from the doorway.

I look up to see my old friend, and I exhale in relief. "Roddy, you're a sight for sore eyes."

"Heard someone tried to poison you, Hunter. You dead yet?"

"Halfway there," I tell him with a grin. "Speaking of which, Miranda—could you go see if Mr. Bishop has arrived yet? I still need to make those amendments to my will."

She stands up haltingly. "Fine. I'll let you boys talk in private. But don't get too attached to the idea of death, young man. You still have a company to run, and there's a whole world out there that needs more of your designs."

When she turns and walks away, I see her lift a hand to her face to flick away some tears. It hurts me to think that my condition is causing her pain. But somehow, I don't think I have a lot of living left to do.

"Are you going to leave me a yacht?" Detective Ricardo Carlos Rodriguez says as he moves to my bedside. "You don't have to, but I won't complain."

"I don't have a yacht," I tell my friend,

covering a cough.

"Fine," he says with a nod. "I'll settle for a duplex. Just a little one."

"How about a ranch where you can retire and raise horses?"

"Sounds good, man. But you have to throw in the horses."

"Done. Now can you figure out who's trying to kill me?"

"Maybe. You look like death," he says as he surveys my bloody hospital gown. "Whoever's trying is succeeding."

"Tell me more good news, buddy."

He grins. "Don't worry. I already sent my team to look at your house, your office, and those three construction sites. And the doctor informed me that you're probably going to live, so you don't have to buy horses for my ranch just yet. Maybe a puppy, though. I always wanted a Siberian Husky."

Coughing and laughing at the same time, I smile weakly. "Having friends is hard when you're rich. You get sick and *they* ask for presents. Why don't I get a puppy?"

"You'll be fine, man," Rodriguez says, suddenly serious. "The doctor said that your kidneys seem to be functioning better than expected, and that your lungs will probably make a full recovery once you finish the chelation. You're tough as Rasputin!"

"Rasputin eventually got killed," I remind the detective with a groan.

"You won't," he says reassuringly. "It's just going to take some time to heal, and you need to rest up and stop working yourself to death. You need to get some sleep."

"I never sleep."

"And that's probably why you collapsed on your goddamn rooftop. You're sick, man. Real sick. You need to take some time off, and allow yourself to get better."

Shaking my head, I frown. "I can't take time off right now, Roddy. You know that."

"Why? Because of problems with your girl? Because you need to work yourself into oblivion to forget about her?"

Closing my eyes, I lean my head back against the pillows. "No."

"Don't lie to me, Hunter."

I exhale slowly through my nostrils. "She doesn't give a shit about me anymore."

"That's bull, and you know it. This is the same girl who tore apart a prison for you."

Nodding, I inhale deeply, which results in me coughing again. In annoyance, I reach for my oxygen mask and take a few whiffs. "That was a long time ago, man."

"It wasn't that long ago. I remember it like it was yesterday. Girls don't commit felonies for guys they aren't crazy about. Then there was that car she stole. Come on—she's committed a *lot* of felonies for you. If that isn't love, I don't know what is."

Smiling slightly in memory, I think about the

ridiculous car sitting in my garage. I lift my
shoulders. "We've drifted apart. We don't talk
anymore. I've tried to give her space. I've tried to
be patient. I even went to therapy to see if I could
sort my shit out—somehow make myself into
someone she could stand to be around again. Things
have only gotten worse."

"It can't be that bad. Let her know that you're
sick, and I'm sure she'll come to see you."

"I doubt it."

"Hunter, you need to let her know. If you
don't, I'm going to inform the press and get some
nationwide-news coverage…"

"Do *not* do that," I warn him with a serious
look. "My company can't handle bad press right
now."

"Okay, okay," he says, patting my arm.
"Don't worry, buddy. I'm just joking around. I just
want you to feel better, and I know—I know that
you'll never feel better unless you get your girl
back."

I press my lips together tightly, trying not to
betray emotion as I stare at the hospital walls. "She
has issues. I always tried to be understanding of
that. I *am* understanding of that. She ran away and
took that job without telling me—I didn't get upset.
She started living with some guy—I didn't get
upset. I know what she's been through, and I know
I screwed up. But maybe I *should* have gotten upset.
I should have… let myself be jealous. When she
dated other guys in college, I should have been

more possessive and showed her that I care."

"She knows that you care! I never realized she cheated on you, man."

"It wasn't cheating," I inform him. "We were never really… together, in the traditional sense. Scar was molested when she was very young, and she is kind of messed up in certain ways."

"Messed up how?"

I turn to look at Rodriguez with a sudden fire in my chest. "You know what happened, a few days ago? I got a call at my office from Zachary Small. I immediately recognized the name as her boyfriend, from her letters. And you know what this bastard has the balls to ask me? If I'll give him permission to *marry her*. Because I'm her foster brother, and I'm the *only family she has*. Closest thing to *a father* she has."

"What the fuck?" Rodriguez asks.

"He wanted my *permission* to marry *my wife*."

There is a silence in the room

"Oh, hell no," my friend mutters. "You gonna let some broke ass mothafucker move in on your woman like that—"

"I know, brother."

"Why would she ever agree to marry some piece of shit, when she is already married to *you*?"

"I don't know. I just thought that there was some invisible line she would never cross. But getting married to someone else? I'm jealous. I'm upset. I don't want to be, but I can't help it. This is too much."

"You're Cole Hunter. Who the fuck is better than you?"

"Thanks, man. But I'm currently coughing up blood and breathing from an oxygen mask, so it's not an awesome day to be Cole Hunter."

"She should be here, by your side." The detective shakes his head. "These bitches. Trifling bitches need to learn."

"She's just scared," I tell my friend.

"What is she so scared of?"

"The truth," I mutter. Thinking about my answer, I turn to gaze into the hospital where all the staff is rushing about purposefully. "She's always been scared of the truth."

While I'm speaking, there is an odd impact on the side of my face—pressure and heat. It is followed by a terrible noise. The noise is blinding, like there is glass shattering all around me blink rapidly. I am confused, and I don't know where to turn first. The windows. My vision is suddenly blurry and unsteady, but I am able to squint and see that the windows are damaged.

But that isn't possible. I built this hospital to withstand earthquakes. Only the toughest of materials were used. I am distracted from this thought by the painful throbbing in my face. I turn to the detective, who is ducking down on one knee, and looking around, similarly disoriented.

"Rodriguez… is there something wrong with my face?"

When he looks up at me, his eyes widen. He grabs the side of the hospital bed, and pulls it forcefully down to the floor, causing the whole bed to topple over with me still in it—but not before I feel another searing impact in my shoulder. This time, an earsplitting yell is ripped from my throat as I crash painfully into the rails of the fallen bed. There is also sharp glass under my hand, which I had put out defensively to break my fall. The metal pole holding my chelation treatment clatters to the floor beside us.

"Stay down!" Rodriguez shouts, covering my body with his own, and using the hospital bed like a shield.

When there is a scream from the doorway, the detective gestures wildly with his arm. "Miranda! Get down! Get away from the windows!"

"What is happening?" I ask my friend, clutching my shoulder and moaning. My face feels like it's on fire. It's like I just got stabbed with a hot poker in the eye. Shutting my eyes tightly, I try to brace myself against the pain so that I can think. I hear the sound of nurses screaming and scattering in the hospital, and people shouting at each other to take cover. "What the hell just happened? Roddy?"

"Your face just got ripped open," he says with a grimace. "Large caliber bullet."

I blink several times, suddenly able to make sense of the burning sensation under my eye. Jesus, it burns. The glass underneath me must be from the flower vase Miranda brought me being hit.

"A sniper?" I ask Rodriguez, my voice a hiss through gritted teeth. I feel suddenly light headed and it is hard to think. I whisper as though it will keep the bad guys from knowing where I am. "Scarlett's boyfriend, that Zack guy, he's a sniper."

"Is he a bad sniper?" Rodriguez asks. "Because this guy missed you by a mile."

"Missed me?" I ask as the searing pain floods my shoulder, causing me to writhe and grip my arm with a moan. "What are you talking about? I feel like I just had my damn shoulder blown off."

"Naw," Rodriguez says, leaning forward to examine the wound. "It's just a scratch. If he were a real sniper, you'd have a bullet in your brain. Here…" Looking around, he grabs one of the sheets from the bed and begins typing it around my shoulder awkwardly, even managing to loop a corner around my face. "This should do for now. A hospital is literally the best place to get shot, so don't worry, man."

The pain is causing my whole body to break out in a cold sweat. "Sure. I'm not worried. Do I look worried?" My breathing is coming in short, shallow gasps, and I push the sheet above my lips so I can breathe better. My injured lungs are not cooperating, and I wish I could take a puff from my oxygen mask.

Reaching for his police radio, Rodriguez studies me with slightly lifted eyebrows. "I'm not the best detective in the world, Cole, but it looks like someone really wants you dead. This motherfucker knew he failed at killing you with poison, so he decided to use bullets. Good thing you're in Rasputin mode."

"Rasputin died!" I shriek hoarsely in reminder, clutching my shoulder with great frustration.

Pressing a button on his radio he begins communicating with his precinct. "10-71 in progress, requesting backup…"

Laying my head back on the floor, I stop listening to him. He ducks as a bullet whizzes by over the hospital bed, and rolls his eyes as if only lightly annoyed by the futile efforts of the shooter. I have always known that my friend was a badass, but I didn't realize he was this calm under pressure.

Using my teeth to pick some glass out of my palm, I wince at the pain in my face. My whole fucking body is a shredded mess. Coughing, I reach for my phone, which has clattered to the floor. My fingers leave a blood thumbprint on the screen, and the sticky wetness prevents me from unlocking the device. I give up and just let my arm lie limply on the cold hospital floor. I feel like I've been punched repeatedly in the eye, the shoulder, and the gut by a three-hundred pound man with brass knuckles.

But all these injuries are only serving to expose my deeper pain.

Underneath the shallow flesh wounds is a sick, empty feeling. A hollowness.

None of this would matter if she was still on my side. If I could just pick up my cell phone and

27

call her, and tell her that I'm hurting. Tell her that I've had a hard day, and I need her. If I could just know that I would see her at the end of all this, when I get out of this hospital, this would be easier to endure.

All of this would disappear if I could only touch her.

If I could just go home and find her sitting there, wearing her librarian glasses, sipping a cup of tea while she does god-knows-what on that laptop of hers. If I could only hold her, and put my head on her shoulder, and breathe in the scent of her hair. Every bad day would be a private joke, easily washed away.

But now, even if I do get better, and get out of this hospital, I will still be going home to an empty house. I will still be surrounded by paintings and furniture we picked out together. I will still have to get dressed in our walk-in closet, which is 95% filled with her favorite clothes, that haven't been touched in years.

I can get the poison leeched out of me, and I can get the bullet holes patched up, but I can't fix the empty shell that my life has become. My therapist was right when she told me that I was slowly killing myself with my inability to let go. I need to be honest with myself.

I'm never going to see Scarlett again.

I need to let go.

"Hunter!" Rodriguez is saying, gently shaking my good shoulder. "Hey, buddy? Stay with me, okay? You're losing a lot of blood."

"It doesn't matter," I tell him quietly.

"What do you mean?" he asks. "Don't get emo on me now, man."

Turning my head to the side, I rest my uninjured cheek on the linoleum floor. The blood from my injured cheek drips down around my nose, and into my eye. I don't even have the energy to blink it away. All the fight has gone out of me.

"Hey," Rodriguez says, shaking me. "We need to get you some medical attention. Help is on the way, and the shooter is probably on the move by now. Do you think you can help me get to the door, holding this bed as a shield?"

I can't bring myself to respond. The distance from where I am to the door feels infinite. There's no way I'm going to make that.

"Cole!" Miranda is shouting, as she sobs from behind the door. "Honey, are you okay?"

I open my mouth to respond, but I can't find the words, or the energy to project enough volume to reach her. I know that she cares. But it's not enough. Something is preventing me from being able to really feel anything. I've already lost so much. My mother. My father. Scarlett. Would it really be so much worse to lose my life?

My head is spinning with these thoughts, and the words of my therapist.

You need to let go, Cole. Let go of the past.

In this moment, I feel suddenly aware of the fact that my whole life has been meaningless. What have I really done? The hospital floor is still cold against my cheek. Is this all there is? These harsh white walls, and these cold floors. These giant boxes are my children—this is what I've created.

This is the only sort of thing I'll leave behind when I'm gone. Coldness.

No love. No photographs on walls. No children to mourn me.

As rich as I have become, it means nothing without family. And if that bullet had struck a few inches closer—if I hadn't turned my head—who would really care? Rodriguez looks concerned, and I know he did his best to protect me. Without him, I probably would have just sat there like an idiot and allowed the shooter to go to town on me as target practice.

"Cole," Rodriguez is saying, gently slapping the lower half of my cheek. "Okay, I may have exaggerated. This is a little more than a scratch. We need to get you some help."

Tightening my hand around my phone again, I try to unlock the device. The blood has dried a little more and it is easier. I go to my favorites and jab my number into the only name there. That's what you're supposed to do in this type of situation, right? Call your wife. I hold my breath as the phone rings. Twice. Three times.

I wait, listening for the sound of her voice.

And then finally it comes, her answering machine. Of course, it's impossible for her to actually pick up. Her cell phone is sitting at home in my nightstand, where she left it when she skipped town. I keep it charged up and waiting for her. And I still occasionally call her, in moments when I really need to hear her voice.

Like when I've just been poisoned and shot by a sniper.

Her soft voice brings tears to my eyes, and the phone trembles in my hand.

"Buddy," Rodriguez says softly, placing his hand on my neck and checking my pulse. "We're going to get out of this. You're not going to die."

"What if I want to?" I ask him.

His brows grow narrowed. "Don't say shit like that, man. Especially when you're bleeding to death on the floor. It freaks me out."

"No," I tell him. "Not *die* die. Disappear. You can make that happen, right? If someone's trying to kill me?"

"Like witness protection?" Rodriguez frowns. "Probably not. We would need to get approval…"

"I'm not asking for government protection, Roddy. I'm asking for *your* help. You did it before, right? With your cousin."

He looks at me in disbelief before shaking his head. "Man, that's insane. My cousin had a criminal record. You are well-respected, with money, a great job, a great life. You would lose everything. I know things seem hard now, but you're not thinking straight. Just let me deal with these assholes who are after you. They'll be behind bars soon, and you will feel safe again."

I smile at him. "Do you ever feel safe, Roddy? Does anyone ever feel safe again after something like this?"

His expression darkens. "No."

"Exactly." I lower my voice to a whisper. "I need to die here today. There are many witnesses who saw me get shot. People are ducking for cover and terrified out of their minds. They don't know what's going on. It's perfect. Can you make it happen?"

"Is this really what you want?"

"Yes."

"You're gonna regret this, Hunter. You have no idea what you're asking me to do. You'll be throwing away everything you've worked for."

"I already threw it away," I tell him. "Besides, you owe me one. Make it happen. Make the phone call. Make me a dead man."

He stares at me, clenching a muscle in his jaw. "This is about Scarlett, isn't it?"

"Partially. Look, I know I seem crazy with blood all over my face, but I'm thinking clearly. This is my decision."

Rodriguez glances to the doorway where Miranda is taking cover, and looking at our whispered exchange with worry.

"Can she be trusted?" Rodriguez asks.

"Yes. Absolutely."

"Fine. What's the safest room in this hospital, Cole? Somewhere private."

I scan my brain for information. "The

32

morgue."

"Okay, good," he says, glancing over the bed-shield cautiously. "We're going to make a run for the morgue. The hardest part is making it safely to the door. That amateur will never be able to shoot us once we're moving if he couldn't even shoot you while you were sitting still."

"Makes sense," I say weakly. "But I don't know how much energy I have."

"Just leave it to me, okay?" Rodriguez says gently, ripping the chelation tube out of the needle in my arm so that the bag won't slow us down. "Stay low."

Glancing up over the bed, he springs to his feet and flattens himself against the wall. The sound of another bullet is heard, but before it has even lodged itself in the hospital walls, Rodriguez is grabbing me and hoisting my arm over his shoulder as he drags me out of the room. I dizzily try to keep up, but my legs are clumsy.

Miranda grabs my other arm for support as soon as we are in the main hallway, and I wince at the pain in my collarbone. She wraps an arm around my waist, crying as she helps the detective lead me to the morgue.

"You're going to be okay," she says between sobs.

"Just think of Rasputin," Rodriguez tells me.

I grimace with pain as they drag me across the hospital floor. "I don't see how that could possibly help."

Chapter Four

Cole Hunter, 2016
After I got shot

Everything is cold. I am being pumped full of O-negative, chelation, antibiotics, and some morphine I tried to refuse. I can hear voices and feel people touching me, but it's hard to make sense of it all. With my eyes closed, I feel only a sort of swaying sensation. I feel like I'm on a metal raft, and it's bobbing up and down in the middle of a stormy ocean.

"You're lucky," says a man's voice. "It barely nicked your bone. You only have a hairline fracture. This could have been very messy."

I pry my swollen eye open to see a small pair of scissors holding a curved needle. It is pulling black thread away from my eye. The needle descends toward my eye again, and I wince as it pierces the damaged skin over my cheekbone. I can't feel it, because of local anesthesia, but it is similar to dental work. No one likes seeing their wisdom teeth being broken with a pair of pliers as they are pulled out of their jaw.

I remember getting my wisdom teeth taken out, years ago, while going to MIT. I tried to ignore it for months, but eventually the gums grew so infected I couldn't eat, and the headaches got so bad that I couldn't study.

Scarlett dragged me to the dentist and insisted that I get the teeth removed. She always took care of me like that. I was eighteen at the time and we couldn't afford to remove all four so I only removed the two impacted lower molars. Due to my anxiety over falling asleep, I opted for local anesthesia only, and watched the whole procedure. I am not sure why watching a thread stitch my face up like I'm a Chucky doll is more terrifying than hearing that grotesque crunching sound of my teeth getting broken.

It might be because it's so close to my eye. It might be because of the traumatic experience that preceded the injury. Getting shot at is no fun—but getting shot by someone you can't see, when you least expect it, is deeply unsettling. A hospital is supposed to be one of the safest structures, a building where healing occurs. I designed this building with that in mind. If I had known the patients would be vulnerable to sniper bullets from nearby buildings, I might have designed it a little differently. It's ridiculous, but I feel somewhat responsible. I didn't build this place to be a bunker.

Some days, I really wonder if every building should be a fortress or a bunker. Our bodies are so delicate, and we all reside in such flimsy structures. It is so easy for harm to befall us. Bullets can pierce glass, buildings can burn or fall down entirely. Not my buildings, not usually. I have tried so hard to create strong structures to protect people, but I can't even protect myself. What good is my work if people still get hurt?

All those subdivisions near forests that I designed to be fire resistant—bad things still happen there and people die all the time. All my work is for nothing.

This is a slightly depressing train of thought, but it hasn't been a great day for me. I was already poisoned and dying before I got shot, and missing an important business meeting. You would think that would be enough to deal with for one day. But worst of all, after getting patched up, Scar isn't going to be there to make me Jello shots to cheer me up, like she did after my wisdom teeth removal. Scarlett could never really cook anything other than coffee, but she could make a mighty fine Jello shot.

"All done," the doctor says, as he ties off the stitches.

"Good," I tell him. "Now stop the morphine drip. I need to drive soon."

The doctor hesitates, but after sharing a look with Detective Rodriguez, complies.

Rodriguez examines the bag containing blood. "On the bright side, the blood you lost was poisoned with cadmium, anyway. You just got rid of the bad blood, and got powered up with all this fresh juice that's sure to make you heal even faster. It's like you got a free oil change! Joke's on you, shitty sniper."

I reach up to gently finger my shoulder, where the bullet tore through my trapezius muscle. The area is completely numb, but I can feel a stiffness when I try to shrug. "Is that really how it works?"

"Not exactly," the doctor says. "Losing blood is never something to celebrate."

"Unless the condom broke," Rodriguez mutters under his breath.

My mind is preoccupied, and it takes me a second to get his joke, but I am too miserable to smile. "Why do you think someone wants me dead so badly?"

"I don't know," Rodriguez says, "but I'm going to find out."

The doctor pulls off his surgical gloves and wipes the back of his hand across his forehead. "We're just lucky that the bullet didn't completely tear the trapezius, or hit the shoulder joint. When it comes to ballistic trauma, the damage is usually extensive. This could have required bone grafts and hours of surgery, but it seems like you're a very lucky man, Cole."

"I am?"

"There might be some nerve damage, and you might have some trouble moving this arm for a while, but it's nothing that physical therapy won't mend."

"He's been shot before, doc," Rodriguez says proudly, patting my leg. "He's a professional at narrowly escaping death."

The doctor shakes his head. "Just don't make it a habit. The swelling should go down in a few days. Until then, you're going to look like you went to Spain for the Running of the Bulls, and the bulls won. But we'll load you up on painkillers, and this will be a distant memory soon."

"Thank you, doctor."

"You should be thanking Detective Rodriguez. That was quick thinking, to shield you from fire and tie up your injuries with the blanket to prevent more blood loss."

"He's my hero," I say honestly.

"That was nothing," Rodriguez says smoothly. "You should see what I can do with a tampon."

"What?" I ask, a few seconds after he speaks. The morphine is clouding my mind, and I hate it. "What can you do with a tampon?"

"Buddy, you have no idea. Tampons are glorious things. They are perfectly designed for stuffing a GSW in the field, when it's difficult to get medical attention. They come out of the package clean, and they help stop the bleeding real fast. Tampons save lives, man."

"Wow. I never would have thought of that."

"The laughter helps too. When a friend has been shot and you have to shove a tampon in his bullet hole—well, it's impossible to do that sort of thing without cracking a joke that's sure to cheer him up."

The doctor nods. "I've heard stories from field medics. When you don't have access to all the bells and whistles, you make do with what you've got. But luckily, we've got everything we could need right here." He gestures around at the morgue with both hands. "Blood, sterile equipment, drugs to make this all more comfortable. This is like an all-inclusive resort for getting shot. Again, Cole, you're a very lucky man."

I don't feel so lucky. Have you seen that movie where the stuffed animal gets ripped apart and loses his stuffing? That's a pretty good visual representation of how I feel. Also, that movie made me cry. I really liked that stupid stuffed animal.

"That's all that I'm needed for here," the doctor says. "Do you have any questions?"

"Do you think I'll be okay to drive tonight? And do you think it's safe for me to stay in a remote location without access to quick medical care?"

"I wouldn't recommend it," the doctor advises.

"And if I do it anyway?"

The doctor hesitates. "I'll put together a pack of emergency items you might need: drugs, antibiotics, and fresh bandages. But I do highly recommend you stay near a hospital just in case any secondary complications arise."

"Understood," I tell him.

"I'll leave you two alone for now," the doctor

39

says, giving Rodriguez a knowing look. "Please let me know if there's anything else I can do."

"Sure thing, doc," says Rodriguez, fishing into his pocket to hand the doctor a wad of bills. "I appreciate your silence."

"I appreciate your business, as always. Should I send the lawyer and that woman inside?" the doctor asks.

"Yes. Just tell them to give us a few minutes to discuss things."

The doctor nods and leaves.

Rodriguez pats my good shoulder and grins. "That wasn't so bad, was it? I bet you're regretting what you said before, about wanting to disappear."

"No," I tell him, pushing myself into a sitting position with a grunt. "That's what I need to do."

Pausing and frowning, Rodriguez examines me. "It doesn't make any sense. You have everything, Hunter. There are men out there who would die to have a *fraction* of what you have."

"They would need to. It's damn near killed me getting here. It's killing me to keep going."

"Buddy," Rodriguez says slowly, shaking his head in disbelief. "I thought that once you got some good drugs in you, you'd change your mind. But you're serious, aren't you?"

"Dead serious."

The detective exhales slowly, scratching his chin as he processes this. "I know you're hurting over this girl, but I think she's making you crazy. Why don't you just try getting some rest for a few days? Go to therapy some more. Go on a holiday. More importantly, bang some other chicks. You can find someone better than her, man. You can forget about her and move on."

I close my eyes as a dull throbbing pain fights its way through the anesthesia in my cheek. "Roddy, you don't understand. She isn't some girl. I built my life around her. She's… part of me. Like, I swear I can feel strands of her DNA floating all around in my body, knotted up with mine, entangled, painfully. I don't know how to keep living my life if she isn't close to me. It's like my soul is being stretched—stretched clean across this damn country, to wherever she is."

"So what are you saying?"

"I need a fresh start. And the only way I can do that… is if I die."

"You need to give up *everything* just to give up *her*?"

"Yeah. Because she is my everything."

Rodriguez nods. "Okay. You've convinced me—that you're completely insane. But I do owe you, so I'm going to do this. I am a homicide detective, after all, so maybe it will be easier to work your case if I pretend you were actually killed."

"Thanks, buddy."

"But if I lose my job over this, you better make it up to me in your will."

"A duplex, a ranch, and some horses," I say dizzily, shutting my eyes. "I'll even throw in a toaster."

"Cheapskate," he says with a grunt. "I save your life and kill you in one day, and all you can think to add is a toaster? Whatever. Should I call the others in?"

When I nod, he moves to the door and opens it a crack, gesturing for Miranda and Mr. Bishop to enter.

"Oh, Cole," Miranda says, rushing over to me and encircling me in a careful hug. "Are you going to be okay, honey?"

"Yeah, I'm fine," I tell her, squeezing her shoulder. I accidentally used my arm attached to the shoulder with the bullet wound, and it sends pain searing up from my collarbone to my skull, but I clench my teeth together to hide this from her. If this is how much it hurts while on drugs, I'm really looking forward to them wearing off.

"Are you still planning to go through with this, son?" Mr. Bishop says, adjusting his wire-framed glasses. "As your lawyer, I must caution you that thoroughly faking your death and dividing all your assets is… well, irreversible."

"Not totally irreversible, but we'll all have to suffer the consequences. I would probably take the fall for this," Rodriguez says. "So you have to be absolutely sure."

"I'm sure," I tell them all. "Make me dead to the world."

"How is this even possible?" Miranda asks. "Are you sure we can pull this off?"

"Roddy has connections," I explain.

The detective nods to confirm this. "I know a guy."

Mr. Bishop clears his throat. "Cole, son, for the sake of the company, I must highly recommend that you not…"

"I have to, Mr. Bishop. I'm so sorry. I know Levi is struggling in Karachi, but I've done all I can for that project. They have my designs, they have my instructions—I can't babysit them anymore and yell at them to do the jobs they were hired to do, and intimidate them into making deadlines. It's destroying my health, worrying about this 24/7. I barely sleep as it is, but now…"

"Are you sure this is the best time to make this decision?" Mr. Bishop asks. "You've just been shot, and poisoned—the physical illness and emotional trauma could be clouding your judgment."

"My judgment is crystal clear, maybe for the first time ever. My whole life, I've just been working myself to the bone. Every single day, work, work, work. I need some time to heal, Mr. Bishop. I need some time away from it all, without my phone buzzing constantly. I need to get away from the company, away from the stress, away from this whole damn city. If I don't get away now, it is actually going to kill me. Sooner rather than later."

"I understand, my boy," says Mr. Bishop. "Your parents would be proud of all you've accomplished. You need to put your health first. If

stepping away from this all is what you need…
well, I will support you."

"Thank you."

"He also just needs to nurse his broken heart
over his wife marrying some other guy," Rodriguez
explains, to which I roll my eyes.

"Honey," Miranda says, stroking my hair.
"Scarlett is going to be devastated when she finds
out. Do you want us to tell her the truth…?"

"No!" I say, a little too forcefully.

Rodriguez echoes, "No way in hell."

"Cole," Miranda says with a disapproving
tone. "Are you just doing this to make the poor girl
upset?"

"No," I say softly.

"Honey, that would be a terrible thing to do!
And you're going to make us lie to her?"

"What makes you think she will even show
her face here, Miranda?" I ask a little angrily. "She
doesn't care about me anymore. She doesn't care
about you, or Mr. Bishop, or this company. She's
moved on with her life."

"So do you want me to cut her out of your
will?" Mr. Bishop inquires.

"On the contrary," I respond. "I want you to
leave her everything."

"Everything?" he asks.

"What about my yacht and my ranch?"
Rodriguez whines.

I smile. "There are already large endowments
in my will for all of you. I want to leave Scarlett

controlling shares of the company. We started Snowfire together—with Miranda, of course. But she left me to run it all by myself. She left me high and dry. So make it her responsibility to take over all this stress that I have to deal with on a daily basis. And if she doesn't come to claim it, you can give it all to Miranda and Levi."

"I beg your pardon?" Miranda objects. "You want to give me the stress?"

"The control. You can sell your shares if you don't want the stress. Mr. Bishop, I would like to leave a million dollars to my therapist, Dr. Annabelle Nelson, or to the charity of her choice. She's been so kind, and she really tried to help me. Tell her it wasn't her fault, and that I just couldn't be saved. I'm a lost cause."

Pausing, I remember another important detail. "I have a note I need to give to Scarlett. Maybe you could just write it down for me before I leave. And there's a manila envelope for her in the top drawer of my desk with some information about her birth family I received recently."

Mr. Bishop is furiously writing down my demands. He glances up over his wire-framed glasses with a pitying look. "You're really upset at the poor girl, aren't you, Cole?"

I give him a sad smile. "It doesn't matter anymore. I'm letting go."

"I understand," the older man says softly. "Do you know where you are going to live from now on? You'll have to lay low for a while."

"I have the prototype of the mobile home we sold to NASA. That thing can take me anywhere. But for now, I was thinking of your vacation home in Nevada? If you don't mind, Mr. Bishop."

"Of course, son. That home belonged to your parents. It was never really mine."

"Thank you. Miranda, have my security team wipe the hospital cameras so that the police can't figure out that I left the hospital alive."

Rodriguez frowns. "That's not going to help us find out who's after you."

"Does it matter? They succeeded. They killed me. They will stop trying now."

"Bad people need to be punished for their crimes," Rodriguez says. "Can I get a copy of the footage before they are wiped?"

"No, Rodriguez. It would put you at risk."

"Fine."

Everyone stands around in silence for a few seconds, and we all seem keenly aware that we are in standing in a room that serves as a walk-in closet for refrigerated dead bodies.

Gesturing behind me, I grin to break the ice. Then I wince at the pain in my face. "As long as all those corpses are really dead, we should have no problems," I tell my friends. "I have complete trust in all of you."

"So we're really doing this," Miranda says softly. "We're saying goodbye to you for good."

"Yes," I say softly. "It's better if you just pretend I'm actually dead so that it's easier to lie."

"I'm going to miss you, honey," she says, leaning over to give me a hug. "Everyone's going to believe you're dead, because I'm going to be crying for days at the thought of losing my friend."

"I'll miss you too, Miranda. Oh, don't cry."

"I can't help it. There's nothing we can do or say to change your mind? You're really going? Do you really have to do this?"

"Yes," I say with quiet conviction.

"We are going to have to lie to the whole world," she says tearfully. "We're going to have to lie to poor Scarlett."

"Yes," I say again, feeling an odd twist in my stomach.

Rodriguez nods enthusiastically. "Bitches need to learn."

Chapter Five

Cole Hunter, 2016
After I died

It's the fourth day since I was officially murdered.

I never knew life after death would be so good. If someone had told me that wiping out my entire existence was the key to happiness, I would have let myself get murdered a long time ago.

Yawning and stretching in bed, I breathe in deeply of the fresh, filtered air in the cabin, and congratulate myself on finally achieving the luxury of not having to look at the clock to know what time it is, and not having to immediately rush off to complete tasks that should have been done hours or days ago by people I already paid to complete those tasks. Delegating never really works as well as it should—no one ever cares about your business as much as you can. It's just a job for everyone else, while for you, it's your calling, your purpose, your destiny. Your raison d'etre. Most people will never understand that kind of passion.

Of course, this same passion, mixed in with an unhealthy dose of perfectionism, usually means you end up polishing up and redoing everyone else's tasks, and carrying the weight of the duties of a dozen or more individuals on your shoulders. Until one of those shoulders gets shot, and you decide to fuck it all. It's really glamorous, isn't it? The high-powered life of a wealthy CEO. So stressed it's impossible to take a dump without coffee or laxatives, and so tense that even masturbating feels like an exhausting chore. If only all those dumb, gold-digging girls who prey upon men like me could understand the levels of anxiety I face, and how unhinged I am, they would think twice about coming near me.

None of this was ever worth the money.

As soon as I finished making arrangements for all of my assets and responsibilities, Rodriguez had a coroner friend come by and give me an "autopsy." I must admit, although I have experienced a lot of unusual things in my life, I have never been autopsied before.

In Los Angeles, everything is truly for sale. Love, sex, beauty, ecstasy, even death.

The coroner even tried to sell me a new face to go with my death certificate. He said he knew an excellent plastic surgeon, and could get me a package discount. Apparently, after faking one's own death, many people like to go the extra mile and totally change their appearance. This makes sense, especially if they were being hunted by the mafia, the police, an abusive ex, or you know, if they were just plain ugly.

I declined the surgery, of course, partially because I'd just been shot in the face. And partially because I like my face. I just couldn't delay or stay in this city any longer. I needed to get away. ASAP. Rodriguez had his friends drive me out to the factory that produced my mobile home, and we took one of the newer prototypes. They helped me to load up the house with supplies, a few personal effects I requested from my home, and enough MREs to last a year.

Then I happily drove the hell away from L.A., out into the middle of the desert. I drove and I drove, with one eye nearly swollen shut, and one arm lying limply in my lap. I didn't even look back once with nostalgia and bemoan the life I was leaving behind.

When I finally arrived at the house on Red Earth Lane, I stared at it for a few minutes, thinking of my parents. They used to bring me here when I was very young, but I can barely remember those days. What I did remember was a secluded geyser, in a mountain oasis with fresh water. Not even entering the house, (which now belongs to Mr. Bishop, since I gave it to him in exchange for taking care of Scarlett when I was in prison) I took a detour back out onto the road, and drove around the valleys and between the mountains to a deserted, well, desert, that I could drive my vehicle across. Then it was time for some serious off-roading.

Driving thirty miles over paved road is easy, but when there is no road, and the terrain is virtually impassable—you need a tank. Or something better than a tank, like my NovaTank. Although it has been field tested, I must admit feeling a great deal of pride from getting the opportunity to really see what it's made of. I have designed a lot of houses in my life, and even partnered with other companies to design house boats and the interiors of luxury airplanes, but this one is my baby.

Upon arriving at the oasis, my good shoulder was in just as much pain as the one that got shot. It took a lot of strength to steer the Nova across all that rocky terrain. But once I saw the geyser shooting up to welcome me, I knew the journey had been worth it.

I need to be isolated and off the grid to totally detox from all the bullshit and stressors of society. I need to leave behind all the artificial constructs of humanity, and reconnect with nature.

I don't care if that makes me sound like a hipster millennial.

Besides, I'm not doing something ridiculous like hiking the Pacific Crest Trail. This is not a sensationalized vision quest, it's a deeply personal choice to set my whole life ablaze, and destroy everything I am like a self-immolating monk. Everything I am is wrong, and flawed. Everything needs to be changed.

I realize that camping out in a tent is probably the preferable housing for reconnecting with nature, but my NovaTank has an endless list of benefits that a tent would never have. (Although, along the drive, I did think of at least five ways that I could improve this model.) I know that considering my weakened state and poor health, it is unwise to be far from civilization and hospitals, but I have no intention of getting sicker or going back.

Somehow, I know that everything I need to heal is right here up in the Great Basin desert.

Since the day I officially died, I have labored to keep a detailed journal of my activities. As any solitary adventurer out into the wild knows, it is customary to keep a diary of your thoughts, experiences, and discoveries—even if mine will be largely internal. Many brave and intellectual men throughout history have chronicled their expeditions thusly. Charles Darwin, Ponce de Leon, and hundreds of much less famous, but equally important, captains of ships venturing across oceans, ice, and outer space. Of course, my writings are not nearly as exciting, but they are important to me.

This may or may not be an exact transcription from my journal:

Day One: Sleep.
Day Two: Sleep.
Day Three: Sleep.
Day Four: Sleep.

Needless to say, it's been the best four days of my life. At least in recent memory. Has it even been four days? It might be more or less than that. I'm not even sure, as I've been too busy sleeping to care. It's a deep, dreamless sleep in my completely darkened Nova. I needed this so bad. Have you ever been to one of those float tanks, the sensory deprivation chambers? I have always been meaning to go, but I just never had time for that sort of thing. The quietude of my house combined with the quality of the mattress, and my painkillers, have simulated my own sort of private float tank.

For at least 72 hours, I haven't been miserable.

No cell phones ringing at all hours because I have business happening on the other side of the planet. No computer lights blinking for my attention because I fell asleep working on my laptop. No conversations with anyone asking me for help, or to fix a problem, or to sign something, or to talk sternly to someone who's been giving them trouble.

Is this what Scarlett felt like when she got rid of all her technology? I always wondered why she would choose to work with the government instead of me. I always wonder why she would accept their ridiculous imposition that she steer clear of the internet. I have found it extremely frustrating that she hasn't owned a cell phone or computer for several years, as it has become nearly impossible to communicate with her.

But now, it makes sense a little. It feels *so damn good* to be so totally disconnected. I can't remember the last time I heard myself think so clearly. I mean, I think all the time at work, but it's mostly utilitarian thinking about immediate actions I need to take. Thinking in the city is like trying to have a conversation with the one person you care about most in an extremely crowded room where everyone is chattering loudly and pushing you around. Your inner self needs to yell just to be heard, and even so, it's never heard clearly. There always seems to be a deep, fundamental misunderstanding.

Now, I can easily have a conversation with myself. I can remember who I am, underneath the suits and ties and deadlines. I can remember who I was before all this—before the money, the fame, the offices, the houses, the cars. Before the bullet wounds, before prison, before meeting Scarlett, before my parents died. If I go back to the very start, and try to remember the little boy I was before life started twisting me up and throwing curveballs and tidal waves at me, I realize that I haven't taken care of him. I sacrificed that little boy's mental and emotional well-being—I haven't let him get a full night's rest without medication in twenty years.

I stopped listening to myself. I stopped caring about my basic needs, so much that I lost touch with who I really am. I pushed him down. I've kept him buried under all the ash and soot and cinders of that fire.

I've managed to skirt by, pretending to function as a normal human being, while very often feeling dead inside. I may have been successful, but it never felt the way I wanted it to feel. I had effectiveness, and the drive to finish what I started, but I was woefully lacking in real human connections. And when Scarlett left...

I think I had just invested so much of myself into building a life with her that I could never imagine anyone else. I was torn apart. No amount of therapy could give me the ability to mend. I don't know how so many people are able to experience the death of loved ones, go through many breakups and divorces, and still continue about their lives as though they haven't been shaken to the core.

I can barely remember a time when I was not grieving for someone. In my experience, losing someone you love is always devastating, and you can never be the same person you were before. My whole life has been lived in a state of grief, cumulative, mounting, escalating grief, until this explosion when I finally realized that if I didn't make a drastic change, I was going to lose myself as well. And I might be willing to say goodbye to everyone and everything I love, but I am not ready to say goodbye to my life.

I love my life: every painful, messy, miserable minute of it. I always have.

Climbing out of bed sluggishly, I place my hand on the wall to flip on the light switch. There is something to be said for how condensed and convenient this living space is. I can almost reach everything I need to sustain my body without taking a single step. The close quarters are cozy, and much preferable to the loneliness of sleeping by myself in a five-thousand-square-foot home, and bolting out of bed to check the security camera footage at every creak and sound.

Reaching out to my very compact bookshelf, I retrieve an old photo album. I sit on the bed rubbing my injured shoulder, pleased with how much better it feels after so little time. Sleep really is a magical thing. I wonder if I would have been able to tolerate continuing on as Cole Hunter if I could have only forced myself to sleep a little more. But it's not as easy as it sounds.

I must confess that I've had second thoughts about my decision a few times today. Now that the bliss and euphoria of being alone and having absolutely nothing to do is wearing off, I can't help wondering how I will pass the time once I feel better. My fingers keep itching to design something, and I don't know how I am going to force myself to just Netflix and chill the fuck out instead.

Maybe I will continue to design things—but won't it drive me crazy not seeing them become real?

Running my hands over the dusty old photo album, I wonder to myself whether I should open it. I haven't opened it in years, because I was in denial that Scarlett was really gone. I figured that if I started looking at old photographs, it was acceptance that I would never see her again.

Now, I found myself sitting here alone in the desert, wondering if I even really remember what she looks like. Sometimes I stare at strange women on the street, because they might have a feature of hers. Pale, clear blue eyes, or unnaturally jet black hair. I stare at them as they walk down the sidewalk, until they have walked far away.

When their backs are retreating from my line of sight, it is then that they look the most like my Scarlett. Sometimes, my chest swells up and I have to fight the urge to chase after them and call out her name.

Smiling derisively at myself, I unlatch the album and prop it open. I inhale sharply at the first picture of her, and I feel pain in my still slightly raw lungs. I am no longer coughing up blood, but my throat feels sore, like I'm recovering from a bad cold. Contrary to the notes in my journal, I have been eating healthy and getting enough nutrients to heal. Rubbing my neck subconsciously, I stare down at the album.

The photo is one I took of her for a school project. It was a windy day, and her hair is covering most of her face. But the striking blue of her eyes is visible, and it still makes my breath get stuck in my sore throat. I developed that film myself in a darkroom. What a useless class that was—if only they had known that film photography would go the way of the dinosaurs! But in the early 2000s, film photography was still what "real artists" did, and it was pretty cool to go through the extra effort.

As I flip through the album I see more photographs of Scarlett trying very hard not to be photographed, and a few of us together. God, I was skinny back then. Regular gym time does wonders for a man's body—I must have nearly doubled in size.

Scarlett basically looks the same in these photos as she did the last time I saw her. The only difference is the development of her fashion sense, ability to afford those fashions, and some new skill with styling her hair and makeup that she usually didn't bother to use unless we had an important meeting. The girl who used to walk around the house wearing one of my t-shirts and singing into a hairbrush looked the same at age twenty-three as she did at age thirteen.

I can't believe I've known Scarlett so long that I took photos of her with *film*. It makes me nostalgic, and I wish I had some pictures of my parents, or pictures of myself from my childhood, but they were all destroyed in the fire. Mr. Bishop has some of me playing with his son in his family albums—those were taken as Polaroids in the early 90s. *Polaroids.*

I can't believe that I just said goodbye, for good, to some of my oldest friends. My family.

And I totally ghosted Scarlett.

What was I thinking?

Sighing and shutting the album, I reach up to flip off the light switch. I lie back down in the dark, with the images from the photographs fresh in my mind. Images of the life I used to have. It all seems so far away now.

I know I shouldn't have asked Rodriguez's goons to bring me this photo album. I should have left everything just as it was, as if I had really died. When people get murdered suddenly, they don't usually have a chance to pack their photo albums in a carry-on for the afterlife. I kind of ruined the authenticity of my death with this tiny detail—but the album was locked away in a fireproof safe with other sentimental items, so I'm sure no one will notice its absence.

Except Scarlett. If she returns to the house, and carefully examines all our belongings, she might notice the missing album. She's a smart girl. The smartest girl I've ever met. Would that tiny clue be enough for her to figure out that I'm not really dead?

Did I leave that clue intentionally? Do I want her to figure it out?

No. Absolutely not. If she notices, she will probably just think I moved it to another part of the house. I don't want her to figure out that I am alive. Ever. She stopped replying to my letters. She's marrying some other guy. I'm already dead to her.

This is just a formality.

Sighing, I put the photo album aside and let sleep wash over me again. But with the photographs dancing across my brain, I know that I am going to dream of her. I try to push the dreams away.

I came out here to detox, to heal, and to truly, completely let go.

It will take some time. It won't happen overnight. But very soon, I know that my mind and heart will be completely cleansed.

I will be renewed.

Chapter Six

Cole Hunter, 2016
My rebirth

Sleep is amazing.

I wish I could sleep on the side where I was shot without too much pain, or on my stomach without hurting my face, but I'm getting there. Regardless of the limited number of sleeping positions, and the limitations of a twin-sized mattress when I'm used to a California King, sleep is amazing.

Sleeping here, in my Nova, is amazing.

I don't think I can adequately describe how peaceful this is.

Enclosed tightly in this pitch black, soundless safety bubble—it's so pure, almost meditative.

I think that for the first time in my life, I can understand the allure of taking a monastic vow of silence. Who knew that silence was so precious? I suppose the monks did. Monks from almost every religion on earth, actually, value contemplative silence. There must be something to it. I guess that relinquishing all my earthly possessions except the NovaTank and a few things I absolutely need is sort of like a vow of poverty. Detachment.

A few times, I have ventured out of the Nova at night to stretch my legs, walking in small circles around my mobile home in the cold desert oasis. I was greeted with a stunning display of the Milky Way that was so powerful it nearly knocked me to my knees. It's the closest thing to a holy experience that I've ever felt. I can't even recall the last time I beheld the immense river of stars stretched across the night sky like this; it's a glittering postcard from my past. I almost forgot it was there.

It is comforting, this celestial blanket wrapped around our little solar system. A reminder that we are all spinning, spinning, spinning, utterly insignificant and powerless.

I think that's the problem with modern day America. Light pollution makes it impossible for eighty percent of our population to properly view the night sky—this makes it easy for us to lose touch with our origins. How can we truly understand what it means to be human anymore if we can't look up and be reminded of ourselves? Many of us are becoming more machine than man. I know I was.

But that's changing now. Sitting up in bed, I reach for a sweater to prepare myself for the cold desert nights. I am feeling the pull of the sky, and I

am excited to go outside and walk around a little.
Even if I only have enough strength for five minutes
or less, that's enough to touch my soul.

The galaxy is absolutely surreal. It vaguely
reminds me of a spiral staircase I designed for a
building in Barcelona. It is evidence that my job is
completely unnecessary, and perhaps ridiculous.
Tectonic plates created these perfect mountains, and
this nearly magical geyser in my idyllic oasis.
Gravity has shaped thousands of galaxies, and
thousands of solar systems inside those galaxies.
Each one is designed a little differently, but the
basic bones of the blueprint are always the same.
Nature already has enough art, mastery, and
functionality. It doesn't need me.

I guess I really am coming to terms with my
retirement.

Smiling, I reach for my boots and tug them
onto my feet. I never intended to retire before thirty,
but I guess life has other plans for me. I'm just
happy to be here, and I'm excited to see another
exquisite clear sky outside my NovaTank.

Just gazing up at that giant arch across the
horizon makes me feel humbled. It's like the perfect
vaulted ceiling, far superior to all of my favorite
Byzantine era architecture. It teaches me how
foolish I am and makes me feel connected to parts
of myself I forgot long ago. So long ago it predates
my parents, my lifetime, my pain. It predates my
ancestors, my species, my planet. I'm remembering
the true scope of things.

In the few days I've been out here, I feel like my mind has expanded and relaxed. My whole perspective has been refreshed. Standing up and stretching my arms out slightly to prepare for my walk, I wince at the pain in my shoulder that radiates up my neck. But everything feels small now. I am beginning to feel different—if I might be so bold as to use this term, maybe even a little… enlightened.

When I started thinking in geological time instead of Google Calendar time, it became a lot easier to breathe. A lot easier to let go.

Someday, every skyscraper I've built will turn to rubble and eventually dust. Everything turns to dust, in the end. But I've done a great deal in my lifetime. Whether I'm dead or alive, my NovaTank might eventually be modified for use on the Moon or Mars, when people are finally able to expand their tiny reach. I've contributed to all of this. I gave all of myself that I could possibly give.

Now, maybe I deserve a little… serenity.

The word makes me feel light instead of heavy. Even though it's Scarlett's birth name, I am able to think of the concept without thinking of her for the first time. It might be too soon to say for sure, but I really think that soon, I will be free of her. I will just be free, in general.

Opening the door of my NovaTank, I step out into the oasis. And I am struck by a few realities. I am struck by these realities fairly quickly, in rapid succession, or possibly all at once. If I try to break down the processing structure of my brain, the realities would probably hit me in this order:

#1. It is not night. It is glaring, blazing daytime, and I can't see the stars I came out here to see.

#2. I guess pretending to be a hippie and not looking at a clock for days has caused me to lose track of time. That's embarrassing.

#3. I'm not alone. There's someone here. Someone is moaning loudly.

#4. Um, how the hell am I not alone? I am dozens of miles from any sort of civilization or even trails. Who could find me out here? Is it a crazy, lost wanderer? Should I get a gun?

#5. Actually, I just need to go back inside and shut the door. The Nova is a Tank after all, and has a built-in arsenal. I haven't tested out the ammunitions aspect yet, and I was hoping to use it to score some wildlife for dinner. But self-defense could be a good field test, also. Not that I need to field test my product, because I'm retired now that I'm dead, remember? Get it together, Cole.

#6. It is a woman's voice. She seems to be crying.

#7. I can't see anything. Stepping out of the Nova from complete darkness and into the blinding sun was a gross miscalculation, and my eyes are still adjusting to the landscape as I shield them with my hand.

#8. I hope I don't look like too much of an

idiot, and I hope there isn't another gun pointed at my head. You never know in rural America, and I've been riddled with enough bullets to reach my maximum lifetime comfort level of bullets colliding with my body. Yes, that's a thing. Everyone has their maximum, and mine must be significantly lower than 50 Cent's.

#9. I start closing the door and retreating into my Nova slightly. Getting shot isn't fun. The mere thought is enough to make me want to slam this door and hide away in here for a year. If you think getting shot is cool, or heroic, or dramatic, think again. It fucking sucks. If there is any way you can possibly avoid getting shot, you should definitely do that instead of the alternative.

#10. The Nova's door is nearly closed when I hear the woman speaking. She speaks one word, over and over in a whisper, between sobs. And I recognize her voice. And it sends chills down my spine. I do not close the door.

#11. Against all of my previous thoughts, reactions, and all of my arrogant ideas about "enlightenment" I swing the door wide open, because I don't care if she has a gun. She can pump me full of bullets for all I care, I just want to look at her, and hold her, and assure myself that she is real. That she is here. I squint, trying to see better.

#12. Hey, how many painkillers did I have today? Is this really happening? It could be an opium dream. I think some of my painkillers are opioids.

#13. Shit! If this is an opium dream, I better move fast and give her a hug before she disappears.

#14. My vision is clearing up. Finally! I can make out an outline of her body, her dark hair… She is kneeling on the ground, crying into her hands. Her shoulders are shaking slightly.

#15. "Knock, knock," she whispers, over and over again. "Knock, knock."

I am no longer thinking clearly enough to know what the hell I am doing as I stumble forward. I come to a sharp halt standing above her, looking down in absolute shock as a lump forms in my throat. And I'm pretty sure it has nothing to do with my recent bout of poisoning.

"Scar," I whisper hoarsely, reaching out to touch her hair. My hand stops a few inches away from her scalp, because I'm sure she's going to disappear as soon as I make contact. That's already happened in my dreams for several years, so I'm familiar with the plotline chosen by my sadistic subconscious psyche. It can't fool me this time. I'm not going to touch her.

But as my vision grows even sharper, I begin to see other details that pique my interest.

Her arms are deeply reddened and sunburnt, like she has been outside all day. Scarlett's skin is naturally very pale, and she burns easily. I have spent a lot of time slathering her delicate skin with a high SPF sunblock, because it was the only way she could go outside without turning into an Oompa-

Loompa.

I would say she is deep into Oompa-Loompa territory, and maybe even passed it entirely on the spectrum and graduated to the realm of boiled lobsters with Rudolph-noses. I notice some other details then, too. Her clothes are dirty and damaged, like she has been walking for a while and she has fallen many times. Her body is bruised, and her hair is frizzy and unkempt. There's even a twig in it.

Reaching out uncertainly, I remove the twig from her hair.

I stare at the twig in appraisal, and twist it between my fingers. It seems like a real twig. It feels like a real twig. It even smells like a real twig. Okay. I think this might actually be happening. And that would have to mean that she drove to my house to look for me, and walked…

The lump in my throat grows bigger. She walked all this way…

"Scar," I say again, tentatively touching some of the frizzy, flyaway hairs sticking up erratically from her head. I can feel the dry, coarse texture from years of hair dye, and the desert sucking away all the moisture and softness. She feels real. This is too real. "Scarlett," I say again, as my heart begins to pound so violently that I fear I'm going to rip an artery open more efficiently than a bullet ever could.

She does not respond. She only shakes her head in refusal. She shakes her head vehemently, as if it is all too much to bear, and it is then that I know she feels exactly as I do.

I fall to my knees and wrap my arms around her body, crushing her against me. I bury my face in her hair as I hold her, swaying slightly from the dizzying emotions. Tears spring to my eyes and I can't hold them back. None of the pain matters anymore. It hurts to breathe, and my shoulder is ablaze at the effort it takes to hold her, but I don't give a damn.

She is crying against my chest, sobbing and clinging to me. I can't believe she's here.

"Honey," I say, hoarsely, a term of endearment we don't usually use. It feels awkward on my tongue, but I don't remember exactly what to call her to show my affection. "I never thought I'd see you again."

"Why," she says, choking on her words. Her voice breaks and mounts to a shriek. "Why the hell would you do this to me? Why the hell would you *do this* to me?!"

It occurs to me then, as I really begin to process the situation, that no one knows precisely where I am. They know I went to the cabin, but they didn't know about the geyser dozens of miles away. Only Scar knew that. Also—my friends wouldn't betray my confidence. I told them not to tell her that I was alive, and I am sure they kept it a secret. They are loyal and trustworthy.

So how did she find me? Was it the picture album? The lump returns to my throat. She must have actually thought I was dead up until this moment. I sort of feel like I have been dead for years, and somehow, in this moment, holding her is making me feel alive again. I release my grip on her body so that I can look at her. Wiping some of her black hair out of her face, I see that the whites of her eyes are heavily bloodshot. There are dark, puffy circles under her eyes, and her lips are cracked and parched. She looks desperately in need of sleep and water.

"I didn't think you cared anymore," I tell her softly.

"You asshole," she mutters, clenching her palm into a fist. I don't have time to blink before it collides with my jaw, making me wince.

"Hey, take it easy!" I say, holding up my hands in a gesture of peace and surrender. Luckily, she hit my good side, but the impact still spread throughout my face. "I might be alive, but I was still shot, you know."

"I hate you," she says tearfully, balling both of her hands up into fists as if she intends to beat the shit out of me.

Catching her wrists in my hands, I hold them fast to keep myself from being pummeled. I gently push her to the ground, and sit over her, using my own body to restrain her the way I used to when we wrestled as children.

Is this really happening?

I stare down into her reddened, tear-filled eyes, and I see the anger and the hurt. I never should have misled her to think that I was dead. But

I'm having trouble focusing on anything other than the utter elation of being near her again, in her presence. If thinking that I was dead led her to come find me, and led her all the way out here, to the middle of nowhere—I would do it all again in a heartbeat.

"I hate you," she says again turning away from me so that I can no longer see the pain in her face. "How could you make me think you were gone?"

Releasing her wrists, I let her hands fall to the grass. Her body is so limp, so weak, so defeated. I don't think I have ever seen her this broken, and it's *my* fault. I never wanted to break her. But I can't deny being deeply moved by the fact that she walked all the way out here for *me*. It must mean she really still cares, right?

I stare at her, hard. So hard. I drink in every curve and edge of her sad Victorian profile, her defiant, rebellious bloodshot eyes, and chapped lips that quiver slightly with vulnerability and emotion. Her face is food for my weary soul, and the sight of her nourishes me more than all the stars in the night sky.

Forget what I said before. The whole damn galaxy can burn. I just want Scarlett.

Letting my face fall forward so that my nose collides with her cheek, I draw in a deep, shuddering breath. I breathe her in. *She is really here. For real.* The tiny spark of joy inside me explodes into electricity that reaches every cell of my being. Tears seep from my eyes, bathing her skin.

"I thought I'd never see you again," I say to her honestly, as I inwardly scheme how to keep her from ever leaving. I can't help it. I place my hand on her collarbone, just above her breast, feeling the soft skin that is nearly transparent. Her blue veins are visible under her skin here, which isn't as sunburned due to the curtain of her hair.

I feel Scarlett's hand sliding up my arm, hesitantly. She seems to be searching for something. When her hand collides with my injured shoulder, she squeezes, and I wince, trying to hide the pain. Her other hand immediately reaches up to grasp my shirt and she digs her hands into my body and clothes, gripping me fiercely as she blinks tears away.

"Cole, you didn't have to be so fucking convincing. I wanted to die."

"What? No!" I pull her hands off my shoulder and hold her firmly, giving her a little shake. "You promised. You said you'd never…"

"How did you expect me to feel?!" she screams, and her words come out in a jumble of gasps. "The morgue—detective—Miranda was crying."

"I probably felt the same when I found out you were getting *married*."

"What?" she says in confusion, lying back in the grass and blinking slowly. "To who?"

It suddenly occurs to me from the dizzy look

on her face that she might have a mild case of sun stroke. I know that I need to run into my Nova to retrieve a bottle of water for her, but it's difficult to pull myself away. I feel her neck and her face and I curse softly. I am afraid that if I get up or step away, I will turn back and she will be gone. She will have melted into the grass and disappeared forever, and I will go crazy and die alone out here, wandering the desert forever and pulling my hair out.

"Just wait a sec, okay, Scar?" I squeeze her hands and kiss her forehead before running to the Nova and grabbing a bottle of water. When I come back outside, I am frightened to see that her eyes are shut. "Scar? Hey!"

Moving to her side, I pry her lips apart and pour some water between them. She coughs on it at first, but then she begins drinking greedily.

"Tell me when," I say softly. But she does not tell me when, and soon enough, she has guzzled down all the liquid in the bottle. A little trail has trickled down the side of her face, and I wipe it off and lightly dab my fingers across her forehead to cool her down.

I lie beside her for a minute, holding her hand, looking at her with worry. "We need to get you inside to the air conditioning."

"I'm getting married?" she asks, with her eyes still closed.

"Yeah, to Zack. He called me."

It takes her a second to respond, but a deep

73

frown creases her features. "No. Zack is a liar, and I never agreed to marry him. He stole your letters from me."

The letters. They never reached her. I exhale in relief. "God, Scar," I say, lowering my head to her chest and hugging her tightly for a minute. Then, I feel something metallic under her blouse, like a pendant, and I am puzzled. Scarlett doesn't usually wear necklaces. Sliding my fingers under her shirt and pulling out the pendant, I am surprised to see something that strikes a chord in my memory.

I remember buying this for her. But I never gave it to her. That was a lifetime ago. Where did I leave it? It suddenly hits me, and the answer makes my stomach fall. It's that sick, exposed feeling you get in dreams where you are naked in public. The vodka bottle. Our high school. All those years ago...

"You found it..." I say hoarsely, hoping she isn't upset at all the lovesick, humiliating words I wrote. I was a stupid, fucking child. I didn't know that you couldn't just plan out the rest of your life with the person you loved and expect everything to happen easily, like in a Hallmark movie.

Life is a constant, back-breaking struggle. Real, worthwhile relationships require effort, and true love feels like you're in a scene from Ben-Hur, rowing madly in a slave ship, rowing your heart out to stay alive.

"I got your clues," Scarlett is saying. "Take the pin out. End of the earth. That's how I found you. You're a real dick, to play games with me like this."

Swallowing back a lump in my throat, I rub my thumb over her cheek. "Scar—I didn't think that you'd find that letter. Ever. And I didn't know it contained any clues or hints to my location. I think you just found me... by accident."

"You're lying. I know you can travel through time, like Future Trunks. Your time machine is right over there."

I blink, glancing over in the direction she's pointing. Upon closer examination of my NovaTank, it does look a bit like a time machine. I will have to add that to my growing list of ways it could be improved. A list that I will never be able to give to my junior architects and automotive engineers, since I'm not in charge anymore. I turn back to the dark-haired girl.

"Scarlett, I only left a note with Mr. Bishop to say goodbye. It was for closure. I'm just... I had no idea you still cared."

"Don't make me hit you again," she says, her eyes flashing with a sudden clarity as she pushes me away with anger. She grabs handfuls of my shirt and glares at me with unbridled fury. "What the fuck is wrong with you? Love other people? I didn't want to love other people! I didn't need any other people! I just needed you, and you were never ready. Over and over, with this 'we're not ready' bullshit. When will we be ready, Cole? When we're both dead? When you get shot in the head, and buried in front of me, and I have to climb over a fucking mountain for you in the boiling hot Nevada sun, and hallucinate that you have a spaceship from 2047, will we be ready then?"

She's rambling so fast that I can't keep up. She's definitely cracked, and I need to get her inside and out of this heat. But she's also so irresistibly adorable that I find myself doing something equally insane. I grab her and crush her lips against mine, kissing her soundly to shut her up and calm her down.

Her body is still for a moment, until her arms slide around my back as she begins to kiss back, arching her body against mine and intertwining our legs. The kiss is fueled by a feverish kind of passion, and I feel like we must both be seriously unwell. I am clumsy and lightheaded from my injuries and my painkillers, and she is burnt to a crisp by the sun. Still, I can't stop kissing her, greedily trying to taste all her emotions, and trying to communicate to her that she is mine.

She must know that, right? If she came all this way—if she read that letter, and if she refused to believe that I was dead—if she hunted me down, she must know that this is a new beginning for us? I won't have it any other way.

Her lips are parched and rough against mine, but I don't care, because she is Scarlett. When she seems too tired to keep kissing me, and grows somewhat limp in my arms, I become alarmed.

"Scar," I say softly, patting her cheek. "Scar?

Jesus, you're so dehydrated. Are you okay?" When she doesn't respond, I consider lifting her and taking her into my Nova. But when I slip my arms under her and try to lift, my shoulder makes me cry out in pain. Instead, I go back into the camper and grab another bottle of water. Bringing it over to her, I pour some water between her lips and splash some on her face to wake her up.

"Scar? When was the last time you slept? Your face looks like death."

"Your face looks like butt," she tells me stubbornly, without opening her eyes. She grabs the water bottle and begins chugging it.

I smile at her fondly, feeling like not a day has passed. She's still my Scarlett.

After drinking two thirds of the bottle, she opens her eyes to glare at me. "I barely slept since I found out you were dead. I'm never going to forgive you for this. Never."

With a small sheepish grin, I glance at my house. "So you wanna come inside my spaceship?"

She smiles at me, before inching closer and resting her head against my leg with a sigh. "You can go to hell in your cool spaceship." Her fingers dig into my leg. "But then, after you go to hell, come back to me."

"Always," I tell her. As she falls asleep again, I know I'm going to have to carry her inside, or let her lay here and get burnt even more by the harsh sun. Shit. Can I carry her? Is my arm capable? I would really like to be the romantic hero in the storybook right now and save the damsel in distress, but I don't think I'm physically up to the task. Still, I'm going to try anyway. I'll just pop a few more Percocets after this, as it seems to work better for me than the Vicodin.

Sliding one arm under her shoulders, and another under her thighs, I grunt as I hug her against my chest and try to use my legs to lift her. Damn. Did she get heavier or did I get weaker? I guess I missed a few gym days lately due to getting shot. I take a step and nearly drop her, but I grunt and shove my knee under her bottom to prop her up. I have to pause and take a breather, with most of her body weight supported on my knee, before taking another step. Wincing and making a face, I am grateful that her eyes are closed and she can't see me struggling pathetically like this.

It feels like her body weight is ripping my arm clean off my shoulder. Grunting and using only my good arm and my knee, I grasp her around the waist and toss her over my good shoulder. Exhaling in relief at the pressure being relieved from my arm, I carry her into the NovaTank tossed over my back like a sack of potatoes.

Real heroic, Cole.

As I try to gently place her down on my mattress, she groans and clutches her stomach. "I'm so hungry," she mumbles. "I want gingerbread. We can be Hansel and Gretel and find candy."

"I don't have candy or gingerbread, but I have some chocolate," I tell her, moving over to my cupboards. "My food is mostly tasteless MREs, but I have a few good things I can prepare… Scar?" I realize that she is fast asleep.

Moving over to the cupboard where I keep all my medicine, I take a Percocet out of the package and wash it down with some water to help my shoulder. I shut the door of my NovaTank so that the air conditioning can cool us down, before going to the freezer and taking out a few pieces of ice. I move over to Scarlett, and place an ice cube against her forehead. She doesn't even stir.

I add another ice cube into each of her armpits, as I remember reading somewhere that that's how you're supposed to lower someone's temperature when they have had too much sun exposure. She mumbles a little in her sleep, something about a witch and a fire, but she doesn't open her eyes. I stare at her for several minutes, rubbing an ice cube up and down her arms.

When the ice cube has disappeared, I move to her feet and undo the laces of her running shoes. Not just because it's odd and surely uncomfortable to wear running shoes while sleeping, but because I want to allow some of her body heat to escape through her feet. When I slide her shoes off, her knees jerk a little defensively. As I begin to peel her socks off, she whimpers in pain.

"Shit," I mutter when I see how raw and blistered her feet are. Just how far did this crazy girl walk? You would think her skin would be mostly protected by the cushiony running shoes—unless she took them off and went barefoot for some reason. I shake my head. While it is flattering that she did this to herself to get to me, I hate seeing her injured and I feel extremely guilty. I feel like faking my own death was just a test, or attention-seeking behavior, which isn't true. I did this for my own reasons, and not to punish her.

Still, seeing her hurt like this makes me have second thoughts about my decisions. Maybe I should have just gone to Washington D.C. instead of coming out here to the desert. Maybe I should have flown out there to confirm whether she was getting married before jumping to conclusions and getting depressed. Maybe I didn't need to take such drastic action.

But I don't regret this. I don't regret being here. I needed this desert as much as I needed her.

Rushing back to my medical supplies, I grab some antiseptic liquid, ointment, and bandages to treat her blisters. Out here, in the middle of nowhere, every little injury feels a lot more dangerous. We can't just drive for twenty minutes, or even an hour to get help. It takes a lot of difficult, slow maneuvering to get the NovaTank out of the mountains, and even then, the closest hospital or doctor's office is probably hours away.

As I sit at the foot of the bed and begin tending to her wounds, I see her facial muscles twitch in pain at the burning feeling of the antiseptic against her blisters. Something suddenly occurs to me.

"Scar, did you see the envelope in my desk that I left for you?" I ask her. When she does not respond, I continue speaking softly. "I found your family. You have a biological brother named Liam Larson living in New York, and both of your parents are alive. Can you believe it? All these years of not knowing who abandoned you, and now you can finally get answers. You have a real family somewhere out there. Do you want to meet them? I didn't give permission to the genetic testing company to release your personal information yet because I wanted to discuss it with you."

She mumbles incoherently in response. I'll have to tell her again later. Carefully applying antibiotic ointment to her blisters, I cover them lightly with bandages to keep them clean.

Getting up from her bedside, I move over to my writing desk, where my mostly empty and decidedly boring journal sits. I am compelled by the urge to write a new entry. Grabbing my pen, I glance at Scarlett, and study her sleeping form for several minutes. Finally, after chewing on my lip thoughtfully, I lower my pen to scribble a few words.

Now my journal looks a little like this:

Day One: Sleep.
Day Two: Sleep.
Day Three: Sleep.
Day Four: Sleep.
Day Five: There's a girl here. Sleeping in my bed. And I think it's my wife.

Loretta Lost

She looks exactly like my wife. Am I going crazy?
Did I take too many painkillers?
Note to self: Stop taking so many painkillers.

Chapter Seven

Sophie Shields, 2016

There isn't enough water in my brain.
It aches.

A person's brain should be like a juicy grape, ripe on the vine, but mine is just a shrunken, shriveled raisin, rattling around in my skull. It's a wonder I can think and feel this at all.

I've been slipping in and out of consciousness for a few hours now. I've been hearing words being spoken to me, but I'm not quite sure who is speaking. I hear all sorts of voices. I see all sorts of people. It's difficult to move. It's difficult to even keep my eyes open.

"Here," someone is saying to me, while pressing something ceramic into my hands. "Water isn't enough. You need electrolytes."

"Zack?" I murmur. "I don't want your stinking electrolytes."

"No, Scar. It's me. It's Cole."

I feel his hand on my forehead. His large, warm hand, brushing my hair away from my face. I sigh. "Okay. I want your electrolytes," I tell him.

He laughs softly as he brings the cup to my lips, and pours something sweet down my hoarse throat. It hurts to swallow. I drink as much as I can before pushing the liquid away.

"How are you feeling?" he asks me. "I made some mac and cheese, if you think you can eat."

Opening my eyes, I peer at him dizzily. "Cole. Are you really here?" I reach out to touch his face, tracing a deep scar with several stitches along his cheekbone. "Did I die in the desert?"

"No," he tells me as he moves to fiddle with a thermostat, possibly turning up the AC. "You're sweating a lot, Scar. I'm a little worried. Do you think we should go to the hospital? It's a long drive, so I should probably start now."

"Hospital? Why?"

"I think you have heat stroke."

Reaching for his arm, I tug him closer to me with a smile. "No. But you can give me heat stroke," I say as I begin pulling off his shirt.

"Scarlett," he says in surprise, grabbing my wrists. "This isn't a joke."

"It's a dream," I tell him. "I'm just dreaming, like always, and when I wake up, you'll be gone. So let's make the most of it, while we're here."

"This isn't a dream, love. It's like you have this massive fever on steroids. Do you think you can get up and come into the bathroom with me?

We can run cold water over you, and see if it cools you down."

Turning away, I feel myself getting pulled back into darkness. "You're boring, and I'm tired," I complain as I drift back to sleep.

I find myself stirring, waking up from a deep sleep.

It is dark. Yawning and stretching, my hand collides with someone's skin. I feel the skin curiously, trying to determine its owner. "Cole?" I whisper.

The skin moves.

The person possessing the skin moves on top of me, raking his hands all over my body. His fingernails are sharp and scratchy, like thorns. My heartbeat quickens. I squint to try and see who it is, but there are only shadows. All I feel is his skin against mine. A leathery old skin, thin and wrinkled, with jagged bones just beneath the surface.

"My darling girl," says the man in a breathless voice, as he slowly clamps a hand around my neck. His fingers are stiff and brittle as digging into my windpipe. "How many years has it been since I've touched you?"

"Benjamin," I whisper.

"Is that any way to speak to me?" he asks, with hurt and disappointment. "I adopted you, Serena. I'm your father now. You should call me Papa."

When I feel his wet, fleshy tongue licking my face, raking over my lips, nose and eyelids, a scream is ripped from my throat. The clammy feeling of his saliva being drooled all over my skin makes me shiver violently, like I have just heard nails on a chalkboard.

He continues to lick my face, like a dog, spreading his saliva all over my eyes, and my lips, until I am choking in his saliva. I am drowning in it. I scream and squirm, trying to get free.

"Scarlett!" Cole says, from somewhere in the distance. "Wake up! Come on, wake up! It's just a dream. Just another nightmare, love."

I find that he is lightly slapping my cheeks.

When I rip my eyes open, I see the look of concern on his face. I am panting heavily.

There is a wet washcloth on my forehead, soaked in cold water. It is dripping all over my skin. I rip it off in disgust, throwing it at Cole with a sob. It must have been this washcloth that made me dream of Benjamin's saliva. Ugh. Disgusting.

Cole sits beside me and gathers me up into his arms, holding me close. I feel a strange sense of déjà vu, like he has done this for me through many nightmares. And I have done this for him.

The familiar sensation of his arms around me is soothing, and begins to help me calm down. My breathing slows, and my heart stops straining to beat right out of my chest.

"You were dreaming about him again?" Cole asks.

I nod as I press my forehead into his chest. "Yeah."

He runs a hand over my hair. "We're dozens of miles away from every living person, Scar. He can't get to you way out here. I'll take care of you."

Clutching his arm, I nod gratefully. These nightmares have always bothered me, but I guess the dehydration, combined with seeing Benjamin recently…

At least Cole knows. At least he understands.

I don't have to explain myself to him.

"Do you think you can eat something?" he asks me gently. "We have lots of food. Please try to eat something, honey."

Why is he calling me that? It makes me feel like a child. My face screws up in frustration. Did he used to call me that, ages ago? I don't think so. I can't remember. I'm only one year younger than him, so I don't need any of his condescending diminutives.

Is that what he called some other woman? Is that what he called Annabelle? Or maybe Brittany?

I'll be damned if I allow Cole to lump me in with all of his other women, and recycle the same basic, boring terms of affection for me. Doesn't he know who I am?

Do you even know? Who are you, exactly? Who am I?

Pushing him away, I let my head fall back onto the pillow, closing my eyes. My stomach growls, but I am too tired and sore to move. Just a little more sleep.

Maybe I'll wake up if he can remember the proper way to address me. But I can't remember, either. What did we used to call each other? What was my name? I think it was Scarlett. But even that wasn't really my name.

As I drift off to sleep, I see various driver's licenses and passports swirling in my mind.

What the hell is my name? What was my name before all of this? Before Sophie, or Scarlett, or Serena? Before people called me all these various terms. Honey, baby, sweetie, *darling* little girl.

I can't remember. If I don't know what to call myself, how can he?

The passports all disintegrate, turning into ash.

I never traveled that much, anyway.

Chapter Eight

Sophie Shields, 2016

Sitting up suddenly in bed, I find myself alert and clearheaded. My dehydration headache is gone, and I feel like myself again. Looking down at my reddened arms, I see that my sunburnt skin looks ridiculous, but I don't care. When I try to move my legs, I feel that the muscles are all very sore, and I see that the blisters on my feet are loosely wrapped with bandages. Cole is sitting a few feet away at the writing desk which doubles as a kitchen countertop, and he seems to be sketching something intently. He must be designing a new building.

I inhale with contentment. He doesn't need to work anymore. He's legally dead, and free from the rat race. But architecture is so deep in his blood that he can't just turn it off at will.

Throwing my feet off the side of the bed, I stand up and stretch, examining the mobile home. I wasn't lucid enough to really study the design of the structure before. I walk up and down the length of the small house, opening doors to examine multi-functional closets and to check out the surprisingly stylish bathroom. My eyebrows lift at the sight of the luxurious steam shower with multiple jets to surround the body, and comfortable seating in the chamber that allows it to double as a bath or hot tub.

Turning back to Cole, I see the smug look on his face. "Do you like it?" he asks.

I roll my eyes at his arrogance. He knows I'm impressed and he wants to rub it in my face. Classic Cole. My stomach growls and I walk briskly over to the kitchen area and begin opening cabinet doors.

"Where's my mac and cheese?" I ask.

"It's in the microwave, in case you want to heat—"

I have yanked open the microwave before he finishes speaking, and pulled the saran wrap off the bowl. Using the plastic fork he left in the bowl, I begin shoveling the cold pasta into my mouth, barely chewing before I swallow.

"Jeez, Scar, at least heat it up first!" he complains, hurt that I'm not enjoying his masterpiece as intended.

"It's delicious," I say with my mouth full, between bites. "Now get me more food. Any food, fast." I sit down on the bed and continue to stuff macaroni into my face until the bowl is clean. Then I scrape the bits of dried cheese off the bottom of the bowl and close my eyes as I savor it. "Mmm, that was really good. What else do you have?"

Cole has opened a compartment in the floor of the mobile home that I hadn't seen before. "I have military MREs mostly, but I've also got some nicer ones from Mountain House that take a few minutes to heat up…"

Reaching into the compartment, I stick my hand in an open cardboard box and pull out the first package I touch. Ripping it open, I use the included spoon to ravenously devour the contents of the pouch with no regard to the taste.

I just need *calories*.

"I forgot you had such dreadful table manners," Cole says playfully.

Glaring at him, I consider throwing something at his head, but I am still so hungry. There are only a few bites left. I don't even know what I'm eating, but I don't care.

"The food is only going to last us a couple months," Cole says. "I have about a year's supply, but with you here, it will go faster. At some point, I'll probably have to drive over to the house and order another year's supply, along with any medicine we might need."

When I finish swallowing the last bite, I sigh with the satisfaction of having a full belly. "You know that I'm not going to be this hungry on a daily basis. I just had an *unusually* strenuous couple of days with a lot more exercise than usual."

I am digging back into the box for another pouch of food when I hear Cole clear his throat.

"So you don't think that we'll be doing any strenuous activities?" he asks me innocently. "We don't have television here, you know. How can you be absolutely sure you won't be getting *a lot* of regular exercise?"

Glancing up at him, I see the mischievous boyish smile on his face.

"Well, that depends," I answer coyly. "Do you have any books?"

"Books? I'm afraid not," he says with mock sadness. "You see, I'm not that fancy sort of fellow who reads a lot of books."

I lift my eyebrow as I grab another pouch of food and sit back up on the bed. I get the feeling he's roleplaying with me. "Not a single one?"

"'Fraid not," he says with a helpless shrug. "You see, I'm just a rugged mountain man, used to manual labor with his calloused hands. I ain't never read me no books. Wasn't expectin' no fine young ladies with edumucation and book learnin' to wander over my way."

"No?" I say, trying very hard to keep myself from laughing.

"No." He closes the floor compartment of the mobile home and moves closer, circling his hands around my ankles. "I'm afraid I don't have much in the way of sophisticated entertainment for a cosmopolitan girl like you. But I reckon I know how to keep you entertained in other ways."

"Do you, now?" I ask him.

He slides his hand up and down my calves.

"Sure. Out here in the country, us cowboys know how to pass the time when we're not riding horses and... chasing cows?"

"Oh, is that what cowboys do?" I say teasingly. "It sounds so dangerous. You must be so brave."

"I am," he says, sliding his hands over my thighs. "It's hard, physical work that gets you all sweaty. Would you like me to show you? I bet I can make you forget you ever read a book in your life."

He's looking at me in a way that makes my stomach do flip-flops. I try to seem unaffected. "That's a lot of big talk, cowboy. You better not disappoint me."

Pushing my knees apart, he moves between them and stares directly into my eyes for several seconds. My throat goes dry as he slides his hands into my hair to drag my face down to his. When his lips meet mine, I sigh against him, and the MRE pouch in my hand falls to the side, forgotten. I allow my arms to reach out tentatively, colliding with his chest, his shirt, and finally wrapping tightly around his neck. My mind becomes a hazy fog as I sink into his kiss.

He lets his hands move lower to grab my bottom, dragging me flush against his body so that I can feel his warmth radiating through my jeans. He bites my lower lip gently before kissing down my neck, nibbling gently and being careful to avoid the sunburned skin. One of his hands moves to grasp and knead my breast while he kisses me, and I

93

moan and tighten my arms around his neck.

He pauses, and I feel his breath leaving his body in a sharp burst.

I release him and pull away, looking at his face. He's in pain.

Looking at his neck where I was holding him, I pull his shirt aside and examine the bandage on his shoulder. There is a little spot of blood visible through the fabric.

"Cole!" I exclaim with worry. "You were shot here? How bad was it?"

"Not bad at all," he assures me. "It didn't even hit an artery. It just tore up my muscle and got lodged in my shoulder blade, but it was easily removed."

"Lodged in your shoulder blade?" I ask him in horror.

"But I'm fine!" he says, patting the spot lightly before reaching out to rub my upper arms reassuringly. "Don't worry. The doctor said I might have some nerve damage and need physical therapy, but I don't. Every part of my body is in working order. *Every part.*"

"For god's sake, Cole," I say, deftly standing up and slipping out of his grasp. "You better be careful or we could tear all your stitches."

"I would be happy if you tore all my stitches," he says, advancing on me. "I've never made love to a CIA agent before. Is it just like the movies?"

Sighing, I feel a pang of guilt that I haven't gotten back in touch with my boss. "You probably will never find out. I went AWOL and off the grid, and I've probably lost my job by now. I've been such a bitch to my wonderful boss."

"No one in their right mind would ever fire you, Scarlett. You're brilliant." He smiles, moving closer to me and hooking his fingers in the belt bucks of my jeans. "I've heard a lot of good things about this Sophie Shields person. I'd love to meet her."

"Hey, you know what," I tell him suddenly, feeling very hot and sticky. I lift my hands to itch at my sunburn. "I just realized that I smell gross. Do you mind if I take a shower in your luxury hydrotherapy spa-sauna-steam-waterfall thing?"

"Go right ahead," he says, with a grin. "Best shower of your life, I guarantee it."

"I'm sure it would be if my skin wasn't all peeling off. Thanks for making me walk a billion miles in the hot sun to find you, by the way. I'm still sore about that."

"You should let me make it up to you. I bet I can make the long walk worthwhile," he says, undoing the button and zipper of my jeans. He slides his fingers under my clothes, gently cupping my sex, and allowing his warmth to seep through my skin. "Besides, it makes sense to get really dirty before you can get clean."

I breathe heavily, unconsciously pressing myself against his hand, but then I remember everything and pull away abruptly. "Hey, do you have a razor? The last time I shaved my legs was for your funeral. Thanks for making me attend your funeral, by the way. You have a lovely tombstone. Did you know it says you were an extraordinary husband? *Extraordinary!* Nobody even bothered to ask *your wife* if she thought that word was accurate. But consider this: would an extraordinary husband pretend to be *dead* and make his poor wife cry for days? I'm not so sure!"

"Scar…" he says gently, with an apology in his voice.

Cole is damned good at apologies and explanations. So since I can't stand here and listen to him apologize or explain without forgiving him almost instantly, I turn my back and walk into the bathroom, slamming the door behind me. There. Let him feel guilty for a few minutes.

Chapter Nine

Sophie Shields, 2016

Pulling off my shirt, I wince at the pain as the fabric scrapes over my scaly, peeling sunburn. Next, I reach behind myself to unhook my bra, and glancing into the mirror, I am vastly annoyed to see a perfect, white imprint of the bra straps on my otherwise red back. I guess I must have fallen asleep on my stomach, and my shirt offered little protection.

Growling in frustration, I rip the bra off, followed by my jeans and underwear. Last, I gently pull the bandages off my feet before stepping into the shower. It takes me a minute to figure out how to open the chamber, which has a watertight seal and high-quality glass. As I shut the door behind me, I am keenly aware of how much my skin is burning as it is exposed to the air. My feet hurt, my legs hurt, and everything generally hurts. I can't wait to get some cool water on my skin to rinse off the dirt.

But when I begin pressing buttons to turn on the water, nothing happens.

There are a lot of buttons. Like, I swear this shower has more buttons than some skyscraper elevators. The buttons are also very fancy, with silver LED lights surrounding each little bubble. I punch a few marked with various symbols for water. One looks like a snowflake, which I assume means cold, one looks like a gust of wind, which I assume means steam, and one looks like a waterfall, while another looks like an explosion of water from all angles.

Nothing is happening.

Getting annoyed, I begin punching all the buttons. Why is this not working? I am usually the person who figures this sort of shit out. Do I need to hack into this shower to get some damn water on my body? I am startled by a voice coming out of the user interface.

Yes. There are actually speakers in this shower.

"Are you having some trouble in there?" Cole asks cheerfully.

I roll my eyes and exhale in exasperation, before hitting the button next to the speakers. "Why is there an intercom in your shower, Cole?"

His voice filters through at once. "While we originally designed the NovaTank for NASA, it might be many years before those applications can be realized. They are testing a few out in simulations as we speak, but we were also designing a second model for use by the military, especially in rescue or aid missions, or disaster zones. The durability is unmatched by most emergency vehicles. So, the idea is that if someone is taking a shower and the Nova comes under fire, or if enemies seem to be approaching, you can tell your partner what's happening from the driver's seat so that he get out of the shower quickly to assist you."

I cock my head to the side, curiously. "That's really neat. How does the vehicle detect if enemies are approaching?"

"I was hoping you could help me with those features."

"Hmmm," I say thoughtfully. "Maybe some infrared or sonar… Cole! Don't distract me. How do I use the damn shower?"

"Do you want me to come in and show you?" he asks.

Sighing, I shrug in defeat. "Sure! But no peeking."

When he enters the bathroom, I step back and use my arms to cover myself modestly. He enters and presses a single button, which begins the flow of a few *extremely* gentle streams of water. They feel like a soft caress. I sigh gratefully. He presses another button to make the temperature a little warmer.

"Why couldn't I get it?" I complain. "I swear I pressed that button."

He turns to me with a smile. "I may or may not have turned off the water while you were undressing, in hopes that I could offer some technical assistance to a certain sexy computer engineer who has never needed technical assistance in her life."

"You asshole!" I say, sacrificing modesty to smack him in the arm.

"I put the pressure on a low setting so it wouldn't hurt your sunburn. Is it okay?"

"It's perfect," I tell him honestly. Hesitating, I brush some of the wet hair out of my face, glancing down with a sudden shyness. "Do you want to join me?"

He looks at me in surprise. "Yes." Reaching for the hemline of his shirt, he pulls it up over his head, but winces at the pain of moving his shoulder that way. I reach out to help him, tugging the shirt up over his back and over his muscled arms. I can't help staring at his golden-brown torso in awe for a second, before reaching down to help him remove his pants.

When he steps into the shower and turns to close the door behind him, I see the crescent moon and star tattoo on his good shoulder, and I reach out to trace it with my fingertips. Familiar ink etched on familiar skin. Memories come rushing back so hard it steals my ability to breathe. For perhaps the first time since I arrived here, the reality of what's happening is beginning to sink in. Cole is here. I'm here with Cole.

I guess I thought I'd never see him again.

All those years ago, I screwed up. I walked out on him, when he really didn't deserve that. He'd always been there for me. I just couldn't deal with all the real emotions, and how serious things were getting between us. I was completely, insanely head over heels in love with him, and afraid of losing him every single day. Afraid of something happening to screw it all up, because my whole life, things have only ever gotten all screwed up for me.

So I screwed it all up myself, trying to preemptively avoid getting hurt.

And I ended up hurting both of us anyway.

When Cole turns to face me, there is so much tiredness and pain in his dark eyes that it's difficult to bear. The young boy I knew all those years ago was so full of strength and energy that nothing could ever slow him down, intimidate him, or wear him out. I know he's been through a lot lately, but it's still shocking to see the toll that life has taken on him. He's definitely gotten older. There are streaks of grey in his hair, and he's only 29. I guess I just always thought that my Cole was made of steel. He was always taking care of me, and being so larger-than-life that I never realized that he was just a vulnerable young boy under all that charisma and bravado.

He kept all his issues buried deep, so no one else would have to worry. He protected us all.

I wish I had protected him a little better. Swallowing down a lump of regret, I reach up to touch the scar on his cheek.

"Are you sure that you can let your stitches get wet?" I ask him. "Isn't it better to let yourself heal a little longer and avoid water?"

"Maybe," he says softly, reaching out to trace the rivulets of water falling down my stomach. "But I just want to be close to you. I'm a little afraid that one day I'll wake up, and you'll be gone. I've been trying not to sleep since you got here, so that I can stop you from leaving if you try. But just in case you manage to outsmart or outmaneuver me— which you always do—I want to spend every waking moment with you, while I can. I'm sorry, I know this is pathetic. But I can't bear the thought of you being in a different room, even just to shower. I was just pacing back and forth out there, wondering if there was some way you could escape, even though I know this room has no exits."

"Cole," I say softly, stepping close to him and resting my cheek against his chest. I feel his arms go around my back, possessively holding me against him. "I understand. That's how I felt my whole life, about everyone I ever cared about. If my mother could just toss me aside, then why would anyone else want to keep me? I just... I'm sorry. It's just something I've always done. Running away."

"But I thought you knew I would never leave you," he says, letting his fingers get tangled up in my wet hair. "I tried so hard to show you that I would always be there."

There is a long silence in the shower,

punctuated only by the noises of water falling gently on our bodies. Tears begin sliding from my eyes, and I try to hold my breath. It feels like there is a balloon in my chest, filled with daggers, and if I don't let some of the air out, it's going to explode all over my insides and destroy me.

"I was pregnant," I whisper hoarsely, trying to hold my shoulders very still so that he can't tell that I'm crying. I wrap my arms around his middle and cling to him tightly, letting the water wash away my tears and secrets. "I'm so sorry. I was afraid."

Feeling his body stiffen in my arms, I hold my breath. I am terrified. I have visions of him dragging me by the hair and tossing me out of his trailer completely naked, and locking me outside to burn in the sun. I imagine him refusing to speak to me again. Pulling away slightly, hesitantly, to look at his face, I flinch when he clamps his hands around my shoulders.

"What did you do?" he asks angrily, his fingers digging into my shoulders. "What did you do? God, Scar! You said it was a false alarm in your letter. You said you were just late, due to the stress of deciding whether to take that job at the CIA. What the hell did you do?"

I shake my head, hating the look on his face. "Don't worry. I didn't..."

"Scar! Why the fuck didn't you tell me?" He lowers his head and takes a few deep, ragged breaths, as though his lungs are failing. I can feel his whole body trembling with rage. There is water from the shower dripping off his hair, obscuring his face, and for a moment, I am certain he's going to hurt me. "Did you have the baby?" he asks in a whisper, sounding completely brokenhearted. "We told each other everything. How could you keep this a secret? Please god, tell me that you didn't have an abortion. Please tell me you didn't give it up. Please tell me… just tell me…"

"No," I say softly, feeling my knees grow unsteady. I pull away from him, leaning my forehead against the shower wall for support. "I wasn't well, Cole. I couldn't eat, I couldn't sleep. I just stayed in my motel room all day, crying and vomiting. I lost the baby, pretty early on. Before I took the job. I only took the job because I couldn't go back to you after that. I was… afraid it would happen again. I was afraid, because I love you, and I can't control myself around you, and I just want you so much, all the time, even now..."

He places a kiss on the back of my shoulder as his arms wrap around me, just beneath my breasts. "You should have told me. I would have taken care of you, kept you healthy. I would have gotten you help, if you needed it. We always knew these things would be challenging for us. I just needed to be there with you, Scar. How could you exclude me like that? I was your best friend. I am your best friend. I understand if you wanted to run away, but why couldn't you just take me with you?"

"I didn't know what you really wanted," I confess softly. "After so many years of just being friends, just being brother and sister, I didn't know if you even wanted to be with me. I asked you a couple times. I asked you for more. Cole, be with me. Cole, just be my boyfriend. Be my husband. Dude, we're already married, what the fuck. Just make it *real*. And you kept putting it off. Maybe after we graduate. Maybe when things are more stable. Maybe someday, when we're older. Maybe, maybe, maybe."

"We were so young, Scar. I was scared, too."

"I needed you," I tell him tearfully, "in every way! Do you know how I felt? Do you have any idea how I felt…" I pause, trying to catch my breath, and lift my hand up to touch the necklace. "When I read your stupid letter, and I saw that you really wanted to be with me? I thought you were dead. Actually dead. And I thought we'd wasted all that time."

"God, Scar," he says, pressing his face into the back of my shoulder. "I was a fucking idiot. I was terrified of hurting you. I was terrified of us. I just wanted to do the right thing, so badly. I wanted to do right by you, so that we'd never be apart. And I made you leave anyway."

His arms are wrapped around my ribs so tightly that it's difficult to breathe. My diaphragm can't expand. But I don't need air; I only need him. I need him close to me, pressed against my body like this. I need him to understand me. "Cole, I just thought you saw me as a friend, or a sister. I really did. I tried really hard to seduce you sometimes, you know? To make you see me differently."

"Oh, believe me, I know. You didn't have to try, Scar."

"But I did. You only had sex with me if there was alcohol involved, and you apologized the next day profusely like you'd made some huge mistake, and you didn't really mean it. Do you know how that tore me apart? I just wanted to be yours. For real."

"Jesus, Scar. We slept beside each other almost every night. We were so close..."

"And that only made it harder. It was *almost* perfect, but you were just holding back. You were *everything* to me, except the one thing I needed you to be. And I tried so hard to make you change your mind..." I pause, shutting my eyes tightly. "This doesn't excuse what I did—leaving you. I was the biggest bitch on earth to you, Cole. I hate myself every day for what I did. But I didn't run away from Cole, my friend, or Cole, my brother. I kept writing him letters. I just ran away from Cole, my half-assed lover. But maybe... maybe if I had known all the shit you said in that letter, maybe I wouldn't have ran away when I found out I was pregnant. Maybe I would have known that things were going to be okay. I would have known that you were going to be there, the way I needed you to be. As my man. As my husband. I just always felt like I needed you more than you could give. I needed you more than you wanted to give. But if I had seen that letter, and known you felt the same, all those years—I would have just said *today*. *Today* is the day that we need to be ready, Cole. Please let's grow up and be adults now. And love each other."

"Scar," he says, releasing me and stepping away.

Without his warmth, I'm suddenly cold, and I turn around to look at his face. The hurt written on his features is too much to bear.

"Are you saying," he asks slowly, "that if I hadn't been such a fucking idiot, maybe we could have been happy together now? As a family? Maybe with an adorable little four-year old daughter running around?"

I feel like I've had the air knocked out of me. The shower begins to spin in my vision. I see that little girl, and all the hopes and dreams I push down so hard, and never let myself believe. I see myself in that girl. I see my own childhood, when I was four, and no one loved me. But I know her life would have been different. She would have been always smiling, always the happiest little girl in the world, because Cole was her daddy. And of course he would have taken care of her, because he always took care of me. She would have been happy. She would have been loved. She would have never gone to bed hungry, not for a single night.

We were millionaires, after all.

I lost that little girl. I stole her from us. Grasping one of the various shower nozzles for support, I struggle to stand. I struggle to breathe.

"Just tell me," I say to Cole hoarsely. "That

you didn't mean any of the words in the letter. Tell me that you changed your mind since then. You grew to just think of me as a sister."

"Are you fucking kidding me?" He looks at me with wide eyes, shaking his head slowly. "Scarlett, I don't remember exactly what I wrote. But I've been slowly dying without you for years. Let me be perfectly honest: I have changed my mind. Because the fifteen-year-old piece of shit who wrote that letter didn't love you a fraction of the amount that I have grown to obsessively, compulsively, neurotically love you over the years. Do you even realize that I just faked my own death and gave away my entire fortune because I thought you were marrying some other jackass? It was basically a fucking temper tantrum! And it worked, because you're here with me—not with him. So I'm happy. And part of me is glad that you were upset when you thought I was dead, because you deserved to suffer! I'm vengeful—and I want you to feel the pain that I felt when you left me. So maybe I pretended to die just so you would see how it feels."

"Cole," I say, crying and shaking my head. "Stop. Just stop."

"And you want to know the very worst part?" he asks me, stepping closer. "Here we are, standing together naked in a shower. You are so sunburnt that you look like a fucking cherry tomato, but you're still the most gorgeous woman I've ever seen. I haven't been with anyone else since we got married, Scar. I lied when I said that it was all pretend. I was pretending it was pretend. I wanted you every minute of every day, and I had to shut it off, because I feared that passion so much. I want you right now. Can't you tell how much I want you? Couldn't you always tell? And you just told me how you lost our baby—and kept it a secret. Do you have any idea how that breaks my heart? Not just because that was my baby, but I hate the fact that you had to go through that alone. What if I lost you, Scar? I should have been there. You never have to be alone in this lifetime, as long as I'm breathing. Thank god you know better than to trust a death certificate. I'm rambling on like a fucking idiot."

He takes a deep breath. "Really, all I want to do is grab you and kiss you and say it's going to be okay. But I want to say even more than that, because I'm a fucking disgusting man. Do you know how hard I have to try to act civilized and restrain myself around you? I just want to tell you we'll try again. Right now in this damn shower, I'll make love to you until you can't walk. I'll make you pregnant again, you better believe it, and this time we'll do it right. We'll have that little girl—or boy, I guess it's okay if it's a boy—and just be really fucking happy like we were supposed to be from the start. I'll show you, Scar. I can be your lover, and your man, and your husband, and not hold back. Not hold anything back." He hits a button on the shower interface that makes a bunch of the nozzles stop spraying and retreat into the walls. He advances on me, pinning me up against the shower wall, and pressing his hardness against my body as he puts his lips against my ear. "I'll fuck your brains out, Scarlett. I'll fuck you so hard you scream loud enough for this whole desert to hear you. Would you like that? Because I just don't care anymore. What do we have to lose? We already lost each other. We lost the baby. I lost my fucking job. We lost everything. So let's make it better. Let's make a new baby, right here, right now. I dare you. I dare you to do this with me."

I shake my head, unable to respond. Tears won't stop falling from my eyes, and my dehydration headache is returning. It's too late. We really have lost everything. We're both too late. He is nudging my thighs apart with his knees and pressing against me a little too aggressively. I find myself sobbing, because he doesn't feel like my Cole right now. He feels crazed, and understandably so after the news I've just given him. What have I done to this man I love? I've destroyed him. Why have I said any of these things? Why did I have to talk so much?

"Scar," he says, putting his fingers under my chin to lift my face. "What do you say? Are you ready? Let's make a baby. But if it's a boy, we have to try again to have another kid, because I really want a little girl so that I can show her Frozen and take her out for ice cream."

I can't take this anymore. I push him away with all my strength as I begin to sob so violently that I can no longer stand up. My knees crumple and my back slides down the wall of the shower until my butt lands on the tiles. I let my body sag to the side as the sobs shake my chest, and I gasp for air and breathe in water from the shower that is pouring down my face. I cough on the water as it fills my throat.

Or maybe I'm just drowning in my own tears.

Cole is immediately at my side, crouching over me and whispering soothing words. He places kisses all over my face and tries to coax me back to him. I can feel myself slipping away, deeper and deeper inside myself. I push his hands away weakly. I can't cope with this. I don't want to cope with this. It hurts. It hurts so much that it rips my insides apart, and it hurts far more than the miscarriage did. I remember the pain like it was yesterday, but I also remember the pain magically shutting off.

I need that now. I need to shut it all off.

I remember the memories. The memories of the things I had forgotten, and how as soon as I began to remember, my mind would shut it all down. I can shut it all down, with the flip of a switch.

I can save me from me. I just have to give her permission.

I've been fighting her back for so long. But I need her now. I had forgotten how much I need her.

I need her to help me survive this man, and these memories.

111

Chapter Ten

Cole Hunter, 2016

"Scar? Scar, look at me. Come back to me. I'm sorry. I'm so sorry. Please." I cup her cheek and tilt her head up so I can look in her pale blue eyes. But her head is limp, and her eyes are empty. Shit, what have I done? What did I say? "Scar," I say hoarsely, shaking her shoulders gently. "I'm sorry. I was just angry. I'm just… it's so emotional, being close to you again. I feel like a fucking stupid fifteen-year-old boy. Please don't be scared. Don't go away."

But it's too late. She's not responding to me. She has totally shut down. I exhale in defeat, moving to sit beside her in the shower stall. The floors are hard and unpleasant to sit on, so I reach to my side and struggle to lift her onto my lap. It kills my shoulder, but I clench my teeth together to brace myself against the pain. Cradling her in my arms, I let her head fall against my neck, and I know that I'm holding her for my own comfort more than hers.

"I never realized how much holding back hurt you," I tell her, stroking her hair. "I was trying to avoid hurting you by holding back, you know? It was just the only strategy I could think of, to cement having us in each other's lives. I was just trying to do right by you, and not take advantage. But I never seem to do the right thing." I swallow. "Scar, I'm so sorry for all that stuff I just said. The baby stuff. I know I probably sounded like a monster. I know what you've been through, and I never wanted to hurt you. I never wanted to hurt you."

Rocking her gently, I place a lingering kiss on the top of her head. "I'm so sorry. I mean, it wasn't a lie, I do want us to have a baby. But not right this minute. I was just trying to do the opposite of what I've always done, saying 'maybe someday,' by saying 'right now.' I wanted you to know that I'm capable of change. But you also know that I'm not a spontaneous person, and I was just being ridiculous and insane. I mean, I just faked my own death—how the hell am I going to raise a kid? Where are we going to live? Here? I just gave away all my money. Okay, some of it was to you. But... I'm not father material anymore. Maybe I was six days ago. But I've screwed everything up, haven't I? I would need to get a decent fake identity, like you did. What job will I do? I loved my job. I loved my company. Maybe we can live in a small town, where no one knows us."

I hold her against me for several more minutes, thinking about everything. The wheels in my head are spinning out of control. When the shower turns off automatically to conserve water, I can still hear it falling all around me. It's so loud, now. All the colors and sounds inside my head are a cacophony. I was peaceful in my silent darkness, for a brief moment in time. Things were easy. I was dead to the world, but now I have to find a way to live again. I have lost my peace, but regained something greater. Love. I wouldn't trade the girl in my arms for anything. I will make this work, somehow. I am the one who messed it all up.

"Scar," I tell her softly. "You're kind of silly. How could you ever think I didn't want to be with you? I have given you my whole life. I always fulfilled the duties of a boyfriend or husband, emotionally. Sexually, I tried to hold back to prevent exactly the issue that ended up separating us. But I couldn't successfully hold back forever, and you knew that. You tortured me, on purpose. You had me completely wrapped around your finger, my love. I would have been anything for you. Friend, brother, boyfriend, lover, husband, even a goddamn circus clown. Do you want me to put on a clown costume and dance around and... do whatever clowns do? I swear, I will. You know that I will."

Sighing, I squeeze her naked shoulders gently.

"Also, I lied earlier. About the books. I was just goofing around, but of course I have books. I have a Kindle loaded up with hundreds of them. We have tons of power from the solar panels, so you can read to your heart's content."

Sitting in silence for another minute, she finally responds softly. "Really? You have books?"

"Yes," I say, my breath leaving my chest in a gust of relief. I hug her close. "So many books."

"Good. Cole? I'm sorry. I just needed a minute."

"I understand. I'm sorry I said all that—"

"Don't even worry about it," she says, standing up and stretching. There is something strange about her voice, and she seems suddenly very energized. She offers me a hand to help me stand, and I take it with my good arm. Once I am upright, she moves to grab a towel and wrap it around herself, studying herself in the mirror.

"You're right. I really do look like a cherry tomato."

"I may have exaggerated a little. You're more like a bottle of ketchup."

She laughs softly, grabbing another towel to dry off her hair. "Thanks."

"Scar, I appreciate you telling me all the stuff you said earlier. I never really knew the reason you went away. It kind of hit me like a Mack truck."

"Well, be prepared to get hit by a few more trucks," she says as she walks into the central room of the trailer and turns around to face me, crossing her arms under her chest. "I have some other bad news."

"Nothing can be worse than the reason you left."

"Really?" She narrows her eyes and gives me a scrutinizing stare. "I thought you had a better imagination than that, Cole. There are a lot of awful things in this world."

"You're worrying me," I tell her, as prickles of dread begins to creep up my back.

She nods, looking down to the floor. "Annabelle is dead."

I stare at her in disbelief for a few seconds. "No. Doctor Anna? My psychotherapist?"

"Yeah. I'm sorry."

"Jesus. She is… she was an amazing woman."

"I know. I hacked into your emails. I thought maybe you were in a relationship with her."

"We spent a lot of time together," I say softly, moving over to sit on the bed. I am still naked and wet from the shower, but that's hardly important. "Scar, what happened? Is it my fault? How did she die?"

She moves to sit by my side, and places a hand on my knee. "I don't know exactly. I just got the call while I was driving over here. It turns out she'd been dead for days."

"No," I say in refusal, reaching up to run my hands through my hair. "Are you absolutely sure?"

"Yes. The detective found her body at her clinic. She was murdered at work."

"But the clinic is so busy," I say in protest, trying to find any way to make this untrue. "How could no one find out for days?"

"Her secretary was calling clients and cancelling all the appointments."

I shake my head, unable to understand. "Brittany, right? Why would she do that?"

Scarlett closes her eyes briefly, leaning against my arm before responding. "Cole, her secretary's name was Brittany *Brown*."

"Oh, fuck," I say, putting both of my hands in my hair. I get up and begin pacing in the NovaTank. "Fuck, fuck, fuck. I didn't know, Scar. We never met her, did we? There were photographs in the house. Was she at my trial? I knew I didn't like the secretary, but I thought it was just because she always wore so much makeup. I mean, those extremely square eyebrows and all that crazy contouring. She was just trying way too hard. Why would she spend like three hours on her makeup every day when she's just a secretary?"

"Because she's also a serial killer," Scarlett explains with a shrug. "The makeup bothered me too, the first time I saw her. It was flawless. But it turns out that it might just be a type of disguise. Contouring can change the appearance of the facial structure. We didn't recognize her as Mr. Brown's daughter, after all."

Growing too tired to keep pacing, and too tired to put clothes on, I crawl over the little bed to lie on my back, behind Scarlett. I think about Anna, and everything I learned from her. She was a good woman. She was only targeted because she tried to help me.

Scarlett reaches for the blankets and tugs them over my naked lower half, before moving into the bed beside me and resting her head on my good shoulder. "I'm so sorry, Cole. I'm sorry that your girlfriend is dead."

I swallow a lump of emotion. "She wasn't my girlfriend, Scarlett. She was helping me get over my issues."

"What issues?"

"Losing you. The stuff we talked about in the shower. The stuff I did to scare you away."

Sliding closer, Scarlett pulls the blanket over herself as well, and rests her leg over my thighs. "You haven't lost me. I'm right here."

"But I keep hurting you," I tell her angrily. "You know what, I think that Anna was interested in me. I was just so emotionally unavailable and fucked up that she had to be my therapist instead of my lover. She knew that I was too unstable and… frankly, too much in love with you to offer her anything."

"And now she's dead," Scarlett tells me softly. "You could have had something wonderful with her, but now she's dead and you'll never know. It's too late."

I look at her in surprise. "Something wonderful, like what you have with Zack? I'm devastated that Anna's gone, but don't say shit like

118

that. I never wanted anyone but you, Scarlett."

"So don't make it too late for us," she says softly, placing her hand on my stomach, and tracing my abdominal muscles. "You nearly died, Cole. It isn't the first time. Then I nearly died finding you. Let's just be together from now on. In every way."

"I want nothing more," I tell her honestly. "That's what I was really trying to say, in the shower…"

"I know," she says with a smile, sliding her leg over my upper thighs, "I would like that, too. No more wasting time, right?"

There is something odd about the way she's behaving. "Scar?" I ask softly. "Are you okay?"

"I'm better now," she responds, slowly raking her leg up my naked body so that it grazes my penis and rests across my hips.

This makes my breath catch in my throat a little, and I gently hold her knee still.

Turning her head toward my skin, she places kisses on my tattooed shoulder, while letting her hand slowly slide up over my chest. "I missed you, Cole."

"I missed you, too," I tell her, groaning a little as her knee moves a little in my hand, causing her thigh to massage my hardening member. "Scar…"

She removes the towel she is wearing so that her body is naked as it rests against mine. She shifts her position a little so that she can place her lips near my ear, and she kisses my earlobe and bites it before whispering something quietly against my neck. "Didn't you say something about fucking my brains out?"

I draw in a breath sharply. Pulling away to look at her face, I see that familiar, frightening glint in her eyes. "You're not Scarlett."

"No," she responds. "Of course not. I'm the one who does what needs to be done." Shifting her weight to her knees, she sits on top of me, straddling my stomach. "Right now, I think that happens to be you."

Sighing, I place my hand on her thighs, a little sad that Scarlett felt the need to send in her pinch hitter. But this girl is an important part of Scarlett, and I love her, too.

"I didn't mean to hurt her with all that talk of making a baby," I try to explain. "I was just overwhelmed…"

"It's okay. She'll get over it. She's way too sensitive sometimes. You're not our enemy, and she knows that. She just needs to hide for a minute. And I don't mind the fresh air."

Looking up at Scarlett's face, I see that old familiar strength. I know this girl well, and we have a certain understanding. We have killed for each other. I reach up to touch her face, and let my hands fall down to her neck, before sliding them over her breasts, and the rest of her body. "I'm glad to see you. I didn't know if you were still inside her."

"Of course," she says with a small smile. "It's so warm and comfortable inside this body. You should join me." She scoots back to rub herself against my erection teasingly. "I miss feeling you inside me, Cole."

I close my eyes and groan, digging my fingers into her thighs. "Stop that. Scarlett's upset with me, and I don't think she wants this."

"Don't you think I know what she wants?" the girl says angrily, leaning forward to glare down at me. "She wants the same things I want, but she's too afraid to go after them. Do you know what a pain in the ass she's been lately? She keeps giving up. I'm always fighting so hard to get past her fears, but I can't do jack shit unless she lets me."

"What do you mean?" I ask her, reaching up to splay my fingers across her breasts. I gently close my fingers together, squeezing her nipples between them. It's so easy for me to touch this girl. I know her so intimately, and I'm never afraid with her.

She bites her lip as my hands massage her breasts. Then she looks down at me intently. "Cole, do you honestly think she's tough enough to walk that far in the blistering sun? She's pathetic. She kept sitting down to rest. She even passed out once. I just got up and kept going. By my calculations, she only walked for seven hours. That was her limit. I walked the other fifteen."

I blink. "Are you telling me you were walking for nearly twenty-four hours straight?"

"Well, it wasn't exactly *easy* to find you. Her phone died and I had to follow the map from memory. The first patch of water was a dud, and I got lost."

"Damn you," I say hoarsely. "Look at what you did to her! She's burned and blistered all over. You hurt her badly. She was so dehydrated."

The girl looks at me in shock before drawing her hand back and slapping me in the face. I cry out, because she slaps the cheek where I've been shot. "Really, Cole? Do you think she gives a crap about these sunburns? She put a gun to my head, did you know that? At your funeral, in front of Miranda and Mr. Bishop. Damn *you* for making her think you were dead, because she really wanted to join you. I fought so hard to stop her, but I can't take control. I can only make her finger hesitate on the trigger. I can't stop her from pulling it unless she lets me. She's getting stronger as she gets older."

"No," I say in refusal, my heart beating erratically. "She didn't really try to do that, did she?"

"Yes. Your house on Red Earth Lane—the ceilings are about eighteen feet, correct?"

I visualize the floor plan, and those ceilings. The number seems correct, so I nod.

"She was calculating whether throwing herself off the banister would get the job done when we didn't find you at the house. She thought about it several times on the way here. I'm part of her mind, Cole. I know when she's serious about something, and I had to find you to save her life. So don't you dare yell at me about some fucking sunburns."

As she speaks, I begin to remember all about this girl, and how much I admire her. "I'm sorry," I tell her, sitting up slightly so that I can wrap my arms around her and kiss her. "I know that you've always protected her more than anyone else. I should never have suggested otherwise."

"I never wanted her to leave you," the girl says with tears in her eyes. "I tried to stop her. I tried to make her call you from the motel room and tell you about the pregnancy, but she wouldn't let me."

"I know you did," I tell her, running my hands over her back. "You were always so honest with me. We understand each other."

She kisses me gently, and it feels different than it did in the past. This girl used to be pure fire and brimstone, but now she's a prisoner in her own body. She pulls away, looking at me as though she can read my thoughts.

"Serena is completely governed by fear," she says, "while I have no fear at all. What an odd pair we are, the two of us. She is definitely not well— after what happened with Benjamin, she can't even think about being pregnant without having a nervous breakdown. She couldn't even tell you about Annabelle, so I had to do it. I'm sorry for all the trouble she's given you."

"It's worth it all," I tell her, resting my forehead against hers. "You're here with me now, and that's all that matters. We'll get through everything else."

"I wish I could be here more," she says. "It's so difficult, helping her stand up when she keeps dragging me down. I keep fighting, Cole. People always say that you need to have hope and faith, but they are idiots. You make your own damn hope by fighting through obstacles. You need to have faith in yourself and your abilities. She thought you left clues for us to find you, but I just made up those clues to keep her going. And I kept fighting to get to you at all costs, so that she could have some hope. I refused to believe that you were gone, that anything could keep you away from me, even death."

She cups my face in her hands and smiles with an unearthly beauty and power.

"I swear to god, Cole. If you were really dead, I would have found a way to bring you back to life. You think this sunburn is bad? It's nothing. I would have walked through hell to find you. I've walked through fire for you before."

Her words wash over me, making my heart swell at the immensity of her love. I wish I could show her that I'm just as devoted to her. I find myself ignoring the pain in my shoulder as I grasp her thighs and pull her legs around me, positioning her hips so I can make love to her. I don't feel the need to ask her for confirmation of whether she wants this, because I can see the need in her eyes. Her words already pierce into my soul deeper than anything we could do with our bodies.

When I prod against her entrance, I find that she is already dripping wet, moving against me, and begging me with her hands, her mouth, the rocking of her hips. I plunge myself into her as I kiss her mouth, feeling her cry out against my lips. I dig my fingers into her waist, dragging her down against me and grinding my hips up against her to drive myself deeper.

She tilts her head back and cries out, and I use this opportunity to take one of her breasts into my mouth and suckle hard as I fuck her, beginning to grow more rhythmic with my motions. I pull her nipple gently between my teeth, causing her to gasp as I lift her hips up and down on my shaft. My shoulder pain is entirely forgotten.

"God, I missed you," I murmur hoarsely, clutching her against me with an achingly tight grip. I really never thought I'd hold her like this again.

My heart is pumping new blood wildly through my veins, and I feel like a brand new man. I don't know where this blood came from, or who it belonged to before it was mine, but I know it has never pumped so madly through anyone's body, or experienced such an emotional, hormonal surge of bliss.

This blood may have kept me alive, but that did not matter until this moment.

Now, I am finally living.

My shoulder is cramping up due to the difficulty of the position, but I keep going. I use my whole body to lift her, rocking back with my hips, and slamming her down to impale her as deeply as I can.

"Cole!" she gasps loudly, wrapping her hands

around my shoulders. Her fingers dig into my stitches. "Harder. Please."

Lifting her body against me with my good arm, I twist and lower her to the bed, following to rest my hips between her thighs. I continue to drive myself into her, as deeply as I can, and as forcefully as I can, feeling like a man possessed. She cries out and uses her legs to pull me closer, arching her back off the bed.

"Don't ever leave me again," I growl against her temple as our sweat mixes together. "I'm sick of being fucking patient with you. I should have just flown to D.C. and beat the shit out of Zack and dragged you home years ago. You're my woman."

"I wish you had," she says breathily. "Cole—slowly, slowly. We don't want to hurt her."

"Speak for yourself. Maybe I do want to hurt her a little," I say as I rest my weight on my elbow and wrap my other hand around her neck, constricting slightly. "She left me."

The girl moans a little and lifts her hips against me. I'm not afraid to be a little rough with her. She's not as fragile as Scarlett, although they share the same body.

"You can take it out on me," she says softly, tilting her chin up to bite my bottom lip. "Give me all your anger and rage. Take all your hate and hurt, and use it to fuck the shit out of me. Then you can give her your love."

I thrust and jerk my hips roughly against her, causing her to cry out. "Like this?"

"Yes," she says, closing her eyes.

I continue to drive myself into her, until I'm getting close. Then, as I see the ecstasy on her face, and her lips slightly parted, I slide a finger into her mouth, feeling the vibrations of her moan.

I can see that she's close, and it nearly sends me over the edge. But suddenly, I stop. A realization occurs to me, and it's terrifying.

"Wait," I say quietly. "Wait."

"What?" she gasps in annoyance. "Don't you dare stop, Cole Hunter. It's been years."

"Exactly. It's been years since I slept with you, not her. You're the one who got her pregnant."

She looks up at me, blinking in confusion. "What the hell? I'm not a hermaphrodite."

With an inhuman amount of resolve, I pull out and roll myself off her. I lay there on the small bed, panting. She whimpers beside me, grabbing my arm.

"Cole…"

I try to catch my breath and explain. "That's why she said there was always alcohol involved when we had sex. Because it was mostly you, wasn't it?"

"Yes. She shuts off sometimes, during sex. She doesn't want to remember it. That's partly why I exist—to protect her from that."

"I need to discuss it with her. I need her to be there when we're having sex, so she can make decisions. I don't want her to run away again."

"Cole, I don't think she *can* be there. She's

not capable."

"Was she there with Zachary?" I ask angrily.

"No," she says softly. "Zack lost a leg, and he was kind of embarrassed about his body, so he didn't usually want to have sex at all."

"I see. Look, I just don't want a repeat of the way things were. Is there any way we can fix this? Can we heal her? I did mention this situation to Anna a couple times, and she talked about 'integration.' Maybe you and Scarlett could *merge* and somehow…"

She sits up and moves away, with hurt on her face. "You want me to go away?"

"No, no, no."

"We're having sex and you just stop and tell me I need to be someone else? You talked to your shrink girlfriend about how to *fix* me?"

"Honey, you *are* someone else, most of the time. Can't you see how I feel? It's like I'm cheating on her with *you*. I feel like… this isn't what she wants. I don't have any condoms here, either. I don't know what the hell to do, but I sure as hell can't get her pregnant again without making sure I'm discussing it with the actual person who's going to have to sustain that pregnancy."

She puts her face in her hands. "Cole, please don't do this to me. I love you, and I'm happy. I'm happy just being near you. We're communicating, and fixing our issues. She just confessed a whole lot of shit to you. Don't demand that I change and be someone else before you can be with me. It might never happen. I might never change, and never be integrated or merged or whatever the fuck all that psychobabble says."

"I want us to be together," I tell her, moving to her side and hugging her close. "I'm not going back on that. I'm not letting you go again. You're mine, and I need you beside me, always. I need you in my bed, every night, for the rest of my life. Okay?"

"No," she says, shaking her head slowly. "We're a package deal. You heard her—she was upset at the whole brother-friend bullshit. You slept in the same bed with her for thousands of nights without touching her. She wanted more from you. And maybe sometimes, if you touch her, she gets scared and I come out, and then you're touching me. That's just how I am, Cole. That's who I am. I'm sorry if it's complicated. I can't control it. This is just how I survived, and this is how I keep surviving. There are still some days—like the last few days—when she wouldn't have survived without me."

"I know," I tell her.

"You don't know anything," she says, pushing me away and standing up. "There is nothing to fear. Every single person in this body loves you. Totally and completely. And if you start holding back on us again, like we're still in high school…" She smiles at me, a sadistic little smile that gives me a cold shiver of panic. "Maybe you don't deserve her, Cole. Maybe I shouldn't have brought her all the way out here. What do you think we are? Your little harem of sister wives, and you need to get permission from your first wife to be with me? You need to discuss it with her? She *just* said that she left because she wasn't sure you wanted to be her man. Maybe I'm not too sure you want to be *my* man."

"Calm down," I tell her, standing up and touching her arms. "Please…"

"Maybe I should poison her against you," she says with a growing smile. "Maybe I should take her back to Zack right now, and accept his marriage proposal just to spite you. Maybe I should let her see you for who you are, a fucking pussy who's scared to touch her!"

Grabbing her shoulders, I slam her body against the wall of my NovaTank, breathing heavily. "Stop!" I shout in her face. "Just stop. I love you, too. Every part of you. I named my company after *you,* not her. You're so strong, and resilient. You inspire me to be a better man. But she *is* delicate, and I'm just trying to do the right thing, so she doesn't get hurt. I'm protecting her, just like you. Please try to understand that."

I pause, reaching out to embrace her, and pressing a kiss against her eyebrow. "Please, don't make me an enemy. We've always been allies, and we always will. I don't care if everyone else on earth is against us—I need you on my team. Okay?"

She remains frozen for a moment, then she nods slowly.

"Help me, Snow. Help me," I say quietly. "Tell me how I can help her heal, so that if she gets pregnant again, it doesn't make her lose her mind. I don't think I can even discuss it with her openly—she always shuts down."

The girl nods in my arms, and takes my hand, leading me back over to the bed, to sit. Maybe it's because I used her name—something I rarely do—but she seems calmer. I feel like I've successfully diffused a bomb. It took me years to even figure out her name, because she considered it a great secret, a source of strength she didn't want to give away.

She breathes in deeply and exhales. "I apologize for getting angry like that, Cole. I know you mean well. I hate to betray Serena like this, but I will help you, for the sake of her health. You might want to write this down. I am never going to say any of it again, and I know you like making lists."

Chapter Eleven

Cole Hunter, 2016

Retrieving the bed sheet, she wraps it around herself like a toga and lifts the bottom to walk back and forth in the cabin. I hold my breath, enjoying the majesty of the way she moves. She has always reminded me of a goddess—although I could never quite put my finger on which one. Today, she is unquestionably Grecian. Every time I see her, she is slightly different. A destructive, screaming Kali, or a sensual, insatiable Aphrodite.

"I've considered this before," she says, "but I didn't think you would ever ask me. I didn't think it would be possible to heal such deep-seated damage, but you are making me think it might be necessary. So, we need to try to make it possible." She moves over to my desk in a flurry, grabbing a notebook and a pen and handing it to me.

"First of all," she says, "if you use any of this

information to hurt her, I will end you." Her smile is dangerous. "But not before giving you as much pain as I possibly can."

"Duly noted," I say with a solemn nod. "You know I would never hurt her intentionally."

She puts her face very close to mine and that familiar fire is back in her eyes. "Cole, there are no loopholes. You can't hurt her unintentionally, either," she says with a hiss. "Second of all, these are only *my* recommendations of things that I think will help Serena, after years of carefully studying her. An 'insider perspective' if you may." This makes her giggle slightly at her own cleverness. "But you should take this all with a grain of salt— or maybe follow my instructions religiously, I don't care. You'll probably need to develop your own strategies to help her. It won't be easy. And it certainly doesn't help that your favorite therapist is dead. I would suggest another therapist, but… I have a feeling that neither of us can stomach that."

I shake my head to indicate the negative. "Not after Anna."

"She isn't a big fan of therapy, either. Me? I might eat a poor little shrink alive. If we're going to do this, it won't happen overnight," she tells me. "It could take a long time for her to get better. It could take years. She might not even be capable of getting better."

"I'm willing to try for as long as it takes," I assure her.

"Me too," she says. "We'll have to work

together to do this. You'll need her cooperation, so you'll want to discuss your bullet points with her."

"Well, don't keep me in suspense," I tell her, with my pen poised to write in the notebook. "I need this information."

"Fine. But one more thing, before I begin. I want to explain the reason I'm doing this." She takes a deep breath, crossing her arms. "You were right. I did get her pregnant, even though you possess the penis. I let you do that to her—to me. I wanted a baby. I knew she desperately, desperately wants a baby, and so do you. I thought I was doing something good. By facilitating this. I thought she could deal with it. I didn't know that she would crack like that, and I'd be unable to help her. I thought… we were older now. I could help her out through anything, but she shut me out." The girl hesitates. "Maybe that means I'm not as okay as I think I am. I always thought I was fearless, but maybe I do share some of her fears in this respect."

My forehead wrinkles. "That's worrisome. If you're afraid, then I should be petrified."

"You probably should be. Parenthood is the most challenging job we could attempt, and there's absolutely no room for failure. Or our kids will end up in the foster system, like we did."

"Uh, no. Over my dead body."

"Exactly."

"So, what's my mission?" I ask her, feeling like Odysseus receiving counsel. "What do you think is the most important thing I can do to help her heal?"

"You've already started trying," she says kindly. Her head is cocked to the side slightly as she studies me. She is a benevolent goddess today. I am a fortunate warrior being visited by Athena before a battle, having her whisper secret strategies for victory in my ear, guiding me, preparing me for the wars ahead.

For the first time in a long while, I am aware that there *will* be wars ahead.

I thought those days were over for me when I left the city.

But Scarlett is bringing the fire back into my world.

"Most of her fears come from the very beginning, from the way she was abandoned. She doesn't think she can ever be a good mother, considering that everything that she has ever known of mothers has been abysmal. I think you need to give Serena her family. Encourage her to meet this brother of hers—what's his name? Larry? Linus? Whatever. And her parents. Go with her, if you can. She's going to be a mess. But she needs to see where she comes from, and she needs answers about her past. She can never completely be at peace unless she understands what happened."

I breathe slowly through my tender lungs. "We're just lucky that there was finally a DNA match in the system, and we can contact her family at all. I only received that notification a few weeks ago—two or three weeks? I'm losing track of time.

135

It was shortly before Zack called me. I was hoping I'd get to explore this with you, but then everything happened…"

"Write it down," she insists. "You might need to show this to Scarlett and explain all this. Without your support, as her brother—the person who's been her brother for half of her life—it could take her years to gather up the courage to meet these people. But maybe having some blood relatives will take some of the pressure off you, and our relationship can improve."

"That makes sense," I say. "But what if her family is horrible? What if they are just as bad as the Browns? There's a good chance they could be terrible people, especially if they chucked a baby into a ditch and left it there to die."

"Ouch," she says softly, holding her chest like she's been punched. "I think it will just make her appreciate you more, and be more determined to start our own family. She just needs to know where she comes from. She will always be incomplete without that knowledge."

I dutifully write it in my notebook:

#1. Meet biological family.

"I just hope it doesn't make her worse," I say quietly.

"Can she get any worse?" the girl asks me opening her hands and gesturing to herself. "It's like she's not even here, in the room with us. She's hiding so far, deep down, under thick, heavy layers of consciousness. I'm always there, just under the surface, beside her with everything she does. I'm ready to step in and be her champion, and beat the shit out of people for her if necessary. But she's just *gone* right now." There is a pause. "She might as well be dead."

This concept gives me chills. I want to reach out and touch her to be comforting, but when she's standing over me like this, her eyes flashing like sharpened daggers, I know it's better to keep my hands to myself.

"What else can I do to help?" I ask softly.

She stares at me very hard, for what must be several minutes. I don't count the seconds as they crawl by, but I can feel the weight of each one.

"I'm going to save the best for last," she tells me. "It's difficult to discuss, so let me get all the other smaller issues out of the way first. Serena needs to start hacking again. It makes her feel alive. It makes her happy. All these years she's been starving herself from the two things she loves most in the world: technology and you—it's been a recipe for death."

"Okay," I tell her. "That's easy enough."

"She also really wants to solve Annabelle's murder and find out who shot you."

"What?" I object. "Absolutely not. That could put her in harm's way."

"Yes, but she is really upset about it. If

Brittany killed Annabelle, she needs to be brought to justice. If it's someone else, we need to know that they are punished, so they won't try again."

"There are others who can do that for us. We're safe here," I tell her. "I just want to forget the whole world exists outside of you and me. Why do we have to bother bringing justice to anyone? Haven't we tried to do enough of that? I just want to fix our issues. I just want to stay here for a while."

She frowns slightly. "You're not yourself, Cole. You've just been through a traumatic experience, and you're avoiding the location where it happened, and anything associated with that location. It's not too different from my own coping mechanisms. You're hiding in a different way."

"What's wrong with that?"

Glaring at me, she steps forward. "Cole, I can only tell you what she needs. You can discuss it with her, or not. It's up to you."

"All right. I'm making notes. Give me more."

"She needs a female friend. She needs to cultivate a relationship with another woman so she can discuss... I don't know, woman things. She's never really needed to discuss woman things, but if she has a baby, she might."

"Like Miranda?"

"Maybe."

"Okay, what else?"

"You need to touch her. You spent so many years not touching her that if you don't try, she's going to think that you just want to be friends. You don't even have to have sex, or risk getting her pregnant. Just… make it clear that you aren't her brother. But if you do have sex with her… I'll try to stay away. I'll try my best not to take over completely so she doesn't remember any of it. But it's difficult," she says softly, touching my arm. "I really like having sex with you."

Grasping her hand, I turn my head to kiss her palm. "I would miss you if you weren't there, at least a little. You're very important to me, Snow."

"Is there any way I could become the dominant personality?" she asks, sliding closer so that her breath caresses my face. "Could we somehow keep her buried deep down, the way she is now—tucked away, safe and sound? Did your Doctor Anna say anything about that?"

Reaching out to grasp her hips, I have to stop myself from pulling her against me. "She said you're the classic violent one. The angry protector. You're unpredictable and dangerous, and definitely not the one who should be in control, because it risks harming the host. The rational one should be in control."

Her face displays hurt. "What the fuck? Aren't I being rational *right now!*" she shouts at me. Then she seems to realize that her outburst is a prime example of her role as the violent one. "But I keep her safe," she protests. "Even from herself. She's not always rational. She's so weak, so depressed, so pathetic. I'm better than her in *every way!*"

Staring at her, I try to think of how to respond. "You are like two sides of the same coin. Parts of a whole. It's really complicated, and I don't totally understand, even though I have done a lot of research. Every case is different. Ultimately, I think things could become way worse if you were in charge 24/7."

She seems frustrated by this response, and she steps away. Lifting a finger, she turns and points it back at my chest. "If I do manage to stay, I'll promise you one thing, Cole Hunter. If you are *ever* fucking me again and you decide to stop like that and leave me unsatisfied, it will be the last time you ever make love to me, or any woman. Because I will cut your fucking dick off."

"See?" I respond, gesturing at her with both hands. "So much anger! This is why you can't be here all the time. You just lash out at everyone before they can lash out at you. You think me stopping meant that I don't care about you or Scar, but I do. I'm in this, one hundred percent. We just need to talk it out, first. Okay?"

She lowers her head and nods. "I know. Maybe you're the rational part of me, Cole."

Her words cause warmth to spread through my chest. Quickly making some scribbles in my notebook, I look back up at her. "Is there anything more, or do you want to tell me that big one you were saving for last?"

"Yeah," she says, as a small smile slowly overtakes her face. That dangerously sweet smile.

Swallowing down a bit of saliva, I feel that I know exactly what she's going to say before the words leave her lips.

"You need to kill Benjamin."

Chapter Twelve

Cole Hunter, 2016

Exhaling slowly, I tap my pen against the paper.

"You have to kill him," she says again, as if it's the easiest thing in the world. "Or at least put me in the same room with him so I can do it."

"Honey, I tried to take him down," I tell her. "I tried to gather evidence to put him behind bars."

She shakes her head. "I guess that could sort of be good. But it would have to be a long sentence. It's not as dramatic as death, and definitely doesn't please *me* as much, but it might be good enough for her. Serena is a nice girl, much less bloodthirsty." Moving closer to me, she fondly ruffles my hair with both of her hands. "I don't care how he dies, or gets put away, but bonus points if I get to see it. That would be deeply satisfying. If you killed him, you'd be my hero for life."

"Aren't I already?" I ask her teasingly.

She rolls her eyes at me. "Not until he's gone. You know... I would really like to get my hands on that bastard. Did you see what I did to his leg?" She giggles lightly.

"You did that to him?"

"Of course, I did. But when I threw him off a hotel balcony, I was hoping to smash his brain open or paralyze him, not just give him a bum leg. Life can be so disappointing." She sighs sadly.

Sliding a hand around her wrist, I squeeze gently. "I really thought Benjamin was behind me getting shot, until you told me about Brittany Brown. He is a piece of work, and he's threatened me on multiple occasions. I am sorry you weren't successful—the world would be a better place without that man."

"Absolutely," she says. "I know this sounds terrible, asking you to kill someone for me. But Scarlett still lives in fear of him finding her, every single day. I feel that fear every time she looks in the mirror and sees her roots showing. She still dyes her hair black, constantly, to look different than the girl she used to be. She wears dark contact lenses if she's going to be anywhere with cameras. She keeps heavy bangs that fall into her eyes, and she wears sunglasses and scarves. Even gloves to conceal her fingerprints! You still can't take a picture of her easily, because she turns away reflexively to hide her face. All her social media profile pictures are so vague and blurry in dim lighting that you can barely recognize any of her features. And she still has nightmares. You know that! How many nights has she woken up screaming, and you had to calm her down?"

I nod slowly, unable to answer.

"Part of the reason she's so afraid to have children comes from years of being molested. How can she easily bring a child into a world like this, without being scared out of her mind?" She takes a deep breath. She looks unsteady on her feet. "I can't ask you to kill every child molester in the world to make it a safer place, but maybe you could help her with this single one. Serena would sleep a lot better at night." She pauses. "We saw Benjamin a few days ago at the police station… and she was not okay."

"You saw him? Face to face?"

"Not exactly. Detective Rodriguez was interrogating him, and I was on the other side of the mirror. But it was like he could see right through the glass." She shivers visibly at the memory. "I could've killed him right there and then, but she wouldn't let me do anything. She freaked out and ran out of the police station. Walked all over L.A. barefoot for hours, in a trance. I don't know how long it was. She shut me out. He said such disturbing things about us…"

When she closes her eyes, I reach out to hold her. I pull her to sit down beside me on the bed, and wrap an arm around her as she leans against me. If this is difficult for *her* to talk about, it's no wonder Scarlett couldn't face it at all.

144

"You don't have to say any more about this," I tell her. "I understand. I think he should die, too."

"Maybe I'm the monster," she whispers. "I can never forgive. I am filled with so much hate."

"Shhh, no. That man violated you for years. He destroyed your mind, made you rip yourself apart into different pieces so you could cope."

"Did he?" she asks with frustration. "Or was I always like this? I can't remember. Maybe this is just how I am. Maybe I'm just as bad as he is."

"No. He caused you irreparable harm. He adopted you under pretense of protecting you, and then made you pregnant when you were twelve years old. He hurt you so much it stole the happiness we could have had. After all you've been through, it makes perfect sense that murdering him would be high on the list of things you need to heal. You need to be free, so that you can someday be a mother, without the shadow of him looming over you, and the memory of that first abortion."

"Abortion," she repeats with a sadistic laugh. She pulls away and closes her eyes for a moment, shaking her head. Finally, she looks at me with the coldest expression I've ever seen. Her eyes are the color of arctic ice, and her tongue drips with words that are roughly the temperature of liquid nitrogen. "I killed it myself. I used a coat hanger."

I think I'm going to be sick.

Standing up, I place a hand over my mouth, rubbing my rough stubble, but mostly concealing my facial expression and fighting down bile. "You could have died."

"I sort of wanted to."

"Scar—" I say, feeling deeply unsettled. Her words have chilled me to the core, and it feels like my organs are growing brittle and shattering to pieces inside my chest. "I—I didn't know."

"No one knows. Not even Serena. It would have been nice to get an abortion from a medical professional, with clean utensils. But he locked me up in my room, refusing to let me leave. I tried to run away countless times, and he kept finding me. He put bars on the windows." She pauses, grasping a strand of her black hair and twirling it around her finger noncommittally.

"But he miscalculated. He shouldn't have locked me in a room with coat hangers."

I can feel the horrified expression on my face as I lower myself to the floor, placing my head in her lap and hugging her legs tightly. I try to speak, but no sound comes out of my face.

"That's the danger of letting a young girl read too many books," she tells me, as she gently tousles my hair. "She learns things. Books always look so innocent, sitting harmlessly on their shelves, but they are the greatest weapons you can find. When I was locked in that room, going crazy, I could only think that I needed to get it out in any way possible, even if it killed me. The more horrible the method, the better—and I had read about the coat hanger thing in a Sidney Sheldon novel, once. I felt like I had the spawn of Satan growing inside me. I know logically that it was just a little hunk of tissue, spongey cells just starting to form a brain and liver... but it was part of *Benjamin! Attached to me* with a cord, sucking the life out of *me!* It was disgusting. It wasn't enough for him to hurt me almost every day, he had now installed a personal parasite to leech away my energy *every single minute*. I couldn't think about anything else, until it was gone. My whole life was completely out of my control. I was filled with so much rage. So I shoved that coat hanger up into my cervix—which was difficult as hell. Painful as hell. It probably didn't actually stab the embryo. It just introduces bacteria which causes the uterus to cramp and expel the tissue later on. But it felt like I was stabbing it, right in the eye. It felt like I was stabbing him. I took out all my anger at him on this little part of him. It was all that I could control."

"Jesus, Scar."

"He tried to put me in an institution after that, but I was gone. I had to become smarter, more evasive, difficult to find. I had to become a master of escape, even from myself, and leave behind that stupid girl who let all those things happen to her."

Lifting my face from her lap, I look up at her with tears in my eyes. "Please tell me that I didn't make you feel that way again, five years ago."

"No," she says softly, looking at me with hurt. "No, no, no. Cole—I love you. You've always made me happy. But it made me *remember.* And all that guilt and horror and fear just came rushing

147

back, and I was twelve years old again, locked in that room." She hesitates, folding her hands in her lap. "Don't tell her what I did. Please? I've never spoken these words out loud. I try to avoid thinking about it so that she can't overhear my thoughts. I know I'm a monster, but I care about her. I did it so she could live, so she could be free. I'll bear this burden alone. I just… I wanted you to know why I want him dead. I *need* him dead. *She* needs him dead."

"You never have to bear any burden alone," I tell her. "Even if you can't tell Scar, you can always tell me." Fuck, I feel like such a piece of shit. I had this complicated plan to send him to prison—but it all seems so small now. It's really not enough. Men like him always seem to somehow escape the law.

Grabbing my notebook and pen off the bed where I dropped it, I scribble down another note.

#2. Kill Benjamin Powell

She smiles, but it's a tired smile. "Cole, this is hard for me. I need to lie down. Can we continue discussing this another time?"

"But when you wake up, you won't be *you* anymore," I tell her in alarm.

"Then you better kiss me goodbye."

Sighing, I lean over her to place a soft kiss on

her lips. "I wish you wouldn't return to being Scarlett every time you fall asleep. I always miss you when you're gone."

She reaches out to squeeze my hand, before lowering her head to the pillow. "You know how to find me," she says faintly, gazing through half-lidded eyes. "I live inside the cracks running through her mind. If you want me, just break me. And I'm yours."

As her eyelids flutter closed, I watch her for a few minutes, processing everything she has said.

When do I get to stop breaking her, and start finally putting her back together?

Chapter Thirteen

Cole Hunter, 2016

I am not sure how long I stand over Scarlett's sleeping form, watching her with my gut twisting up in knots. Finally, I sit on the bed and grasp her hand, sighing as I interlace my fingers with her. I am definitely not going to be able to sleep tonight. Looking down at the notes I've written down in my notebook, I begin to wonder about the practicality of each item.

Almost all of her recommendations would require us leaving the desert and returning to society. I know that I'm not ready to do that, at least not so soon. Reaching up to touch the bandage on my shoulder, I can still remember the impact of the projectiles hitting me. I keep replaying it over and over in my mind. It was more shocking than it was actually painful. But now, it's extremely fucking painful.

After the physical exertion of our lovemaking,

my shoulder hurts so much that I want to rip it off. I ignored the pain while overwhelmed by pleasure, but I think I've aggravated the injury. I want to take a hammer and smash my shoulder to make it stop. I want to take a pair of scissors and sever all the nerves, tendons, and muscles so they are no longer attached to me.

Breathing deeply, I leave Scarlett and move across the cabin to grab a few pain pills, which I've been trying to avoid since she got here. I don't want to miss a moment with her, or have any of my senses dulled. But the pain is growing so intense that I can no longer think. Popping the pills into my mouth, I chase them down with a bit of water.

If we go back into the world, we will both be exposing ourselves to harm like this again.

I am ashamed to admit how much I still think about the moment I got shot. The memory of a bullet is far worse than the bullet itself. It is similar to rape. Long after the foreign object is removed from your body, the feeling of being victimized remains, torturing you endlessly.

I was not feeling my best before getting shot, or even before getting poisoned, but now I wonder if I will ever be back to 100%. The cadmium has left my lungs raw and sore as if I have permanent bronchitis or strep throat. I have been trying not to complain so that Scarlett doesn't worry. But my shoulder injury has compromised the speed and strength of my arm, and the giant gash across my face would make it very hard to disguise myself if I ever needed to go out in public. Looking down at my notebook again, I rewrite the list and organize the points in estimated order of importance.

#1. Meet biological family
#2. Kill Benjamin Powell
#3. Justice for Annabelle
#4. Work on our intimacy
#5. Hacking is life
#6. Female friendship
#7. Therapy?

It's not enough.

I am vaguely reminded of the labors of Hercules, and I wonder if my trials will be even more difficult. Physical strength is one thing, but many of these challenges are psychological. I should keep contemplating this and add some more tasks.

I know that if I succeed, my prize will be greater than the immortality promised to Hercules by the gods. I mean, technically I'm already immortal. I've already died, and proven that my legacy will live on. But there are different kinds of immortality. There are different kinds of happiness. And there is only one kind of love that endures.

That is what I'm fighting for. I am still young, and I could live many more decades than the three that I've seen. Four more decades? Another six? If I'm really lucky, I could push it to six or seven. With the wonders of modern medicine, some people my age might even get to see another eight.

But none of those years will mean anything if they aren't lived right, and if Scar isn't beside me at the end of all that, surrounded by our children, grandchildren, and great-grandchildren.

That's the kind of immortality, happiness, and love, that truly matters.

So I study the list. Number two gives me some concern. Killing a senator is a massive undertaking, and will attract a lot of attention. Even if we wait until he is no longer a senator, he will still be a public figure and an important businessman. This step will require a lot of planning and deliberation so that we can execute it successfully without compromising our own freedom or our lives. We would need to get it right the first time, and there is absolutely no room for failure. If he figures us out, he could come after us.

I really don't want Scarlett to go anywhere near that man. She has been through enough. I should just figure out how to deal with Benjamin myself. It won't be easy, but I know I can manage. Maybe I can ask Roddy for some help, with his connections. But I've already cashed in a lot of favors lately.

And what about Scarlett's family? From what I understand, they are in New York. I would need a solid new identity and a passport to fly—it's an extremely long drive. Although I do seem to recall her mentioning that she drove the Bugatti here, we probably should try to be more inconspicuous than that. Should I encourage her to go alone? I can't bear the thought of separating from her now. As it is, I want to handcuff her to my wrist so that I can get some rest and not worry about her disappearing.

But I know she could find a way out of those handcuffs, if she really wanted to.

As I stare at the list, I try to develop a plan of action, but I just feel immobilized.

I feel like I'm suffocating in this mobile home, from all this thinking.

Moving to the door and turning the handle, I walk out into the dark and starlit night. I put both of my hands into my hair as I look up at the sky in frustration, hoping that it will recharge my emotional batteries. I find myself thinking about my parents, and missing them powerfully in this moment. I also think about the unborn child I lost that I never even knew about, never had a chance to grieve. I think about what could have been. I think about what still could be.

My body is weighed down by a heavy melancholy, and I can't seem to move in any direction.

Between my pain, my fear of going back to society, and my fear of losing Scarlett, I don't really know how I'm going to be able to help her. I wasn't even able to help myself lately. The only way I could be healthy was to physically run away from it all. Although her preferred method of escaping is usually psychological, I think that I am growing to understand her need to run a little too well.

I hope I'll be able to help her, but it worries me that I am such a mess. I don't know what scares me more: being unable to really accomplish any of these goals to try and help her, or successfully making everything on the list happen, and still failing. Many of the items are out of my control. When I was younger, I never had any fear of failure, but now I know that even succeeding doesn't always have the desired results.

I'm still going to try. All I can do is try.

Life is a little like architecture, and this is what it means to be a man: you are the foundation on which the whole house stands, and you must be absolutely unshakeable. Everyone needs to lean on your shoulders and borrow from your strength. So, if there's a flaw in your design, a point of weakness, damage from years of weathering storms and earthquakes—you can't let them know.

If they realize you are also broken, they will sacrifice themselves to help *you* get better, and they never will. It becomes a sick cycle, for if they never get better, *you* never will. It is wrong to take from those you are supposed to protect. It is wrong to emotionally drain those you are supposed to uplift. It is wrong to let your loved ones experience any suffering that you could have shielded them from, and absorbed on your own.

Maybe, just maybe, after everyone else is well, you can tend to your own fractured soul. Maybe, by virtue of tending to others, you are already rebuilding yourself.

I know that if Scarlett can even begin to heal after everything she's suffered, witnessing her progress will strengthen me vicariously. No, actually, it's not vicarious at all.

Her progress is my progress. Her life is my life. And every crack running through her mind also runs through mine. When we mend, we can only mend together. When we break, we can only break apart.

Just like she always has, I'm going to reach deep inside myself and somehow find the strength to do what needs to be done.

Chapter Fourteen

Sophie Shields, 2016

I don't know why I've been so depressed. It should feel like paradise to be here with Cole, but I can't seem to get out of bed since that day in the shower. I don't even remember getting into bed, but a faulty memory in moments like those is something I have grown to expect—and appreciate. Telling him about the reason I left must have brought up a lot of issues I preferred to keep buried. I mean, if my guilt and fear of his reaction bothered me so much that I stayed away from him for years, I can't expect to get over it all easily and quickly. Frankly, I'm glad I don't remember his reaction.

My body feels unusually sore, as though we might have had sex, but I can't remember. I feel like we did, in a faraway dream, but that is a fairly common dream. I want to ask Cole whether or not we did, but I don't want to insult him. That's probably the sort of thing I should remember.

Besides, my whole body is sore, especially my legs and feet, and I don't think another sore part really makes a difference.

Cole has been applying ointment to my blisters and keeping them clean and bandaged, so my feet are slowly getting better. The sunburn still looks terrible, and it's only itching and peeling worse than before. I haven't really gotten dressed in days. My only clothes are my jeans, and I haven't felt like putting them on since I took them off for the shower. Wearing only the bed sheet loosely wrapped around me feels the best for my sensitive skin.

As always, Cole has been kind and attentive. He's been preparing MREs for me and encouraging me to eat them. I finally gathered up the courage to tell him about Annabelle, and while he's been upset, he didn't react as strongly as I thought he would. It's almost as if he already knew.

Cole has been doing what he normally does when he receives bad news, and doodling pictures of houses. It makes me even more depressed to watch him, knowing that he will never get to see those houses made. I know it's not totally my fault, but I feel responsible for all this.

To distract myself, I tried using Cole's Kindle to read, but I was surprised to find that he had books from most of my favorite authors loaded up on the device. In fact, he even had a new release downloaded from just a few days ago—the day he was shot. I can't help wondering if he really expected me to be here. If he unconsciously planned for it.

That makes me feel a little tricked into coming here, and a little trapped being here.

Tossing and turning in bed, I think about everything I left behind.

I feel a weight on the bed and I know that Cole is sitting beside me. He checks my forehead for a temperature before placing a hand on my arm and squeezing gently.

"What's wrong?" he asks me.

"I don't know," I tell him softly, without opening my eyes. "A lot of things. I feel guilty for leaving L.A. in the middle of an investigation."

"You solved your investigation. You found me."

"I know. It's just… so much unfinished business. Annabelle, Brittany, the detective."

"We don't have to worry about anything, Scar. It's like we are on our own private island, and the bad guys can never get to us."

I open my eyes to study him. "I hope you're right about that. You can really sleep at night knowing that someone seriously wanted you dead, and you just ran away? Are you never planning to go back to the world at all?"

"I don't know," he answers. "But I *can* sleep at night. At least, I was able to sleep quite well, until you got here. Now I'm a little too wired to sleep."

"That's not good," I tell him. "What if we're

not healthy for each other?"

"Bullshit. How could we not be?"

Shaking my head, I try to explain. "I just miss my job, Cole. It was challenging, and it kept me busy. I couldn't think so much when I was focused on other things and always rushing around. Now that I have so much time to hear myself think… well, it's frustrating. It's scary. It's painful."

"So you're upset that you have run away from running away?" he asks me.

"Yeah. Zack doesn't know where I am, and I feel guilty about that. And I think I'm experiencing caffeine withdrawal."

He smiles. "I can fix you some coffee, but I think I have a natural stimulant that works better."

"Oh?" I ask him coyly, glancing down at his bare chest. He hasn't been wearing much real clothing either, and has been going around in a pair of silk boxers covered in Pokémon. I have to try very hard not to laugh every time I catch a glimpse of his ass.

"You have to come outside with me," he says, grasping my arm. "The night sky is just breathtaking. Have you seen it? Did you see it when you were walking here?"

"I saw the moon."

"Let me show you the stars," he says, standing up and trying to pull me off the bed. "We can walk around a little and get some exercise. Your feet are really bandaged up, so they should be okay."

Yawning, I resist his pull. "Cole, is it even

night outside?"

"I don't know," he says cheerfully. "Maybe. We should find out, and stretch our legs a little. If you don't enjoy the exercise, I promise I'll just make you some really good coffee instead." Moving to the door of the mobile home, he swings it open.

His whole body grows tense and frozen. I am confused for a moment before I peer around him and see that he is staring down the barrel of a gun. My heart rate doubles. There is a silhouette of a person standing in the doorway, pointing a gun directly at his face. I think it's a woman. Who is it? Brittany? I can't see in the darkness of the night— for it is night, after all.

Cole moves a little protectively, to put his body between mine and the shooter, which removes her from my line of sight and further conceals her identity. I find it suddenly hard to breathe. Why doesn't Cole just slam the door to the NovaTank? Isn't this thing bulletproof? I can see the muscles in his back have grown all rigid and tensed to their limit, which is probably hurting his injury.

Moving slightly and gripping the blanket around me, I try to whisper, "Cole…"

"Don't move a *fucking* muscle," the woman commands sharply. "I'll blow your brains out. From this range, I would have to be a Kardashian to miss."

Chapter Fifteen

Scarlett Smith, 2003

"Scarlett, these SAT scores are amazing," Mr. Bishop says with a kind smile as we sit around the dinner table. "With your grades, you can get into any college you want. I wish my Levi had half the drive and dedication you have."

"Thank you, sir," I say as I finish up my dinner. Mrs. Bishop is not a spectacular cook, but you can really feel her love for her family in every meal. There are hearty portion sizes, and it feels good to go to bed with a satisfied and warm feeling in my stomach, instead of an empty gnawing. But the warmth might be more due to the pleasant family atmosphere, especially in contrast to my last foster home...

"She's just being a show off," Levi says as he shovels mashed potatoes into his mouth. "Scarlett loves making me look bad."

"No," I say, lowering my head. "I just want to make Cole proud. He derailed his whole life for me. Now, he's in jail instead of going to college, and he wrote me a letter that conditions there are dreadful and unsanitary. I better be worth it."

"Oh, sweetie, he saved your life," Mrs. Bishop says. "He only got two years in juvie, and that time will fly by. Two years of his life is a small price to pay for you getting to live decades! He may have *delayed* going to college, but he's only fifteen anyway. He will still be one of the younger kids at MIT, I'm sure. Maybe he can even get out sooner with good behavior."

"But he lost his scholarship," I say quietly. "He has a full ride starting in September. Everything was going so well, and this is all my fault."

"Don't beat yourself up about it," Levi says, eating Cheetos from a bag that is poorly concealed under the table. "Some prisons are pretty great and give educational programs, right? Maybe he can get some college credits."

"Not this prison, son," Mr. Bishop says, standing to take away Levi's Cheetos and place them in a cabinet. "Your mother worked hard on dinner, Levi. Don't be rude by eating this trash instead of real food."

"It's okay, dear," says Mrs. Bishop with a wink at her son. "He's a growing boy, and Cheetos are delicious."

I stare at them all in amazement. What is

happening here? Is no one about to get their face smashed in? They just had a normal conversation instead of screaming and smashing beer bottles? I have definitely spent too much time living with the Browns.

"Isn't there anything you can do, Mr. Bishop?" I ask him with frustration. "Can't you… appeal the judge's decision? Can't we try to shorten his sentence? What if I confess? I could say that I did it all, if it saves him…"

Mr. Bishop shakes his head. "I'm afraid that's unwise, child. The judge is very harsh, especially to children. You could get even more prison time than Cole. It's best we just accept his fate."

"I'm going to do some research," I tell them. "Levi, can you drive me to the courthouse in the morning tomorrow?"

"Sure," he tells me. "But my car won't start, so we'll have to take the motorcycle."

"That's fine."

"You're very determined, my dear," says Mr. Bishop. "Have you ever considered pursuing a career in law? I know a lot of powerful men in firms around the city. I could definitely get you internships to help build up your resume, and almost guarantee you a great job once you pass the bar."

"Oh, no, Dad!" Levi groans loudly. "Don't pay any attention to him, Scar. He's tried to pressure all his kids into becoming lawyers, but none of us were interested in such boring lives."

"Being a lawyer is not boring, son," Mr. Bishop says with a slight frown.

"It's kind of you to suggest that, Mr. Bishop," I say gently. "Unfortunately, I do not have much respect for the law. It has never been good to me. And now Cole's in prison when he really shouldn't be. I don't think I believe in justice anymore."

"Being a lawyer isn't about justice, Scarlett. It's about the truth, and your ability to make people perceive things a certain way."

"I can't do that. I see things in black and white. Good or bad, right or wrong. The justice system is so subjective and arbitrary. There's so much luck involved. I like working with computers. They aren't nearly as complicated as people. I like cold, hard facts."

Mr. Bishop nods. "I understand that perfectly, dear. Let me know if you ever decide to change your mind. You'd make an excellent lawyer."

"Thank you, Mr. Bishop. May I be excused to use the Internet?"

"Certainly, dear."

Taking my empty plate and moving to the kitchen, I leave the family eating their dinner in the dining room. As I begin washing the dish, I feel a tapping on my shoulder.

"Hey," says Levi.

When I turn around, I see a punch headed for my chest, but I am too startled to do anything about it. "Ow!" I say in annoyance, clutching my breast with a sudsy hand. "What the fuck, Levi?"

He frowns. "Why didn't you use the block I showed you? I'm not supposed to be able to land a hit."

"I wasn't expecting you to hit me! I was doing the dishes. And you were moving too fast!"

"Krav Maga is street fighting, Scarlett! An assailant on the street isn't going to move slowly when he tries to attack you. He isn't going to wait until you're *expecting* it."

"Well, could you at least not hit me in the boob? It hurts!"

"Again, this is *street* fighting! An attacker goes for your weak and sensitive spots. He's not going to play nice and only hit you where it *doesn't* hurt that much."

"But you're not an attacker. We're friends, and we're just practicing. Let me finish the dishes, okay?" I ask him, turning back to the sink.

As I soap up the plate to remove the glued-on bits of potato, I feel some breath on the back of my neck. "What if I'm not your friend?" he asks me softly, sending chills through my body. "What if I am an attacker?"

"Levi…" I say with warning.

He brushes his lips against my neck, standing close so I can feel his erection against my body. "What if I want to do very bad things to you?" he asks.

"You don't," I tell him, swallowing back the fear that's rising in my chest with a familiar heat. "You promised Cole you wouldn't touch me."

166

Levi reaches up to grab my hair, collecting it all together into a ponytail and twisting it up around his fist so that he tugs on my scalp. "Who ever said I was the type of guy who keeps his promises? I take what I want—when I want it. And I've wanted to fuck you since the moment you walked into this house."

When his hand snakes around my body to grope between my legs, I find myself growing dizzy. My vision begins to spin and my head aches. I shut my eyes tightly to fight against the pain, and my world goes black.

A few seconds pass.

Or maybe a minute.

Maybe several minutes.

I have no idea, but when I open my eyes again, my hands are tensed up and shaking, with raw energy coursing through them. Is that energy even mine? Levi is lying sprawled across the kitchen floor with blood all over his face. The dinner plate is in my left hand, smashed in half, and the other half is lying in pieces on the floor.

"Jesus!" Levi says, rubbing his head. "Damn, girl. That is exactly what I'm talking about!"

"What?" I ask, feeling horrified. What have I done?

"You *can* fight!" he says gleefully. "I knew I just had to push the right buttons. How come you can pack such a punch when I piss you off, but other times you're worthless?"

Looking down at my right hand and turning it

over slowly, I see that the knuckles are bruised and red. My hands is throbbing and painful and there are imprints of my nails pressed into my palms.

Levi stops clutching his head and moves his hands down to hold his side as he groans in pain. "You got me good this time, Scar. Just try to remember exactly what you did there, for next time I sneak up on you. It was awesome!"

Shit. What did I do? I know that there's something terribly wrong with me, but I am not sure what it is. There are so many chunks of my life that I'm completely missing—usually the parts with the most action.

I think I have superpowers.

That's the only possible explanation for this. Okay, I'm sure there are many more logical explanations, but this is the only one that makes me feel good instead of guilty. I must be like one of the characters from Cole's anime's, who has a secret heritage.

I mean, we don't know who my parents are. I could be from outer space.

If I was sent to earth as a baby in a spaceship, then it's not so bad that I landed at the side of the road in a ditch somewhere, to be found by an old woman. Of course, they never recovered my spaceship, but this is the story I'm sticking with.

I could be a Saiyan or a Kryptonian, and in those moments I can't remember, I channel the strength of my ancient, alien warrior race to do battle. But immediately after the fight has concluded, some fancy alien technology wipes my memory of the event. The processing speed required for such battle calculations is far too advanced for a puny human brain to comprehend.

Smiling proudly at the way Levi is wincing on the floor. I stand over him with a hand on my hip, feeling a little like Wonder Woman. I just need a lasso on my belt, or a cape blowing in the wind. Maybe I'm an Amazonian princess or a Sailor Scout, and I'm powerless in my human form, but I need some kind of transformation to realize my true strength.

The idea makes me smile.

I really need to work on some sort of costume.

"Tell me your secret," Levi says as he sits up, whimpering as he gathers the pieces of broken dishes. "I've trained in Krav Maga for years, and you've just had lessons for a few weeks. You weigh 115 pounds soaking wet, and I'm close to 170. How can you kick my ass like that?"

Lifting my chin, I imagine a ray of sunlight hitting my form-fitting body armor. "What can I say, Levi? Sometimes, I guess I just go Super Saiyan."

He groans as he takes the broken half of the plate from me and tosses the debris away. "That is not a valid explanation! But I don't think Cole needs to worry about you, Scar. You can take care of yourself."

"What is going on in here?" Mrs. Bishop asks as she enters the room, holding the rest of the empty plates. "Levi, sweetie! You're bleeding."

"Just a surprise sparring session gone wrong, Mom," he explains with a shrug and a grin, wiping some of the blood off his chin, as it drips down from his nose. "I should really stop sneaking up on Scarlett, she's getting stronger every day."

"Well, then," Mrs. Bishop says with a satisfied nod. "Good girl! You can kick my son's lazy butt whenever you feel like it, darling."

"Mom!" Levi says in embarrassment.

I laugh softly, feeling a little less guilty. I love this family—even Levi's very frustrating training sessions. I know he only means to help.

Is this how Cole grew up, around sweet and loving people like this?

No wonder he turned out so amazing.

And now, after a few months of being around me… he's in prison.

Chapter Sixteen

Cole Hunter, 2003

I am lying on the top bunk, on top of a thin mattress that mostly feels like metal bars under my back, when my roommate dives into the lower bunk, causing the whole bed to shake.

"Fucking bullshit!" he shouts, and the bed shakes again as he punches or kicks the metal railing. "This place is a fucking shitshow. I hate this place. I fucking hate this place! Everyone in here deserves to go to hell."

Luckily, I never sleep, or his carrying on like that would have really startled me. Folding my hands over my stomach, I wonder whether I should speak to him. At least he's speaking English, and I can understand him, unlike most of the boys in here. I haven't really been big on introductions—I figure that the less I speak to people, the better.

But then I hear a whimpering sound, and I realize that the boy is crying.

Taking a deep breath, I begin to wonder what is wrong. It's only been a few days, and we haven't exchanged names. I have tried to remind myself that this is temporary, and it will pass. I really don't have to get comfortable and make friends.

I still don't really understand how I ended up in prison.

Sitting up on the cold, hard bed, I stare at the metal toilet in our small room, wondering how I'm going to survive the next two years in here. I was so psyched up for the architectural program at MIT. It felt like everything was going my way, until Mr. Brown decided to get drunk and try to choke Scarlett to death.

While I was found not guilty of manslaughter, I was convicted for arson, due to the fact that my parents' home burned down when I was very young. While they didn't have evidence to convict me for that crime, they said that the fact that I stand to inherit a large sum from their death showed motive, and a pattern of behavior.

They also said that even if I killed in self-defense, to save myself and Scarlett, it was unnecessary to start the fire. Mrs. Brown was also in the house, along with all of the family's belongings. They said it was an enormous destruction of property and I had little respect or value for people's homes, or lives, or safety.

Now, my whole life is ruined. I am forced to eat my meals in the cafeteria with dozens of other young boys who are actual murderers and drug dealers. I suppose they are not *too* different from some of the people I've already encountered in foster homes, but these boys are the cream of the crop.

So far, all I've done is try to look down and avoid eye contact. I've read books and written to Scarlett, and tried to ignore my surroundings. But I know I'm going to have to talk to someone sooner than later, and find my place in this little social ecosystem. I am not the kind of person who can stay hidden forever. I know I need to come to some understanding with the other boys.

Besides, I'm sure they have interesting stories, and I can learn a lot from them.

I just need to focus on getting out of here soon, and getting back to Scarlett.

When my roommate continues blubbering quietly, I sigh, turning to dangle my legs off the side of my bunk. "Hey, what's wrong? You okay?" I ask.

"No," he says tearfully. "That fat guard keeps following me around. He won't even let me take a piss without watching me. And that's fine, but I had just taken my shower and I went to use the urinal. He smashed my face against it while I was taking a piss. For no reason. That thing is disgusting, it hasn't been cleaned in weeks. My teeth cut the inside of my lips, and it hurts. But worse, I can still taste the urinal. Johnny and Marco were there and they thought it was hilarious. They stuffed my whole body into the urinal," he says with a quivering lip.

The kid is smaller than most of the boys here. I would guess his age at being around ten or eleven? He is tiny. I hate to think of the older boys picking on him, or ganging up on him. My heart hurts for him, and I wonder what the hell I can possibly do to help.

"They kept kicking and pushing me back into the urinal every time I tried to get out," the boy says. "The guard just stood there and laughed. I can still feel that shit all over me, and now I can't take a shower until tomorrow. I can still smell it."

I find my face twisting up into a grimace. I still haven't gotten used to the restrictions of three-minute showers only once a day. What can you really clean in three minutes? It's enough time to get some soap on your sweaty underarms and your balls, and maybe your ass. That's about it.

It's barely enough time to wash the soap off.

Using the ladder to lower myself to the floor, I retrieve a piece of paper and a pencil from my mattress. "Write it down," I tell the boy. "Every incidence of abuse that you face—write it down. You need to also see if you can get corroborating witnesses, especially other guards. How long do you have left in here?" I ask him.

"Fourteen months," he says.

"That's not much more. It will go by fast.

When you get out, you can sue the guard, maybe for discrimination. Maybe, I can try to find out if he's hurting other boys, and we can complain to the warden even sooner than that."

"Nobody's gonna snitch on the guard," the boy says. "He threatens us. He says he can do a lot worse if we complain."

Frowning, I shake my head. "What can he do? There are rules. We have basic human rights. A lot of the kids in here have had really awful lives, and prison shouldn't make that worse. This should be a positive experience that teaches us discipline and responsibility so that when we get out, we can live our lives better."

"No," the young boy says. "It's about breaking us, so that we know that we're all alone and no one cares. And even if we get out, we'll probably end up right back here soon, because we're not smart. We're not good at school. We're all poor. So we keep stealing shit, or doing whatever led us to be in here in the first place."

"I'm smart," I tell the boy with a smile. "And when I get out, I'm staying out."

He glances up at me. "Probably. You're white, so I bet it's easier."

Sighing, I nod slowly in acknowledgment. "Probably."

"Sometimes, I think I just get in trouble for walking down the street with my friends, or my brothers, being not-white. My friend got arrested for possession, but he ain't ever done no drugs or touched them in his life. He's a good kid. He swears the cop planted the drugs on him to get him in trouble on purpose. How fucked up is that?"

"That's messed up," I say honestly, wondering if it's true.

The boy sniffles and wipes his hand across his snotty face. "And I didn't do nothing either. I shouldn't be in here. I just miss my mama."

I move to sit down beside him on his bunk, to try and be friendly. "I miss my mom too. She's dead."

"Mine's a whore," he confesses. "But she's really nice, and she's an amazing cook. She always makes the best tacos on Taco Tuesday."

I stare at him for a moment, trying to think of how to respond. "Better a prostitute mom than a dead mom."

"Totally," he says, and we both laugh.

It might be the weirdest way I've ever started a friendship.

Is that what I'm actually doing? Maybe the word "friendship" is going a bit too far. We are roommates, so we need to be cordial. We need to communicate. I might be so desperate and lonely in here that I'm just clinging to any kind of humanity. I'll probably never talk to this kid again once we get out of prison. I'll probably forget his name.

Actually, I don't even know his name.

"So, what are you in here for?" the boy asks.

"I killed my foster father and burned down his house," I answer.

The little boy's eyes grow wide. "Wow. I won't mess with you. Hey, if we're gonna be friends, you hafta promise you won't kill me or kill other people randomly all the time. I find that very stressful."

"Don't worry, I don't do that sort of thing often," I assure the boy. "He was a bad man. He was hurting my sister."

The boy nods enthusiastically. "Good. That's why I did what I did, too."

"What did you do?" I ask him.

"I stabbed my mom's pimp and his whore wife a bunch of times, and took all their money. But they stabbed my mom first and took all her money, so I did the right thing," the kid says, sticking his chin out proudly. "Except my mom survived. They didn't. You have to stab the right places, if you're going to stab someone. It's basic anatomy."

"Damn, kid," I tell him, impressed. "I'm lucky you're my roommate! You're probably the toughest guy in here."

"I totally am!" he says, puffing out his little chest. Bless his heart. "That's why they shoved me in the urinal. They're just scared of me."

"Damn straight," I tell him. He's so adorable. I kind of want to give him a noogie. But that might lead to me getting murdered in my sleep, so I probably shouldn't do that.

"Hey, I don't even know your name," the kid says.

"I'm Cole," I tell him.

"Sweet. They call me Little Ricky," he says with a grin. "But my dad was really tall, so I'm going to hit a real big growth spurt any day now. Then they'll regret teasing me."

"Do you want me to call you something different?" I ask him.

"Sure," he says, thoughtfully. "You can call me Rodriguez."

Chapter Seventeen

Cole Hunter, 2003

Does everyone in prison honestly believe they shouldn't be here? This is the question I ask myself as I sit in the cafeteria, eating my slop. Yes, the stuff I am eating is literal slop, like out of Oliver Twist, or a pig's pen. I don't know why I ever expected being an orphan in the twenty-first century to be any better than nineteenth century Victorian England.

At any rate, at least prison has given me a lot of time to read. I also write regular letters to Scarlett, and work on sketches of a house I'd like to build someday. A fireproof house. Dreaming about a future accomplishment gives me hope that I'll get out of here someday and be able to live my life again. Soon, this will be a distant memory.

As the weeks have passed, I've made more

friends and talked to more of the guys here. So now, I am sitting at a table surrounded by my peers. They are good kids, and they are making the most of this bad situation, cracking jokes, and trying to keep smiles on each other's faces. I've learned a lot about their families and their lives, their bad experiences and their dreams. Little Ricky and I have gotten close, and he says he wants to enlist in the air force someday, like his father.

But as I sit here, trying to force myself to swallow this slop, I can't help thinking that some of their stories sound vaguely familiar.

"There was no evidence against me, but Judge McFarlane sent me here anyway," one kid is saying.

I lift my head to better hear what he's saying. I think his name is Daniel, and he's new here. Judge McFarlane is the reason I am here as well, although I secretly suspect that Benjamin had something to do with it.

"Man, it was also McFarlane for me," says another one of the kids, Nathan. "There was evidence that I was innocent, but he found reasons to throw it all out."

"Me too, guys," I say suddenly. "I think someone else had a similar story? Matthew, with the possession charge?" When they all nod, I frown. "He swore that he'd never touched drugs and didn't even know any drug dealers, and the cop and the judge just had it out for him. Do you think—maybe they had it out for all of us?"

"Not all of us," says Little Ricky. "There's a

couple guys here who are real trouble. Like Marco and Johnny." His voice has lowered to a whisper when he speaks their names, and we all glance over in their direction. It's true, we've all been terrorized by those kids, who eagerly brag about the terrible things they've done. Marco seems like the evil mastermind while Johnny is his willing sidekick. Some of the boys have even begun calling Marco by the nickname "Marco Polo Loco" because how much he loves to torture us.

As if they are just waiting for the opportunity, Marco gets up from his seat and walks over to us, proceeding to slam Little Ricky's face down into his slop. He then bursts out laughing and returns to Johnny to share a high-five of victory.

Sighing, I hand a few of my napkins to Ricky to help him out, as do a few of the other kids, mumbling apologies. The guards, as usual, do nothing to help. Later on, in less public settings, they will probably do even worse to us.

This isn't fair. I know some of us have done terrible things. I sure have. But they were done in self-defense. I had stab wounds in my body to demonstrate that. Scarlett had burns all over hers, including the older burn wounds and bruises that indicated a history of abuse. In fact, there had even been a domestic abuse call to the house in the past, from Mrs. Brown, although she never charged her husband.

Why do women never charge their husbands? They call the police in a moment of fear and anger—and clarity—immediately after the damage is done. But while the police are on the way, the man begs and pleads until the woman begins to slowly break down and realize that her love for him is stronger than her need to protect herself. Or her children. I have seen this sort of thing too many times in my foster homes.

But the problem with taking pity on a man who does harm to you, is that he will eventually do harm to others. Other women, other children. And without that original conviction, it's a lot harder to prove that he deserves punishment. There are so many people who deserve to be in prison right now, who aren't.

And instead, I'm here. We're all here.

"Guys," I say, leaning forward. "I'm going to write to my girlfriend and ask her to look into this." I've started referring to Scarlett as my 'girlfriend' instead of my 'sister' because mentioning a sister always seems to make everyone ask for details about her appearance and whether she's single. Mentioning a 'girlfriend' stakes a claim that they seem to respect.

"Your hacker girlfriend?" Nathan asks.

"Yeah. I'll ask her to do some digging on Judge McFarlane and see if she can find any evidence of him being biased against kids or something. It's a long shot, but I might as well try. I also have a good friend who's a lawyer, so maybe he can help."

Little Ricky stands up in frustration. "Cole,

I'm sick of your positive attitude. Things are easy for you, compared to some of us. Don't give us false hope, okay? It's hard enough, waking up in this place every day, wondering if we're gonna spend the rest of our lives in prison. Do you know what the recidivism rates are like?"

Recidivism is a word I recently learned from Little Ricky. The kid is surprisingly smart. It's also a depressing word and concept I wish I hadn't learned.

"Just shut up sometimes and let us vent," he tells me gruffly. "You don't have to try to fix everything. Sometimes, you just can't fix things."

With that, he walks away to toss out his uneaten gruel. I'm still not sure if it's supposed to be porridge or oatmeal, but it's definitely where healthy appetites go to die. Oliver Twist would not be wanting some more of this shit.

I know that I shouldn't be comparing youth prisons to orphanages, as they are very different beasts. But as someone who has lived in both, I can honestly say that they are not too dissimilar.

In this world, it is a crime to be alone. If a child is unlucky enough to be alone from the outset, the world will already view them as having committed a crime by merely existing, long before they are old enough to realize that they have done nothing wrong.

Standing up to dump out my own porridge, I wonder if Scarlett has always felt the way that I do now, in this prison. I wonder if she will ever feel differently. I hope things are pleasant for her in Mr. Bishop's home, and that Levi is treating her well. Swallowing, I feel a bit of jealousy surge in my body, and I somehow know that he isn't behaving himself. He never behaves.

Chapter Eighteen

Scarlett Smith, 2003

After receiving a disturbing letter from Cole, I am sitting in bed with Levi's laptop and examining the personal emails of Judge McFarlane. I find nothing suspicious, and after scanning hundreds of emails, my tired eyelids begin to droop. Sleepily, I drag them open, and push my glasses closer to my face as I examine some of the personal accounts of the prison administration, starting with the warden. Finding nothing, I decide to go a little higher. It turns out that Cole's prison is privately owned, and makes a lot of money from federal contracts. A lot of these private juvenile detention centers are reputed to have atrocious conditions for the kids, especially ones operated by this company.

Chewing on my lip, I find a small list of people who stand to benefit most from attracting more inmates to Cole's prison. It's a long shot, and it could take a while to find anything. I am growing disheartened and tired of searching, and my eyelids are closing again. But when I finally come across a certain email offering a payout for "bodies to fill the beds" I sit up straight. Rubbing the sleep out of my eyes, I begin searching in earnest, and I soon find exactly what I'm looking for.

"Yes," I whisper, in utter disbelief. "Yes! Yes, yes, yes, yes, yes, *yes!*"

I am so pumped I have trouble sitting still, and I want to get up from bed and do a happy dance, but Levi chooses that moment to burst into my room. "I knew it!" he says, pointing at me with conviction. "You weren't fooling anyone with this good girl act, Scarlett Smith. I'll take my laptop back now, if you're done watching *porn!*"

Rolling my eyes, I swing my legs over the side of the bed and rush to Levi's side. "Look. Can you believe this? We need to show your dad!"

Levi blinks. "Damn. I thought I was going to walk in and find you naked and masturbating furiously, but now you're making me read…"

"Shut up and check this out!"

Trying to conceal his disappointment, Levi studies the laptop. He is silent for a few seconds as his eyes scan the screen, but then his eyebrows jerk upward. I watch the reflection of the words in his pupils as his eyes grow narrowed and more focused. "No! Really? Are you fucking kidding me? McFarlane? That's the same judge who sentenced

Cole!"

"Exactly," I tell him victoriously. "The judge is crooked. He's receiving money from the juvenile detention center to have kids convicted and sent there, so that the prison can be more profitable."

"He's getting paid to send innocent kids to jail?" Levi repeats slowly.

"As many as possible."

"So Cole is literally a victim of the system. If he hadn't had that judge, he probably would have gone free."

"I had a feeling something was off," I tell him. "Benjamin threatened Cole before and he mentioned judges, so I was looking for some kind of connection between Benjamin and the judge. But my dear adoptive father is too smart for that, and they probably didn't exchange more than a few words. I should have gone deeper and looked into the prison."

"Does Benjamin have connections to the company that owns the prison?" Levi asks.

"I don't know, but I don't have time to look into that. We need to focus on getting Cole out quickly, so that he can go to school. Will you help me?"

"Of course," Levi says, giving me a funny look. Then he shakes his head. "Cole has no idea how lucky he is to have you, Scar. There aren't many girls out there who would spend every spare minute digging for dirt to take down *a judge* to get her foster brother out of prison."

"It's nothing," I say softly. "He's in prison because of me, remember?"

"You say that like you're doing this out of guilt instead of love."

I make a face, unsure of how to respond to that.

Levi smiles. "You're special, Scar. I would kill to have a girl like you. Sexy, smart, and tough as hell."

"Okay," I tell him, blushing a little. "Stop hitting on me. Let's go talk to your dad."

"It's the middle of the night," Levi says. "He's sleeping. We should probably wait until morning."

I want to grab him and shake him. "Are you kidding me? This can't wait!"

Moving out of my room and across the hall to Mr. Bishop's room, I knock on the door softly.

"Yes? Come in," he says at once, and it doesn't sound like he was sleeping.

I open the door and see that he is sitting up in bed and reading with bifocals and a small lamp while his wife sleeps beside him. He is such a sweet old man.

"There's something important I need to tell you," I say, moving forward with the laptop.

"What is it, dear?" he asks.

Levi follows behind me as I show his father the information on the computer screen, and begin to explain what I've found in detail. Mr. Bishop adjusts his bifocal lenses to get a closer look, and at some point, his wife wakes up and begins to read the screen as well.

I feel guilty for disturbing their sleep, but this is too important to wait.

"That bastard," Mrs. Bishop finally says when I am finished. "How could he do this to these poor children? Being sent to prison will ruin so many of their lives."

"Especially a shitty prison like this one," Levi adds.

"This information is shocking, Scarlett. I am deeply offended to know that a judge would behave like this." Mr. Bishop sighs and removes his glasses, closing his eyes as he pinches the bridge of his nose. "All right, dear. I will file an injunction against the detention center to cease operations first thing in the morning."

"Thank you so much, sir. I would also like to send this information anonymously to the press. Once the public knows what's happening to these kids, they are sure to be outraged."

Mr. Bishop nods. "Some press could be good. A story like this could even get some sort of protest going at the prison."

I chew on my lip slightly. A protest? That could be interesting.

"It looks like we might get our boy out in time for school after all," Mr. Bishop says with a smile. "But—there is still the matter of his scholarship. When he deferred his admissions to MIT, he lost his scholarship. So even if we get him out of prison, he might not be able to afford the tuition."

My face twists up in frustration. "I know it's a lot of money, but can't he apply for financial aid?"

"Maybe," Mr. Bishop says. "A lot of these deadlines have passed, so he might be in a bit of a pickle. But we'll do our best to help him out." The older man pauses. "You know, there is one other thing to consider…"

"What's that?"

"His inheritance," Mr. Bishop says, turning to share a look with his wife. "Cole's father had a bit of a playboy youth, and he didn't really settle down and become successful until he got married. To deter Cole from having a similar adulthood, wasting a lot of time and money partying like he did, he decided that Cole wouldn't receive his inheritance until he got married. Married to a good girl, someone supportive of Cole's career choices, with the intent of starting a family."

"But doesn't he need to be eighteen to receive that money?"

Mr. Bishop chuckles to himself. "Cole has asked me about that a great deal. Technically, he needs to be an adult to receive the money. And Cole has his own special ideas about what being an adult means. I thought it would be impossible with the conviction, but if we get it overturned… then there is still a possibility. We just need a young lady who loves Cole enough to marry him! Do you know anyone like that, Scarlett?"

The way that the older man is smiling at me

makes me a little uncomfortable and embarrassed. "Do you mean…?"

"Dad!" Levi interjects, sounding annoyed. "She's only fourteen. You can't get married at fourteen."

"Actually—" Mr. Bishop begins.

"No!" Levi says strongly. "They are too young. I'm almost nineteen and I would never even think of getting married."

"I married your father at age sixteen, sweetheart," Levi's mother says. "He was your age. And look, here we are, perfectly happy all these years later."

I clear my throat. "Um, I'm not even sure that Cole likes me that way."

Levi rolls his eyes. "What? Of course, he does! He killed a guy and burned down a house for you."

"But it doesn't even have to be a real marriage," Mr. Bishop explains. "As long as you can convince a judge to allow the marriage and Cole's emancipation, he can receive his inheritance and attend MIT. We could use Scarlett's spectacular SAT scores and grades, and some references from her teachers and employers to demonstrate her maturity. We can say that she intends to apply to the same college and attend with Cole, living together as his spouse."

"That makes sense," I say quietly, as I do want to attend college with Cole. Does it matter if I have to pretend to be his wife? I'm already pretending to be Scarlett Smith. My whole life is a lie.

"Dad, this is sick," Levi is saying. "You're forcing them to be together! Even if they don't want to be married, they're going to have to pretend for how long? Years?"

"Levi, my boy," says his mother. "Do you think a marriage of convenience is a new concept? For thousands of years, people have been getting married for reasons other than your naïve notions of romantic love. Your father and I got married due to an immigration issue."

"Cole and Scarlett seem to genuinely care for each other," Mr. Bishop adds. "They should be able to convince any judge."

Levi turns to me with a shocked look on his face. "Scarlett, I apologize for my crazy parents. This is obviously a horrible idea."

It must be nice to be Levi, and to have this home and these wonderful parents. It must be nice to have so much privilege and luxury that you can't even comprehend what it feels like to be desperate. To have a limited number of choices. Cole is the closest thing to family I've ever had, and he's been ripped away. I don't know if marriage is really that effective in keeping people together, especially compared to superglue, rope, or barbed wire. But I will do just about anything to get Cole back and ensure that I never lose him again.

Marriage is a small price to pay.

And hey, it could even be fun. Slowly, a smile

creeps over my face as I begin to formulate an epic plan. Nodding at Mr. Bishop, I give him my assent. "I actually think marriage is a great idea. If we could make it work for the next few years—we wouldn't need to ever be in foster care ever again. I would no longer be a burden on you."

"You're not a burden, dear," Mrs. Bishop says, "but we won't be able to help out much when Cole's in Massachusetts. You two need a long term solution, and you need to be extremely careful with money. The cost of education in this country is insane."

"I think we're going to be okay," I tell the Bishop family. "I can work hard, and so can Cole. We're resourceful. As long as we don't have to live with anyone who causes us harm, I think we'll be fine. I'll suggest this marriage thing to him, but first let's work on getting him out of prison."

"Scarlett, you're insane!" Levi says. "You can't seriously be thinking of getting married at age fourteen?"

"Levi, I have absolutely nothing to lose."

"Cole will never agree to this. Marriage is a just another kind of prison."

I make a face. "You're wrong. This is the perfect strategy. You can't possibly understand what it means to be free if you've never been trapped. In this unique situation, marriage means freedom instead of containment."

"This decision could ruin your life, Scarlett."

"My life has already been ruined, more times

than I can count. Now, Levi, it's nearly morning and I need a ride to the mall to buy a few things required for my engagement. Will you take me?"

"Sure," he says with defeat. "Cole's a really lucky guy."

Chapter Nineteen

Cole Hunter, 2003

It is early morning, and I am sitting at my desk and sketching a house. One of the kids in here, Matthew, has a father who owns a construction company, and he sent some of my sketches home for appraisal. His father sent back a letter with some very positive feedback on my designs, saying that they were practical and attractive homes that could be built at affordable prices. He even expressed interest in working with me at some point in the future.

Maybe prison isn't so bad after all, if I can make valuable contacts for my future career. I have started thinking about creating a business proposal to present to the banks, in hopes of getting a loan so that I can build my first house. But I would probably have to create a company first, and I have no idea what I'd even call it. It would have to be something really cool and meaningful.

Hours spent locked away with no sunshine are perfect for dreaming.

Speaking of being locked up, I am a little puzzled that none of the guards have come around to let us out of our cells at the usual time. Most of the kids have taken the opportunity to sleep in, and don't really care. But as I get up from my desk to stretch and look around, I start to get an odd feeling. I begin pacing in my cell and growing restless. Where are the guards? The detention center is unusually quiet today.

"Can you stop walking around in circles like that?" Little Ricky says with a groan as he pulls the blanket over his head. "I'm trying to get some beauty sleep, bro."

"Sorry," I say, standing by the bars and staring out into the empty prison halls. "Just… doesn't it seem like something is different today?"

It takes Little Ricky a few minutes before he drags himself out of bed to join me, shuffling his feet. His eyes are half-closed, and he yawns as he struggles to peer through them. "It looks like a ghost town in here," he says in surprise. "Like in those Westerns, before a duel, with dust flying everywhere."

Nodding, I notice that a few other kids are standing by the bars, and looking out in confusion. Some of them are quietly chattering with their roommates.

"Is something wrong?" Little Ricky asks. Then louder, he suggests to everyone, "Maybe the apocalypse happened and we all got stuck in here forever. We're going to starve to death!"

"Man, why'd you say that!" says a boy in the next cell over. "Now I'm freaking out. I'm really hungry."

"What happens in the apocalypse?" another boy asks. "Is it war, or like, a plague of locusts or something?"

"Great," I tell Little Ricky with a frown. "Widespread panic is exactly what we need right now. Good job."

He grins at me. "What can I say? I always had a gift for telling a scary story."

Everyone continues to complain about the lack of breakfast, the absence of guards, and the impending apocalypse, when there is a peculiar sound in the hallways. It's an odd clickety-clack sound, like a rhythmic drumming, that echoes off the walls and grows louder by the second.

All the boys in their cells grow quiet as they try to peer down the hallway and see what's happening. There are some murmurs from some of the guys, and I find myself growing curious. As the sound grows louder, it becomes clear that there is a person approaching, and that person is wearing high heels. A female person.

But there are no female guards in this prison. There are no female inmates.

And even if there were any, none would wear high heels.

My curiosity grows as I hear louder whispers,

and a few whistles from the guys in adjacent cells. Finally, by pressing my face against the bars, I am able to catch a glimpse of jet black hair, so black it's almost blue. My breath catches in my throat, and I nearly want to sit down and cry. But I try my hardest to remain standing, and grip the bars for support, just watching her approach.

As she grows closer, I see that she is wearing *red* high heels. I didn't know she even owned a pair! I have never seen her in heels before, and I think my heart skips a beat. She is also wearing large sunglasses, tight-fitting jeans, and red, long-sleeved shirt. She stands in front of my cell, crossing her arms over her chest as she stares at me.

"Cole," she says softly.

It takes all the effort I can muster not to smash myself against these bars with my arms outstretched through them, trying to touch her. I feel like I have been dying of thirst, and there's a glass of water just out of reach. Grasping the bars, I press my forehead between them, looking down and closing my eyes to try to be cool. I try to gather my senses and quell the ridiculously happy feeling in my chest.

"Scar," I whisper in response.

She steps a little closer, and I can see the pointed toes of her high heels in my line of sight.

This is a dream. I'm dreaming.

"You're not allowed to visit," I tell her, looking up with eyes narrowed in confusion. "It's family-only—parents or guardians, and I don't have either of those. So no visitors for me."

"I'm not visiting," she says, as the corner of her lips curl slightly, in a mysterious smirk. She knows something I don't know.

"Scar," I murmur, extending my hand through the bars a little desperately. Is this a dream? It must be a dream, so I might as well try to touch her.

She smiles and extends her own hand so that our fingertips touch for a moment, and I am shocked to find real soft flesh against mine. I try to grab her hand, but she pulls away.

"I thought we could hang out," she says with a shrug. "Go somewhere, get some pizza, talk about life."

My eyebrows lift in puzzlement. Has she noticed that I'm in a prison cell?

Little Ricky whispers from a few feet behind me. "Cole, is that your girl? She's crazy hot."

"Do the guards know you're here?" I ask her. "Scar, you're making me worried. Have you been sentenced to do time here? Please tell me you're not going to be in prison with us."

"Guards?" Her little smirk of a smile turns into a full blown self-satisfied grin, and suddenly, I somehow know that everything is going to be okay. "There are no guards."

I find that I'm smiling too. I'm smiling so big it hurts my face. I shouldn't be, but I can't help it, and I don't care if it isn't cool. "Scarlett," I say quietly. "What did you do?"

"Just a little research," she says, stepping closer. "Did you know that the prison made this huge scheduling error today and didn't ask any of their employees to come into work? And I guess the guards who *were* scheduled to come in received mysterious phone calls that their shifts had been cancelled due to certain... circumstances."

"Circumstances?" I ask her.

"Yeah. No one even questioned it—they must all really hate working here. And there was also this crazy glitch where all the security cameras were disabled. I could just walk right in the front door. It's a bad day for prison security."

"Scar..." I say with warning. "What's going on here?"

Reaching into her back pocket, she pulls a key ring out, identical to the ones used to open our cells. She twirls it around her finger flirtatiously. "I just found this lying around somewhere. Someone must have dropped it. Do you know what this is for?"

My heartbeat is acting erratically. "Come on," I tell her softly. "Stop teasing me and tell me what's going on."

Walking forward, Scarlett picks a key off the keychain, and uses it to open our cell door. She slides the bars open and steps away, allowing us room to exit. We continue to stand still and stare in amazement.

"Scarlett," I say in a harsh whisper. "I can't just walk out of this prison with you. I'll be a fugitive. I have to serve my sentence."

"Not if your sentence was wrong."

"What are you talking about?" I ask her.

Turning and moving into the center of the prison, Scarlett looks around at the other kids in their cells. "Were any of you sentenced to be here by Judge McFarlane?" After a bunch of nods and assenting speech, she continues. "It turns out that he's been charged with conspiracy, fraud, endangering minors, and a whole host of other offences. Judge McFarlane received money from the people who own the prison to send as many kids here as possible. So, some of you are going to get retrials with a better judge. But *all* of you are going to get removed from this prison, because they have received a cease and desist order for all operations."

She turns to look at me with a huge smile on her face. "Cole, you're going to MIT in the fall."

I can't think of anything to say, so I just walk forward in quick strides and gather her up in my arms, kissing the hell out of her. She seems surprised and resistant at first, but soon she relaxes and kisses back, laughing lightly at my enthusiasm. When our kiss finally breaks, I pull away to see that familiar spark in her eyes. What I always thought was a glint of wickedness was actually something else entirely. It's a deep sense of righteousness and justice.

"Cole," she says in admonition, blushing a little.

I only then realize that everyone in the prison is whistling, cheering, and banging their hands against their cages. We're the center of attention, like a couple from a romantic comedy embracing in the middle of Grand Central Station and confessing their feelings in the climactic scene.

My cheeks are burning, partly from embarrassment and partly from smiling so hard. "Sorry," I tell her. "I've just never had a girl take down a judge for me and then shut down an entire prison so I could leave."

"We better hurry before someone finds out."

"Let's take a few of my friends, the good guys." When she nods, I turn and gesture to my cell. "This is my roommate, Little Ricky."

"Nice to meet you, Little Ricky. Thanks for taking care of Cole for me."

"He took care of me," the small boy says shyly. I can tell he gets nervous around pretty girls.

"Come on," I say to Scarlett, guiding her over to the cells, freeing some of the other kids who had complained about McFarlane. But only the guys who I'm *sure* don't deserve to be here. Some of the kids give Scarlett hugs in thanks, and a few of them are crying.

"Let us out, too!" Marco shouts from his cell. "This isn't fair. Me and Johnny shouldn't be in here neither."

She looks at me and Ricky for confirmation, and we both shake our heads.

"No way," I tell her.

"Those guys are bad news," Little Ricky whispers.

"Let us out of here, Cole!" Marco shouts. "Please? Come on, we're friends right?"

"Ignore them," I tell her.

"Look," she says softly. "There are a bunch of protesters outside. We leaked the story to the press yesterday, about the crooked judge who accepted bribes and put tons of underprivileged kids in jail for personal monetary gain. So today, an *anonymous* hacker saw that story, and took down this prison. As part of the protest. Okay?"

"Okay," I respond, and Ricky says, "Gotcha."

Many of the other guys echo this sentiment.

"Let's get out of here," she says with conviction, and we all begin heading toward the exit. I move in a daze, kind unable to believe this is happening after the months of torture in here.

As we step into the sunlight, I feel euphoria wash over me as it really begins to sink in that I'm free. And I haven't lost too much time. I thought I was going to be stuck in here for two years, but it looks like my life isn't going to get totally ruined after all.

When Scarlett takes my hand, I find a cold metal object being pressed into my palm and I look at her questioningly.

"Wanna get married?" she asks with an unbelievably angelic smile.

Opening my palm to look at the ring she has placed in my palm, I suddenly feel like this whole experience of being in prison, and being rescued by a gorgeous teenage hacker girl in red high heels has all been for this moment. It was all just an elaborate marriage proposal.

I am sure there is some extremely logical reason she wants to get married, and she's about to explain all those logical logistics posthaste.

But for now, I'm just going to pretend that I'm a wrongfully accused knight who was captured and held in an enemy dungeon, tortured and close to starvation. But just before his spirit could be broken, his warrior princess slayed a dragon and took down an entire kingdom to rescue him from the throes of evil.

How would you respond if faced with similar circumstances?

The only possible answer is obviously, "Hell, yes."

Chapter Twenty

Cole Hunter, 2016
About to get shot again?

"Don't move a *fucking* muscle," the woman with the gun hisses. "I'll blow your brains out. From this range, I would have to be a Kardashian to miss."

As she steps closer to shove the gun into my face, I feel the old injury on my face begin to throb with the anticipation of being shot again. I am suddenly frozen, waiting for the bullets to pierce my skin.

Scarlett sighs behind me. "So much for your private island, Cole."

I try to think. My muscles have instinctively tensed up, trying to get so hard that they create body armor to protect me from future bullet wounds. Willing myself to move, I try to get my limbs unfrozen. I know I need to think fast, but act faster.

Rodriguez isn't here to help me, so I try to remember what Levi taught me long ago.

"Look," I say to the woman holding the gun, lifting my hands in a gesture of peace. I hope that she doesn't see the slight tremble in my fingers. "We'll cooperate with whatever you want. Just tell us what you need. We have food, cash, jewelry, the complete series of *Breaking Bad* on Blu-ray—" I pivot mid-speech to grab the woman's gun and disarm her. Tossing the gun to Scarlett, I groan as the woman slams her knee into my side. I counter back with turning and punching her in the face, which she successfully blocks. Damn, I'm slow. But I manage to grab her wrist and twist it, using Aikido to wrestle her to the ground.

"You have Breaking Bad on Blu-ray?" Scarlett asks me, sounding annoyed that she hadn't previously known this. "Where do you even have the TV?"

"Just pick up the gun and help me out!" I say, grunting as I struggle with our attacker. The woman slams her palm into my nose before hooking my leg with hers to knock me to the ground. She shoves her knee into my back to keep me down, but I am a lot bigger than her. I twist my body and grab a handful of her hair, jerking her forward as I put my knee in *her* back instead.

"Who the fuck are you?" I demand as I yank her arm up with firm pressure, intending to break it. "What do you want?"

She laughs softly, which puzzles me and

reminds me of Snow. She also holds up her hand in some sort of signal, which makes me anxious. I scan the desert for any sign of other people. Alarmed, I turn to look into the mobile home to see Scarlett approaching the doorway, dressed in her bed sheet and holding the gun. But she is not pointing it at the woman—the gun is merely sitting in her palm. What the hell is she doing?

"I thought you'd be more of a pencil-neck, pencil-dick paper pusher," the woman on the ground says. "Didn't expect you to fight back. I'm impressed. How did you manage to get shot twice with moves like that?"

"Who the hell are you?" I ask her again, growing impatient and putting more pressure on her arm.

Wincing in pain, she looks up to see Scarlett standing in the doorway. She lets a low whistle escape from her lips. "Agent Shields, haven't you ever fucking heard of sunscreen?"

"Haven't you ever heard of pasty white hackers who never go outside?"

The woman sighs and shakes her head. "This is what happens when you send agents into the field without proper training."

"Yes, I think I missed the training session where they went over proper sunscreen use. Is there a PowerPoint presentation I can download? Also, when *someone* gave me a trunk full of cool spy gear, including automatic firearms, cellphone jammers, bugs and keyloggers, she forgot to include emergency sunscreen."

The woman laughs, and I feel awkward about not releasing her. She doesn't even seem to notice that she is being restrained, and Scarlett obviously knows her. But my whole body feels stiffened to the point of immobility. I am not taking any chances.

"To be fair," the woman says, "when I said you should get some field experience, I didn't know there would be so many actual *fields* involved."

"Cole," Scarlett says with amusement. "This is my boss. You can release her. Unless she's about to fire me for getting a really bad sunburn."

There. Now I feel slightly more comfortable letting her go. It is difficult to make my muscles move, as they are locked so tightly I feel like my body is made of wires and steel. I have to take a deep breath to get enough oxygen into my arms so that they can relax and get out of kill mode.

Scrambling off the ground, the woman immediately rushes over to Scarlett and gives her a hug. "Oh, Sophie. Thank God you're okay! I was sure you'd either been killed or captured."

"No, no, nothing like that," Scarlett says, returning the hug with surprise. She seems genuinely happy to see this woman. Looking at me over her friend's shoulder, she smiles. "Cole, I'd like you to meet Agent Luciana Lopez."

When the woman turns around to shake my hand, I frown.

"It's really not a huge pleasure to meet you," I say with annoyance. "Why would you point a gun

208

in the face of a man who's just been shot?"

Luciana rolls her eyes. "Relax, Mr. Pikachu shorts. I had the safety on the gun the whole time. Men of your generation are so sensitive."

"Sadist."

"First of all, I couldn't be 100% sure that either of you were alive and in this vehicle—I got the specs on it, and this thing is an armored, military prototype for a *new tank* that contains built-in ammunitions? Are you fucking kidding me? This thing could waste me from miles away if the people inside were paying attention to their surroundings instead of each other's bodies. It would be stupid if I *didn't* go in guns blazing. My 'field agent' here failed to keep me updated."

"Hmmm," Scarlett says, stepping out of the tank in her bed sheet and studying the exterior. "We really need to work on the monitoring systems and alarms for intruders. At least some visual and audio mapping to check for anomalies in the area."

"We?" Luciana repeats. "Um, last time I checked you had a job. Working for *me.*"

"Yeah, well I had her first," I tell Luciana, stepping toward Scarlett possessively. "And due to the tragic death of a really swell guy, Scarlett has inherited an empire. That comes with tons of responsibilities. So, I think I win."

Luciana laughs. "I think you're confusing your Scarlett Hunter with my Sophie Shields. And *Sophie* chose working for the CIA over working for you."

"Only because of personal circumstances," I say softly. "Also, she worked *with* me, not for me."

"Aw, shucks. Please don't fight over me and my technological talents," Scarlett says, pretending to be embarrassed. "Actually, just keep on fighting. I feel so appreciated right now."

"Speaking of personal circumstances," Luciana says, raising an eyebrow and looking at Scarlett. "I only really flew out here because your boyfriend is worried sick about you. He called me saying you'd disappeared and begged me to send help."

"Zack? Dammit."

"He sounded like he was crying. He was so worried."

"Yeah, that's my bad. I should have let him know I was safe."

"And I probably *shouldn't* let him know that I found you naked in your brother's fancy mobile home, while your brother was also in a precarious state of undress?"

"For god's sake, Luciana. Cole is my *foster* brother."

"Clearly," she says, studying my build from head to toe. She walks around me appraisingly, and I can feel her eyes burning into my glutes. "Mmm, and thank god for that."

I clear my throat, feeling like a piece of meat. "We're also married, and she's broken up with Zack."

"Does Zack know that?"

"Yes," Scarlett says. She hesitates. "He's just not totally willing to accept it."

Luciana nods. "Okay, look, guys. I need your help. There's some shit going on in L.A. that's getting really out of hand, and we gotta go check it out. There were explosions at two of Cole's worksites, and while we suspect it's probably just whoever shot Cole trying to draw Sophie out, some of my superiors want me to investigate whether it's possible that we've stumbled onto some kind of terrorist activity. Especially since Cole ran an international business and has connections to the Middle East and problems in Karachi."

"Whoa," Scarlett says softly. "That's… escalating quickly."

"You want us to physically go somewhere?" I ask the woman, afraid to have our little bubble popped before we've even gotten a chance to get comfortable here. We haven't even had the time to binge watch a single season of *Breaking Bad!* "I can't really travel right now. I don't have any identification—because I'm dead."

Luciana sighs loudly and dramatically. "You do realize that you're talking to two CIA agents, right? Do you think my name is really Lucy Lopez?" She rolls her eyes. "God, men are so whiny. I got shot, wah, wah, don't point guns at me, it's scary. I'm dead now, I can't get on an airplane, I don't have a driver's license in the ten million dollar loveshack I designed for the military and NASA, but really only use to bang girls like it's a

211

Volkswagen Bus from the 70s. I'm such a poor boy, I have a papercut on my face, please pity me, Mommy, kiss it better."

I stare at her, blinking.

She snarls at me. "Get over yourself. Grow up. Shit happens! Now, I'd appreciate if you invited me inside your war machine and made me some tea."

Walking into the NovaTank without waiting for her invitation, she peeks inside curiously. "Whoa, this thing is amazing! I need to get me one of these someday. How does one pathetic businessman have cooler toys than the CIA?"

Scarlett is biting her lip to conceal her amusement at her boss's rant, while my eyebrows are lifted extremely high. No one has dared to speak to me this way in a long time.

"Hey, Cole," she says softly. "I think if I were actually your sister, that's how I'd talk to you."

"Scar—what makes you think that isn't how you talk to me?"

"Do I?" she answers with a grin. "I guess it's been a while and you haven't really annoyed me yet."

Luciana pops her head out of the NovaTank with excitement. "Holy shit, I just saw your shower! Damn, boy, are you an architect, or the fucking reincarnation of Michelangelo?"

Suddenly, I don't dislike this woman as much as I originally thought I did. She's growing on me.

"Please tell me you guys had sex in that

shower," Luciana demands. "This house is like a magic castle on wheels! Can I see the built-in guns, please? Sophie, you've got a good one—he's a keeper. Men are allowed to be whiny little bitches if they are also magnificent artists. You can't have it all!"

"Thanks, I think?" Scarlett says, making a face.

Sighing, I move into the Nova, heading for the ultra-compact kitchen. "I better make the woman her tea."

213

Chapter Twenty-One

Sophie Shields, 2016

"So, that's the gist of what's been happening in L.A.," Luciana says as she sips her tea at a table I didn't know was there. "Do either of you know who might be behind this?"

I glance at Cole, knowing that we are both thinking about Benjamin. But there is also Brittany. But would she really set off explosives at Cole's buildings? I am sure Luciana already knows about these suspects, if she's been in touch with Rodriguez at all…

"We have some ideas," I tell Luciana. "But I need more information, especially about Brittany Brown, and what she's been up to all these years. I need to talk to the detective about Annabelle's crime scene. I need a computer. I need the internet, and I can find us answers."

"What about that whole terrorism angle?" Luciana asks. "Cole, is that bullshit or do you have enemies abroad?"

"I don't know," he says honestly. "I have enemies everywhere, I suppose. I would have to talk to Miranda and Levi."

"Okay," Luciana says. "Then we'll do that. This tea is great! Hey, did you guys like my one liner about the Kardashians? I thought of it on the helicopter ride over here."

"It was okay," Cole says as refills the coffee cup that I have just drained. Earlier, he flipped the bed up into the wall to reveal pop-up chairs that were folded into the floor below the bed, and a table that drops down from the bottom of the bed. The NovaTank is rather small, but the amazing design of the space is so versatile that it feels perfectly cozy, and it isn't terribly embarrassing to entertain here. Cole has thought of almost everything.

And we've put more clothes on.

"I think I was more scared of the gun than the mention of the Kardashians," Cole admits. "But I still have fresh bullet holes in my body that haven't finished healing. I might be a biased sample. What did you think, Scar?"

"Hmmm," I say as I deeply inhale the scent of my fresh coffee. "I was worried for a second when I saw there was a person outside, but once I heard Lucy's voice I felt better. I had a good comeback about how a Kardashian would probably still miss from point-blank range because she'd pause to take a photo of herself with the gun—but then you two started fighting. Cole, I was worried you were going to break her arm."

He nods sheepishly. "It's not a great time for practical jokes. Sorry if I'm a little tightly wound."

"It's okay," Luciana says, patting his shoulder—his injured shoulder—and making him wince. "We've all been there, bud. The first time you get shot is the worst. After that, it gets easier."

"This isn't the first time I've been shot," Cole says. "But I was also in the hospital receiving treatment for being *poisoned* when I got shot, so it was all a little much to handle."

"Poisoned?" I ask him with concern. "No one told me about that. It wasn't in your files..."

"Roddy may have doctored my files a little to try to conceal the truth from you," he explains.

I bite my lip at this. "Do you mean Detective Rodriguez? He knew that you were alive?" When Cole nods, I lean back in my chair and let gust of air pass slowly through my teeth. "He was in on this?"

"He kind of orchestrated the whole thing," I say with a smile. "He's a really good friend."

"That motherfucking bastard. He misled me so much—when I told him I thought you were alive he had this fake conversation with me about spirituality." Clenching my coffee cup tightly, I take a large swig of the brew. "I'm going to punch him in the face."

216

"You met him a few times, years ago, but I don't think you'd remember. My roommate from juvie?"

My jaw falls open. "Oh my god. Rodriguez is Little Ricky?"

"Yes. He grew up a lot, didn't he?"

"Cole! How did I not recognize him? He was at our fucking wedding!"

He laughs softly. "Roddy has changed a lot over the years. After some guy named Ricky Rodriguez died in a tragic murder-suicide, he didn't want to go by Ricky anymore. So we used his middle name until some dude named Carlos Rodriguez smashed his car into a tree while on drugs in Florida, and flattened half of his head. He literally has half a head. Roddy got teased about that for a while, so he ended up just shortening it to Roddy. Most of his friends called him that already."

Luciana yawns. "While your detective sounds *so* very fascinating, I'd like to get back to the murders and explosions? At least five people were killed in those explosions, and over two dozen more are in hospitals. Some of the victims were just pedestrians nearby."

"Dammit," Cole says softly. "You didn't say that there were casualties. Miranda is probably dealing with a PR shitstorm and legal nightmare. I feel so bad for not being there to help out."

"You need me to be bait," I say suddenly, slamming down my 90% empty coffee mug. "It has to be about me, right? If they think Cole is dead…

then why keep doing this? Why else would Brittany try to impersonate Annabelle after her death, and show up at Cole's funeral? That bitch claimed to be his girlfriend and requested that I give her his semen sample."

"What?" Cole says, making a face of disgust straight out of a horror movie. "Please tell me you didn't!"

"Of course not!"

"Hmm," Luciana mumbles. "Maybe she just wanted to destroy it so you'd be like, really and truly dead—to kill out any potential for you to have an heir to your throne. She was destroying your whole bloodline, because only a Hunter can rule Winterfell and hold the north. I mean, Snowfire Industries Ltd.."

"What?" Cole says in confusion.

"Babe," I say teasingly. "Next time someone puts a gun to your head, if you really want to live, offer them the *Game of Thrones* Blu-ray discs, okay?"

"I don't have any."

"Well, we definitely have to go back to society now."

Luciana frowns. "Since you're not actually dead, why don't we just give her the semen and see if it will calm her down. You can make more, right?" She turns to me. "He can make more, right?"

I shrug. I honestly don't know.

Luciana finishes up her tea and hands the

empty container to Cole. "Here's a cup. Give us your sperm and we'll save the world."

I can't help grinning a little, but then I begin thinking. Isn't the semen he made at age 20 better than the semen he is currently making at age 29? It doesn't work that way for guys, does it? There is probably only a slight difference in quality, since they have constantly generating sperm factories. I wonder if I should get my eggs frozen?

Cole coughs awkwardly and pushes away the cup. "I don't know about that, but Brittany was definitely the person who poisoned me," he says with a frown. Reaching up, he runs a hand through his hair, as he often does when upset. "There's this gym and relaxation spa at Annabelle's clinic—I designed it for her. There's a sauna, a steam room, a hot tub, massage rooms—I usually use the gym and steam room after my sessions, to wait out the traffic before heading home. I used the steam room the night before I got sick. I could have inhaled the cadmium there."

"You inhaled cadmium?" I ask him softly. "Is that why you've been coughing so much?"

"Yes, but they got it all out of my system. I'm going to be fine."

"That's an *extremely* clever poisoning," Luciana says with worry. "The attacker knew that was a chemical Cole could have been exposed to at his construction sites, so the foul play could have gone undetected. But then why ruin all that careful planning with a very public sniper shooting?"

"Unless there are multiple assassins," I suggest. "Arguing about their methods. Pulling in different directions. Didn't Professor Brown have another kid—a son?"

"Or it could be Benjamin," Cole says quietly.

Just hearing his name said out loud makes me visibly flinch. It's been like that for years. His name in a book, on a street sign, in a movie, on the news…

"Who's that?" Luciana asks.

"A child molester," Cole begins. "Scar, do you mind if I…?"

"Not now, please. Lucy, you said you brought a helicopter? Can you take us back to civilization?"

"Sure!" she says, standing up and stretching. "Let's get going. It's been a while since I've done any field work myself, Shields. Thanks for getting me out of the office."

"Wait," Cole says. "Wait. I don't agree with this. It's not worth the risk. Scarlett, you can't use yourself as bait for these crazy murderers. Just trust that Rodriguez will take care of it, and Agent Lopez here. We don't have to do anything. We can just stay here, and be *safe*. Luciana found you because of the special phone she gave you, but no one else will have any idea where we are. *No one* else."

"I've spent so much of my life running and hiding," I tell him. "It's time to fight." I reach out to touch his hand. "Let's fight against this, together."

"No," he says firmly. "I can't let you put yourself in harm's way again. You've been through too much."

"This is my job, Cole. I feel that it's important to do this."

"No. Scarlett—you're not well. You can't…" He pauses, breathing heavily. "Luciana, please— she's too close to this. If you care about her at all, you won't let her leave this desert. This world is filled with good hackers who can help out without being in danger. I guarantee that if Scarlett comes with you, she's going to get hurt."

"You're asking your wife to quit her job?" Luciana says slowly, with narrowed eyes. "Because it's too dangerous? That's kind of controlling, buddy. It's her choice to make."

"Look, you don't know the whole story," Cole says. "Luciana, can we have a talk in private about Scarlett's mental health? I think there are certain issues you need to be made aware…"

"What the fuck, Cole!" I say crossly, feeling anger mounting in my chest. "Are you trying to sabotage my life? Because contrary to what you think, I have been perfectly fine without you for *years!* I love working for Lucy. Okay, so it would be a little easier if she let me use a fucking computer. But I do fine."

"Then go back to *that* job, Scar. Work behind a desk, in a secure building, under your false identity. But do not go back to L.A., and get involved in this investigation as Scarlett Hunter. Not right now. Your husband was just killed—" he points to the scar on his cheekbone, "—and his attackers are seriously gunning for you. I happened to turn to the side before this happened, or it would have gone right through my head. I just want you to be okay. Please. We've been apart for so long, and I'm not willing to let you go. Just stay with me until Rodriguez has a suspect in custody."

Feeling deeply uncomfortable and confused about this whole thing, I rub my eyes. I look to Luciana for help, and she shrugs.

"This is a domestic dispute, hun. I never thought you were the kind of girl to let a man tell you not to do something. But he does have a point. I'd rather you sit this one out, and take a long vacation, than get hurt. I don't want to lose one of my best agents. But even if you quit—I'd rather you be alive and happy somewhere in the mountains, with your incredibly hot dead husband, than lying in a pool of blood in L.A.."

I sigh at this, turning to look at Cole.

I wish I were not the type of girl who obsessively needed to find answers. To finish what she started. And as much as I have run away, I have also stayed. I wish I were not the type of girl who was drawn to danger. I wish I did not feel most alive when I was a whisper away from death.

I know that Cole's right. I know it in my heart. I'm going to get hurt.

But I can't live with myself if I just sit back and do nothing while people are getting hurt. Everyone sat back and did nothing when I was younger, and I was getting hurt. I was utterly powerless then. Now I'm capable of actually doing something to help—why would I choose to save my own skin instead of making a difference?

Clearing my throat, I smile at Cole. "We don't have *Game of Thrones* on Blu-ray. And I don't have internet access here to illegally download or stream it."

"That's a huge deciding factor," Luciana adds.

"Scar..." Cole says softly, reaching out to grasp my hands pleadingly. "Please don't go."

"I have to. Will you come with me? You don't have to. I know that you've been badly injured, and you're tired. I totally understand if you want to stay here and rest up. I'll come back for you."

He laughs softly, pulling me close and kissing the tip of my nose. "There's no way I'm letting you out of my sight, ever again. Besides, I do want to see Anna's killer go down. I know my company better than anyone, and there's a lot I can do to help out."

"Okay!" Luciana says, clapping her hands together. "Looks like you know some real men after all, Shields. Let's go, chop-chop! You guys get your stuff, and I'll be waiting in the chopper. See what I did there?"

"Mmmm," Cole says. "It was almost funny."

"I have some spare guns waiting in the helicopter," Luciana says. "I would offer you guys some protection, but I think what you really need is sunscreen."

"Okay. That was a sick burn," Cole says. "Get

223

it? Sick burn?"

"Shut the hell up, both of you," I say with a groan.

Chapter Twenty-Two

Cole Hunter, 2016

My stomach is in knots.

We're on a small plane now, after transferring over from the helicopter. I can see the desert landscape disappearing as it is replaced with the coastal greenery and cities. Scarlett seems happy, or at least focused. She has a computer in her hands, so she is in her element, and watching her is the only thing that is making this situation tolerable for me. It's been so long since I've seen her like this, and it's still magical. Perhaps I should find it more magical now that she has hacked into some of the toughest security systems across the planet—but whether she's hacking my bank account to reverse a

$10 overdraft charge, or saving the world, I find myself equally mesmerized.

Maybe it was a blessing in disguise that she had to leave me. The experiences she had at her new job obviously helped her grow as a person and as a professional, and I couldn't offer that much of a challenge to her. I feel jealous of Luciana, as I miss working with Scar every day, but I am happy that she has succeeded in such a coveted position, where her work is important and deeply valued.

I just don't know how to tell her that I'm not strong enough to do this. I have a very bad feeling in my gut. But I promised Snow that I would try and help her heal. If leaving the NovaTank to return to the city that tried to kill me is what she needs, then that's what I'm going to do. She is the woman I love, and she has suffered from a great deal of pain, some of which I contributed to inflicting upon her, unknowingly.

I'm going to do whatever I can to make this right.

Scar has had internet access for about forty-five minutes, and I'm sure she already knows more than the detective, and anyone else working on this case. She hacked into the police files first, upset that Roddy gave her incomplete information before. She has taken everything into her own hands, as she often does.

"It looks like Levi called the police and gave a statement of a few people and companies he's having difficulty with. Ugh, this is a long list. Do you recognize anyone, Cole?"

"A couple of them. Do you want me to make some notes on what I can remember off the top of my head?"

"Yes, please," she says, handing me her new phone while she continues to search for information on the computer. "Something I didn't do before is access the traffic cams around the area where you were shot, because I didn't know what to look for. But I could access the traffic cams around the two worksites with the explosions, maybe shortly before the detonations happened. I'll cross reference them with each other, and then the area around the hospital, just before you were shot. It looks like the bombs were homemade, if I'm reading the police reports right."

She looks over at me and smiles sadly. "They did very little damage to your buildings. Your structures are so tough and well-secured that they could probably only set the bombs up to harm the construction workers in the unfinished buildings. They aren't fitted with security cameras yet. Maybe I can look up the style of bomb used and see if there's any history of someone using that same technique elsewhere. Or any specific elements required to make the bombs that may have been purchased somewhere."

"You should make Roddy do that," I suggest to her. "Call him up and ask him to help out. You'll cover more ground, faster, if you're working together."

"I will," she says absentmindedly, while she continues looking up information furiously, and pushing her black glasses up higher on her nose. (We had to fly the helicopter back to the house on Red Earth Lane so that she could grab her purse containing her glasses, gun, and ID, and retrieve her laptop from the Bugatti. We also tucked the car safely away in the garage.) When Scarlett is doing research, she sometimes gets so completely in the zone that she blocks out all her surroundings. I should call Roddy to help her out.

"Okay, guys," Luciana says, walking into the plane. "I ordered some things to help keep you incognito. Wigs, contact lenses, some facial hair, prosthetics, and a fake ID for Cole. Also, some makeup to cover up those sunburns for Scarlett, and some aloe vera cooling lotion."

"Thanks," Scarlett says, itching miserably.

"I also got us set up with a great safe house location. We obviously can't go to Cole's house."

"We have other places we could stay," Scarlett tells her. "We could crash with Miranda?"

"It's better not to involve them and possibly make them unsafe. They all have known connections to you two, especially Cole. The safe house is best," Luciana says. "It's not as nice as your tank, but few things on this planet are."

"I have some more tanks," I tell her. "In the warehouse. There are a few models we built to test certain features. No one is currently using them."

"Cole, the tanks might be sturdy and safe, and

228

bulletproof, but they just aren't practical for the city. Where would we even park them?"

"Okay, what's this safe house like, Agent Lopez?"

"It's an underground bomb shelter below a stylish home. Since there have been explosions, and you two seemed so nervous about coming back here, I really wanted to get you something solid. You can use either the house itself, which has four bedrooms, or the bunker below. It's definitely secure. Cole, it's probably recommended that you remain there indefinitely for now, to avoid being seen."

"Can Scarlett stay with me? Can she work from there?

"Of course."

"Guys, I found some really messed up stuff about the Brown family," Scarlett says, pushing her glasses up higher again. "

"She works so fast we might have this case figured out before we even arrive at the safe house," I tell Luciana.

The woman nods. "I've never seen her with a computer before. Her fingers are moving so quickly, I keep wondering if they might set the damn thing on fire."

"My hands are hurting a lot, thanks for asking," Scarlett admits with frustration. "I haven't done this in a while. I'm out of practice."

Turning to Luciana, I give her the sternest look I can muster. "No matter what happens from now on, Scarlett should never be banned from using computers again."

"I agree," Luciana says kindly.

Thinking about Snow's list, I begin to feel a tiny bit of hope that we are moving in the right direction. If only the next few days can progress smoothly, and we can all avoid getting shot or blown up, things will definitely be looking up. I suddenly remember that I am holding Scarlett's phone, and I unlock it to dial the detective.

Chapter Twenty-Three

Cole Hunter, 2016

"Oh, no," I say when I see the house, shielding my face from the eyesore. "Oh, no, no, no, no. Who would build such a disgusting monstrosity!"

"You don't like it?" Luciana asks with hurt as she drives into the parking lot.

"It's an architectural nightmare! Look at all those ugly, useless windows. Look at that hideous roof. And what is up with that portico? If all the houses in this neighborhood are pimples on the face of the earth, this one is a giant, honking tumor. I can't look at it. Scarlett, save me." I try to bury my face in her shoulder, but she pushes my head away.

231

"Stop it, Cole. I'm working," she says softly. "Are you still so structurally sensitive? You need to get over that. Elitist. I just found some extremely large deposits in Jeremy Brown's bank account. That's Brittany's brother. I'm trying to trace them. I also found out that Zack served in Afghanistan around the same time as Jeremy Brown. I wonder if Zack could know of him? I should ask."

"Zack is already waiting inside the safe house," Luciana tells us. "You still want him on as your security detail, right? I highly recommend keeping him. Bodyguards are always better when they actually care whether you live or die."

"Oh, shit!" Scarlett says, blinking. "Yes, I want him to stay on, but I didn't know he was already here. Lucy! Do we have to do this right now?"

"Of course," Luciana says, rubbing her hands together. "This job is so depressing. So many people are dead, and we're always in danger. I had to orchestrate some romantic drama to keep myself entertained." She grips the steering wheel with excitement and dances a little with her shoulders when she says 'romantic drama.'

Scarlett growls audibly as she slams the screen of her laptop down. She grabs her purse before stepping out of the car heavily. "This is why we never hang out, Agent Lopez! You're always doing shit like this, getting involved in my personal life, encouraging me to get a boyfriend, setting me up with guys until I give up and pick one, constantly pestering me with questions about my sex life. What is wrong with you? Do you have no life of your own, and have to get your rocks off by messing with mine? And by *always* making things more complicated!"

Luciana begins to respond, but Scarlett has already slammed the car door shut and is walking toward the house. I see Luciana's shoulders sag, and I feel bad for her. But she turns off the vehicle, and in the next moment, she is opening her car door and yelling right back at Scarlett.

"Do you realize that every single thing you just accused me of doing is just normal shit that girlfriends actually do? What's your damage, Shields? Have you never had a friend in your life? Do you hate women? I get it, girls are complicated. Men are easy to manipulate, because they'll basically do anything for you in order to get laid, until they either give up and move onto the next girl, or get a little taste and keep trying forever. Do you not know how to have a friend without sex involved? Do you not see that our relationship isn't purely about money, and the fact that I'm your boss, and want you to stay alive, but I actually think you're really cool and give a shit about you?"

Scarlett pauses and turns around, with surprise in her eyes. Her lips, as usual, are expressionless. "We have work to do," she announces to us both, with narrowed eyes.

Luciana sighs and begins following her, and I follow suit.

Suddenly, Scarlett turns around with a frown. "I give a shit about you, too," she tells Luciana, before ringing the doorbell.

I notice that Luciana pauses for a moment, surprised by Scarlett's admission. Then she briefly turns back to me and flashes a quick, excited thumbs up on both hands with a giant, goofy smile. It's gone a second later, and I have to bite my lip very hard to keep from bursting out in laughter and betraying her.

I like this girl. I don't know a lot of women who have the balls to even try to keep up with my Scarlett. That friendship item on the list seemed almost impossible to achieve until Lucy dropped into our laps. Although, I do worry about whether she could handle every aspect of Scarlett. Would she freak out if we got into some sort of bad situation, and she happened to meet Snow? Although Snow has matured a lot, over the years. The first time I met her, she was ripping apart a man's neck with her teeth. Snow only existed for a few reasons: sex and fighting, more sex, and more fighting. But now, these days, she can actually stick around long enough for us to have a conversation.

So, if she had to kill someone with her teeth, she might be more polite and friendly afterwards.

That's character growth, if you ask me.

When the door is ripped open by a very large man, he reaches out to hug Scarlett at once. He holds her a little too long, a little too tightly, and I find myself sizing him up. I try to stop, but it's just human nature. I want to say something, or step in, or clear my throat, but I feel a little… guilty.

He was obviously worried about her. He's spent a lot more time embracing her in recent years than I have, so maybe this will be good for her. Comforting.

"Soph, I thought you were dead," he says softly. "I called and I called, but I couldn't reach you. Don't ever do that to me again. I was so fucking worried! You should have taken me with you."

"I'm sorry," she says, pulling away awkwardly. "Hey, let's go inside and talk."

As we all move into the confines of the atrociously designed house that is just as hideous on the inside as it is on the outside, Zack turns and begins to appraise me. I move forward, meeting his gaze, and shut the door behind us all.

"Zack," Scarlett says, "I'd like you to meet my brother, Cole."

I clear my throat slightly. I try to stop myself, but I can't help it.

"Okay," she says with a roll of her eyes. "My ex-foster brother, Cole. Who is also my dead husband."

"Hey, man," I say, stepping forward to shake his hand. I try to use a firm grip, not too threatening, with a friendly smile.

"So, you're Cole," Zack says, returning the handshake. He makes the face you can only make when you are being forced to shake the hand of the guy who is stealing your woman away—when actually, she never belonged to you in the first place. "You could have mentioned that you were married to her when I called you on the phone and asked for your permission to marry her."

I chew on my lip, thinking of how to respond. Scarlett has gone to sit down on the nearest sofa and has already returned to hacking. She is ignoring us. I clear my throat again. "Well, I certainly could have mentioned that, but I didn't want to deter you from trying in case she really did want to marry you. I hadn't heard from her in a little while, and she didn't seem to be receiving *the letters I wrote her*—so we didn't have much in the way of communicating with each other."

Zack pauses, as if considering his next chess move. "I apologize for that. It was very low and insecure on my part. But you need to understand, Sophie is my girlfriend…"

"*Was* your girlfriend," she corrects from her chair as her fingers fly across the keyboard.

"And I made a mistake," Zack says, "which has made her understandably upset with me. But I intend to try my best to be a good man, a good friend, and win her back."

Oh, really. Buddy, don't even try. I am reaching for my non-existent gauntlets and sword to challenge him to a duel when Scarlett speaks up.

"I'm with Cole, now, Zack. He's my boyfriend." She doesn't even pause in her typing to say this.

"What the hell? Sophie, you can't punish me like this. I know I screwed up..."

She looks up suddenly. "Wait—Cole, you *are* my boyfriend now, right?"

"Yes! I thought that was very clear," I tell her with a laugh.

"Okay," she says, returning to typing.

"Very clear?" Zack asks, taking a step closer to me. *"Very* clear? Why is it *very* clear!"

"Well," I say, thinking of how to explain. "She found this letter I wrote when I was fifteen which outlined my plan for our future together, which I intended to conceal until I felt she was ready. We never really seriously gave it a chance, but we're trying now. Especially since I got shot and nearly died, we've had a real wake-up call and talked in detail about our issues. I think ultimately, we've both grown up a lot, and we're going to try to be together."

"You fucked her, didn't you."

"Guys, this is so entertaining," Luciana says, clapping excitedly. "I love excessive displays of masculine bravado. Are you going to beat each other up now?" She snaps her fingers. "Damn, I knew I should have sold some tickets and taken bets. At least get out rulers and measure the diameter of your balls. Let me get popcorn real fast."

"Wait," Scarlett says, lifting her head from her computer. "What did I miss?"

"Don't worry, hun. Your boyfriends are just

figuring out who has the bigger dick and the bigger claim on you. But they don't need to measure, do they? You can just tell us? Everyone in the room is wondering, don't keep us in suspense."

Scarlett makes a face of disgust. "People are getting murdered, guys." She stretches out her fingers, which seem to be getting sore. "Does anyone have a nail clipper or a sharp knife? I've been typing so much that my nails are starting to feel really heavy and difficult to move. I only have a few long nails that haven't already broken off… Actually, forget it. We have shit to do. Zack, do you know a Jeremy Brown?"

"I've heard that name. Oh, shit. From Afghanistan?"

"We think he's the one who shot Cole."

"With a sniper rifle?" Zack scoffs. "I wouldn't have missed."

"Zack!" Scarlett says in dismay.

"No, no," Zack says, lifting his hands. "I don't mean I want to kill Cole. Definitely not with a sniper rifle. Or any type of rifle! Or like, at all. Seriously. I just meant that I'm a good shot, and Jeremy Brown sucks ass."

"Okay. Well, Jeremy, Brittany's brother, received a large sum of money deposited to his bank account recently. I can't trace where it comes from. Like, it's rerouted through several different offshore accounts. I wouldn't say it's completely untraceable, but… it's taking me a while. It's also… it's divided into thousands of smaller sums? That are then divided into even smaller sums? What the fuck is this sorcery! Someone is *really* good at hiding money trails."

"What does that mean?" Zack asks.

"I don't know yet. It's easier to see what he did with the money. Ohhhh, shit."

Scarlett falls back on the sofa, making a guttural groan.

"What's wrong?" Luciana asks, suddenly all business.

"He hired an architect to design a special mausoleum for his mother and father."

"Oh," I say quietly. "Oh, no. Oh, crap. Crap, crap."

"And he only hired that architect after Cole refused."

"I didn't even know who was asking for that project! I look at the project profile, not the developers, most of the time. We're booked solid for years! We also have to prioritize our own developments. We don't have time for petty personal sculptures when the world's population is massively exploding, and there are people everywhere in need of decent places to live for decent prices."

"Dude, we killed his dad. Then you refused to build him a mausoleum."

"And is that a good reason to try to put a bullet in my head?" I ask her.

"No, of course not," she says, sighing. "But that might not be the reason either. He could have

239

received that money as an advance payment for killing you. Or attempting to kill you." She sits back up and leans forward, gazing at her laptop closely. "What if a pissed off competitor didn't actually want you dead, and just wanted you broken? Poison him *almost* to death. Shoot him *almost* to death. Make him need a vacation. Scare him away, so I can pick up some of his market share. Does this sound crazy? I think there are people out there who would prefer to watch someone suffer forever than die."

"That's a really sexy theory," Luciana says. "I like it."

Zack clucks his tongue. "Except for the fact that Jeremy Brown can't shoot for shit, and if he was trying to almost kill anyone, he'd probably actually kill them—or kill someone standing ten feet away from them."

"I think someone should check out the architect's office. M. Williams Flawless Design," Scarlett says.

A little burst of mocking laughter comes out of my throat. "Flawless. I hardly think so."

"You know them?" Scarlett asks.

"One of the worst firms in the city," I tell her. "They don't get much work, but the stuff I've seen them do looks worse than this house. I should probably go and check out their offices."

"Go with Detective Rodriguez," Luciana suggests, reaching for a suitcase and pulling out some facial hair and prosthetics. "He will be here

240

shortly. But you'll have to wear one of these disguises, because I doubt there's an architect in this city who doesn't recognize you. Or hate you."

"Looks like fun," I say, grabbing some crazy facial hair.

Scarlett shuts her computer. "Okay. In the meantime, I'm going to check out this mausoleum. Anyone wanna come?"

"You don't have to do any field work, Shields," Luciana reminds me with a frown. "I can go with Zack, or take other agents if necessary. You figure out where we need to go, and we'll send people while you stay safe and cozy in the safe house. Deal?"

"Is this because of my sunburn?" Scarlett asks, itching at it.

"That's a sunburn?" Zack comments. "I thought someone dropped you in acid."

Scarlett sends him an unimpressed look. "I can handle myself out in the big bad world. Besides, this one is personal. How often do you get to spit on the grave of someone who used your body as an ashtray when you were thirteen? I think I'll bring champagne."

I hesitate. I don't know how I feel about splitting up with Scarlett, but I do know that I would be more useful at the architect's office.

"Do you want me to come with you?" I ask her.

Luciana clears her throat. "I don't think either of you should leave this safe house."

241

"That would be boring," Scarlett says. "Cole, I'll be fine. Zack will come along and keep me safe. You go with Little Ricky."

"He doesn't like being called that anymore," I tell her.

"Well, I doubt there will be much action at an architect's office or a mausoleum," Luciana says. "I guess it's not that dangerous for you guys to help out. I already told that detective of yours to start looking for Jeremy Brown in addition to Brittany Brown, so hopefully his team is all over that. Shields, can you find a single most likely origin country for those funds?"

Scarlett frowns deeply. "I'm sorry, Lopez. It really looks like the money just came from… everywhere. I don't see any other purchases other than the checks for M. Williams Flawless Design. There are some cash deposits though. Bet you guys fifty bucks there's cash sealed away in the mausoleum."

"I'll take that bet," Luciana says. "Fifty bucks on drugs or illegal firearms. We need to be careful—it could be booby trapped or something. Anything that's easily found is dangerous—it might just be waiting to be found. They might actually be finding us, without our knowledge."

"Well, that's ominous," Zack says as he heads to the door. "But I'm ready."

"We don't have to go right this instant," Luciana tells him. "We could strategize a little—"

The doorbell rings at that instant, and Zack

pulls his handgun out of his belt. He carefully checks the peephole before lowering his weapon and opening the door.

"Hey, it's a party!" Detective Rodriguez says, opening his arms. "I should have brought beer and pretzels. Knew you weren't serious about staying dead, Hunter."

"He was," Scarlett tells the detective. "He is. He just came here because we had some loose ends to tie up."

"Roddy... how did Anna die?" I ask my old friend.

The smile disappears from his face and his expression falls. That tells me everything I need to know. This man can stand over a dead body while drinking a peppermint mocha latte, eating a festive donut, and cracking jokes. It must have been really bad if he's giving me *that* look.

"Well, let's just focus on catching her killer," I say, walking out the door toward his police cruiser.

Scarlett exits behind me, and I hear her tease the detective. "Hi, Little Ricky."

He groans. "You told her, man? Everyone needs to forget that nickname *forever.*"

"Strange," Luciana says as she walks out behind us, studying Rodriguez carefully. "You don't seem little to me."

Chapter Twenty-Four

Cole Hunter, 2016

"She walked for how long?" Rodriguez says, turning to me in shock.

"Nearly twenty-four hours. Focus on the road, man."

The detective turns back to look at the street as we drive through the city. "I can't believe she found you."

Nodding, I stare out the window at the familiar buildings. "I had a feeling she would."

"I grossly underestimated her," the detective says as he makes a right turn that causes the car's tires to squeal. "That was foolish of me. She is the same girl who broke us out of prison, after all."

244

"She is."

"I guess when you said she was getting married to someone else… I thought she'd changed."

"Yeah, Roddy. I thought so, too."

"She was so loyal to you back then. There's no way that girl would go off and marry someone else."

"It turns out she never planned to. I had bad information."

"Good," Rodriguez says. "Because if you two split up, after everything you've been through together—there isn't a couple alive who has a chance."

I look at him quizzically. "Are you a romantic, Roddy? Underneath that hard exterior?"

He shakes his head and rolls his eyes, as if that's not possible. "I just wanted my roommate from juvie to live happily ever after with the girl of his dreams. Is that too much to ask?"

I find myself grinning at this answer. He's totally a romantic.

"Forgive me for asking," Rodriguez says in a low voice. "But what happened between you two? You were kind of vague about it before. What could you have done to scare away someone who loves you *that* much?"

Leaning back against the headrest with a sigh, I close my eyes. "Some other time, buddy. It's still kind of fresh, and I still… don't know if I can fix it."

We drive in silence for a few more minutes as he navigates to the architect's office. I chew on my lip, thinking about Annabelle. Thinking about my job. The life I've left behind.

When Rodriguez pulls the car into a parking lot of a derelict-looking building, I frown and lean forward to check if it's the correct address.

"This is M. Williams Flawless Design?" I ask in stupefaction. "What self-respecting architect would do business from a place like this? That's a cross between a toolshed and a…"

"Crack house?" Rodriguez supplies cheerfully. "I should know. It reminds me of my childhood. I'm getting warm and fuzzy feelings inside, man. I bet it smells just like my mama baking cookies on Christmas Eve in there. Let's go!"

As I watch the large man unlatch his seatbelt and pull his gun out of its holster as he moves toward the rundown shack, I shake my head slowly. If someone had told me thirteen years ago that Little Ricky Rodriguez would grow into such a badass, I'm not sure I would have believed them. I don't know anyone quite like my eccentric friend, the detective.

Chapter Twenty-Five

Sophie Shields, 2016

I am not sure what I am expecting to find at the mausoleum, but I feel slightly unprepared. I am still wearing the same torn, dirty jeans that I used to walk across the desert, and I feel disgusting. My sunburn certainly isn't helping. Since someone put a computer in my hands earlier today, I haven't had anything to eat or drink, and I've been typing constantly. I haven't really been focused on anything or anyone around me. I believe that's why it's called an addiction.

Now, Zack and Luciana are chatting in the front seat and cracking jokes. They are both armed with weapons, and I'm still just holding my laptop. What am I going to do, hold it up as a shield? I feel more than a little pathetic. Maybe Luciana was right, and I'm just not cut out for field work.

I'm a little worried about Cole heading off to that architect's office. He did not seem happy to be here—he was quieter than usual and very tense. I watched him in Rodriguez's car as they drove away, and he saw the hard set of his jaw, even under his fake facial hair. I feel so guilty for dragging him back here with me. Maybe I should have put his needs first, and stayed so he could get some rest and heal up.

But in that time, the body count could continue rising.

The problem with making decisions is that you're never really sure if you've made the right one until long after the plan has been executed, and you can finally start to see the longer-term repercussions. On a day like today, I am second guessing myself every minute.

I'm just a girl with a computer, used to living in a virtual world, but these are real people in the car with me—people I care about. If my intel is bad, it could risk their lives. Luciana is driving this scary, black SUV while Zack polishes his gun. I have mostly been just sitting here, hoping this day goes well, and acknowledging to myself over and over that I do not feel ready.

But I am not even sure exactly what I am not ready for.

Soon, I find out.

We have to navigate some rush hour traffic to

get to the cemetery where Jeremy's mausoleum was built, and I spend all this time on my computer. Zack and Lucy chat a little, but I don't really get involved. Until we arrive at our destination.

Putting my laptop down, I grab my gun out of my purse, determined to be of use. I haven't ever really cared whether my friends thought I was tough or cool, but I respect Luciana and want to be involved. I would be deeply embarrassed if I led them to useless information, or if I behaved uselessly now. The sunburn is embarrassing enough as a display of my incompetence.

But as I move to exit the vehicle, she halts me.

"Stay here, Agent Shields," she tells me, all professional. She is no longer Lucy, my friend. She is Agent Lopez, my boss. As the former is fairly knew, I haven't learned where to draw the line yet, and when to listen to her. To err on the side of caution, I close the car door with myself inside.

"I'm going to check out the cemetery and search for the mausoleum. Zack, I'll radio you if I need help. You protect Agent Shields."

"That's my job," he says enthusiastically.

It is only when Luciana has left the vehicle and disappeared from view that I realize I have been left alone in the car with Zack. When he gets out, and moves to sit in the back seat beside me, I swallow, dreading this conversation.

We sit in awkward silence for a few minutes, both of unsure of what to say.

Finally, he begins. "This is a practical joke,

right?" he asks me.

I turn to look at him with a question on my face.

"You and Cole. You're just mad at me about the letters, and you guys decided to prank me that you're together, as some sort of punishment. But it's not true, right?"

His eyes look so hopeful. I stare at him, unsure of how to respond.

"Sophie," he says, releasing his gun with one hand and grabbing one of mine. "You said… at the police station a few days ago. You said we might be going home together after all this? Back to our apartment in D.C.. Back to our lives?"

I did say that. "Zack…" I begin.

"No," he says quietly. "Don't dump me, Sophie. I don't want to hear it. We were happy, weren't we?"

"Sure," I tell him. "Kind of. You're a great guy, Zack, but…"

"Don't give me that bullshit."

"Listen. If Cole really had died—you would have stolen my last few months of communication with him. If he had died… it would have been partly my fault, because you kept me from knowing what was going on with him. In some ways, the only way our relationship worked was by me being a prisoner. And I need to be free."

"I screwed up, Soph. I made a huge mistake with those letters, and you know I'll never do anything like that again. I know how important Cole is to you, and I would never try to keep you away from him—"

"But you did. And I did. I let you."

"Soph," Zack says, taking my hand. "I know you love him as a brother and only married him for the money…"

"No," I tell Zack, closing my eyes. "You know that I'm completely in love with him. I have been afraid, and lying to myself about it for a long time. But I can't do that anymore, after all this mess. I can never let anyone keep us apart again. Not you, not me, not anyone."

Opening my eyes and giving his hand a little squeeze, I smile at him sadly. "You're just not the one for me, Zack. You must know that."

"So we're never going home together," Zack says softly. "You're staying here, and I'm going home without you. To sleep in our bed alone."

"I'm so sorry. You'll find someone better…"

"I don't want anyone else! Sophie, how can you actually be saying all this to me? I may have lied about a few letters, but he lied about being *dead.* How can someone who claims to love you do such a thing?" Zack rips his hand away from me and places it on his gun, stepping out of the car and slamming the door. He walks forward a few steps, pretending to be vigilant and scan our surroundings. Sighing, I shift uncomfortably in my seat before getting out of the car. I hear Luciana talking to Zack on the radio.

"*…found the mausoleum in the north west*

corner, over."

"Don't go in there alone. We're on our way," Zack tells her. "Over."

"You guys can stay with the car," she says. *"The detective said he's on his way."*

Zack turns to me and gestures to the cemetery. "I don't feel like staying with the car. Fancy a midnight stroll?"

"Sure," I say, as we walk forward into the darkness, over the rows of dead bodies.

"I'm not going to stop fighting for you, Sophie."

"Zachary, please. You need to stop. Leaving Cole was the biggest mistake of my life, and I'm not going to leave him again."

A voice from behind the gravestones speaks up. "Did you say Cole? As in Cole Hunter?"

I turn around in surprise, and find a man pressing a gun against my stomach.

"Zack," I say softly.

"Drop your weapon!" Zack tells the man, lifting his rifle. "Put the gun down, now!"

"No, I don't think so." Laughing softly, the man shoves the gun into my bellybutton, pushing me forward. "Tell me more about Cole Hunter. Everything you know."

"I don't know anything. I heard that he died." I can already feeling my insides twist with the impact of the bullet. If he shoots me here, what will it do to me? It could hit my spinal cord.

The man steps forward, and I am able to see

his face for the first time. "I know you," he says with a guttural laugh that can only be described as a cackle. "You're the girl with the red shoes."

"Fuck," I mutter to myself.

When a gunshot echoes through the night, my mind goes blank.

Chapter Twenty-Six

Cole Hunter, 2016

"Roddy, we have to get out of here," I tell my friend as he uses his flashlight to scan through a box of files. "What do you expect to find?"

"I don't know," he answers. "More details about this guy working with Jeremy Brown."

Sighing and looking around, I try to ignore the sickening state of the room. "What are these vials?" I ask, nudging a pile with my toes.

"Oh, those are crack pipes," he says, after a quick glance.

My foot recoils. "Seriously?"

"It looks like he wasn't just an architect, Cole. He was a serious drug dealer."

"Well, that explains why he failed so badly at design. A complete lack of focus! I mean, look at these sketches. I could do better when I was ten years old. Did this guy even go to school?"

Rodriguez gestures behind himself to a degree on the wall as he continues to hunt through the files. "Chances are his whole business is just a front for the drug dealing. He might be smuggling drugs into the country, and distributing them by putting them into the houses he builds or something. I don't know, but I'll figure it out. I just don't know what the connection to *you* could be."

"Oh, shit," I say quietly, peering closely at the photo on the wall. "I think I know what the connection is."

"What is it?" Rodriguez asks tiredly, following my line of sight. "I don't have time for more of your complaining about his lack of proficiency in architecture, Cole, so if you're going to whine about what school he went to…"

"No, no, Roddy. Look."

"Yeah? I'm looking. What am I looking for? He obviously didn't graduate summa cum laude like you…"

"Roddy! His fucking name."

"Okay. Marco Williams Jr.. What's so special about his name? Wait," Rodriguez says, his eyes growing narrowed. "Where have I heard that name before? Marco Williams. Marco Williams… Marco…"

"Polo," I respond.

"Loco," Rodriguez says with a sigh. "Seriously? Marco Polo Loco? The same guy who used to beat the shit out of me when I was twelve? His last name is *Williams*?"

"Junior," I add.

"He was in juvie for selling meth, right?"

"Yeah, and he used it too, from the looks of his teeth back then."

Rodriguez shakes his head. "I never got a good look at his teeth. I was always too busy having mine smashed in."

"You probably couldn't tell this, Roddy, but all his buildings are cheap copies of mine. They are also built shortly after the originals that I designed. Basically, he's been shadowing my career…"

"Stalking," Rodriguez corrects.

"Yeah. I guess when you have no creativity, and your brain is fried by drugs… trying to design flimsy replicas of someone else's hard work is all you can manage. It's sad, really."

"Well, I've seen all I need to see," Rodriguez says, stuffing his flashlight in his belt and heading for the door. "I can't wait to bust this guy. I doubt I've ever enjoyed an arrest as much as I'm gonna enjoy this one."

"Arrest?" I ask him. "If you think you're going to have the patience to arrest Marco Polo Loco, you don't know yourself very well, my friend."

"I guess we'll see," Rodriguez says. "But one thing's for sure. I sure as hell ain't getting my face smashed in by no washed up meth head today."

By the time we get to the mausoleum, Luciana is already there, sitting on the steps and smoking. Seeing this slightly lowers my very high opinion of her, and makes me less inclined to encourage her to be Scarlett's bestie. I don't want Scar picking up any habits that could make her sick.

Rodriguez, on the other hand, moves forward and rips the cigarette from Lucy's hand, before putting it to his lips and taking a drag so long that he nearly turns the entire length of the small cylinder into ash.

"I really needed that," he says, tilting his head back to allow smoke to waft upward, out of his chest.

"Jesus," Lucy says. "With lungs like that, you should play the flute or the clarinet or something."

"My talents are mostly for sucking and not for blowing," Rodriguez answers as he smashes the cigarette under his foot. Then he frowns. "Wait, that came out wrong. I meant to say—"

"Where's Scarlett?" I ask Luciana, and Rodriguez is grateful for the interruption. He always blabbers on and on like an idiot around pretty girls.

"She's on her way over here with Zack. I'm not sure what's taking them so long," she says in frustration.

"They are probably arguing," I suggest. "Have you checked out this mausoleum?"

"I was waiting for someone to join me," Luciana says. "This building gives me the creeps, big time."

"I can see why. The roof is designed all wrong, and these pillars are attached in different places. See? This one is an inch to the left. It could be the fault of the construction workers, but I doubt it. It's very poorly designed."

"It's not as bad as the crack house we just came from," Rodriguez says. "It turns out that the only thing M. Williams Flawless Design was any good at was designer drugs."

"Really?" Luciana says, suddenly brightening. "Well, we'll probably find more drugs inside this mausoleum. And I'll win fifty bucks!"

"It seems to be locked," Rodriguez says as he struggles to open the door. "Hello! Anyone in there?" When there is no answer, he shrugs and turns to Luciana. "Can you do some CIA magic and unlock this?"

"What magic? I usually work at a desk in an office just like Soph—"

I interrupt her by slamming my boot into the weakest part of the door causing it to crack open. Luciana and Rodriguez look at me in surprise, and I shrug.

"Shitty architecture," I explain. "You just kick it and it falls down."

"You're just full of surprises, aren't you?" Luciana asks as she fumbles with the door to push it completely open. But as soon as she does, she lifts her arm to cover her face and begins coughing violently.

I find my body suddenly petrified with fear. Is there some kind of chemical agent protecting the mausoleum from intruders? I can still feel the way that the cadmium shredded my lungs, every time I breathe. I won't survive breathing any more poisons in my current state. As I watch Luciana doubling over and coughing, I take a step back warily, afraid of being killed in some kind of sick chemical warfare.

But Rodriguez moves forward to place a hand on her back reassuringly as he peers through the cracks in the broken door.

"Holy fuck," he says softly, as he covers his own face with his sleeve. "Holy motherfucking fuck."

Chapter Twenty-Seven

Sophie Shields, 2016

It takes me a few seconds to figure out if I have been shot. There is a splatter of blood on my arm and my shirt. I rub my hands over my stomach anxiously, where the gun was pointed, but I feel no pain other than the ringing in my ears.

"Come on," Zack says, stooping to pick up an item and stuffing it in his pocket. He grabs my arm. "We gotta get to Luciana."

Only then do I realize what has happened. Zack shot the person who was holding the gun up against my body, forcing him to drop his weapon before fleeing into the darkness. "How did that happen?" I ask him breathlessly, as he guides me swiftly through the cemetery.

"It's always so easy to deal with people who don't really have any military training or experience abroad. Anything that can happen here, at home, is usually pretty mild in comparison to what I've seen," Zack says.

As I run behind him, I feel my eyebrows lift in surprise. Maybe I never really appreciated what Zack went through in Afghanistan. He doesn't talk about it much, but I know that it haunts him, far more than just the loss of his leg.

Cole has been deeply affected by his recent injuries, and they can't really compare to the permanent crippling feeling of losing a limb. Maybe I should forgive Zack a little more easily for hiding the letters and being insecure.

Or maybe my judgment is clouded by the fact that he just saved my life.

I don't know how long we spend running through the cemetery, but my legs begin to feel like jelly and the blisters on my feet begin to burn. I have to pause and sit down on a tombstone to let my legs rest for a second, and keep them from collapsing under me.

"Come on," Zack says, pulling me up and not allowing me to rest. "He's still out there, only wounded and not killed. We need to find Luciana and take cover."

"Okay," I say, standing weakly and trying to keep moving. I am not really walking any longer—I am constantly falling and stumbling forward in a slightly controlled manner. Zack is offering me

261

some support, and I feel guilty.

How can my legs be so weak that I need help from someone who is entirely missing a leg? Zack is surprisingly athletic on his prosthetic, and focused on the mission. He even seems cheerful, like he would rather be here, shooting at people than cooped up in our apartment.

"What was that thing about red shoes?" Zack asks as we keep moving. "I've never seen you wear red shoes."

"Sophie doesn't," I say, wincing at the pain in my feet. "Sophie wears black, but Scarlett wore red. It was part of my hacker persona. I was known as the Red Stiletto in certain online communities for a while."

"Seriously? That sounds like a superhero."

"That's exactly what I was going for!" I say happily, feeling nostalgia for my hacking days. I always felt like such a femme fatale when I put on those shoes, but I knew I was going to get myself in trouble someday. In the distance, I see the mausoleum up ahead, and Luciana is not there alone.

I am worried that she has run into trouble for a moment, but then I recognize the outline of Cole's body in the darkness. Also, I see him step forward and slam his foot into the door of the mausoleum, causing it to crack open.

"Whoa," I say in surprise, although we are too far away to be heard. I want to make a joke about how death has made him more masculine, but I don't think Zack would appreciate such a joke. Also, the pain in my collapsing legs is distracting me from my ability to have a sense of humor. "Can we stop for a second?" I ask him, moving to lean against another tombstone.

"No," he says at once, scanning the area with his gun pointed out at the cemetery before slipping his hand around my back and dragging me toward the mausoleum. "We need to warn them, and get better cover. Come on."

As he drags me forward, I see Luciana and Rodriguez both covering their faces and coughing. Cole is just standing there and staring.

"Hey!" Zack shouts, waving his arm as we approach. "Get inside! There's an armed man out here."

They all turn to look at us, and Rodriguez begins to fumble to open the large mausoleum doors. By the time the doors are fully open, Zack is guiding me between them. I don't even have time to ask why the others were coughing before it hits me.

That smell.

Oh god, that smell. I lift my hands to cover my face, but it does nothing. It causes my eyes to water, obscuring the darkened mausoleum from view. The smell is startling at first, but then it builds and builds, until it's suffocating. Covering my nose and mouth with both hands, I blink to clear my eyes so that I can focus.

And then I see where the smell is coming from.

There are dozens of dead bodies in here. Dozens.

They are all in various stages of decay. Some of the bodies seem freshly killed, like they may have been alive earlier today. As I gasp a little at the scene before us, the odor continues to build and intensify. Some of the bodies have decayed to the point where the flesh is sloughing off their bones. There are large flies buzzing all around us, and maggots squirming in empty eye sockets. I feel like after entering this room, we might crave sticking our faces in buckets of rotten eggs or portable toilets to get some fresh air.

The smell is so loud and jarring that it takes me a minute to hear a woman calling for help. She is seated at a table. I walk forward, carefully, examining my surroundings, but there is a slight ringing in my ears. I turn back to look at the others, and they are all gagging and coughing, placing their sleeves over their faces.

I can't hear what they are saying, through all the noise that isn't there, so I try to read their lips.

"What the fuck is this?" Zack asks, with a look of horror on his face. He steps around the table carefully, his gun pointed at all the bodies, checking for signs of life.

"There are name cards at each seat," Luciana points out.

Rodriguez is focused on advancing on the living person in the room who is screaming for help. People? Person. It's hard to tell. Everything is swirling around me in a bevy of confusion and chaos. And death. I feel Cole's hand on my arm, and I realize that I am standing numbly and just staring at everything in horror. I suppose I should try to accurately describe the scene before us.

There's a dining table in the center of the mausoleum. It is very long. It has about ten seats? It's hard to count right now. There's a dead body sitting at each of those seats, poised as if eating a meal. Only at the far end of the table, is a familiar fake-looking blonde woman, screaming her head off for help with her perfect eyebrows. So there was some sound in here, after all. She is tied to a chair and gagged, so it's difficult to understand her. Rodriguez is removing the gag from her mouth.

"He's going to come back!" she shouts. "You can't be here. He'll be back anytime soon. Please…"

"Who will be back?" Rodriguez asks.

"Jeremy!" she screams. "I'm so sorry I did all those terrible things. He forced me to. He was going to hurt our mother if I didn't. She's so weak, and I can't bear to see her get hurt anymore."

"Is that your mother?" Rodriguez asks, gesturing to a wheelchair in the corner.

Brittany nods.

I can't tell if the woman in the wheelchair is dead or alive. She fits right in with all of the other dead bodies. There are skeletons designed cleverly to appear as if they are pouring drinks for the people at the table, who will also soon be skeletons.

It's actually set up in a somewhat artistic way. If you stare at the gruesome and grotesque long enough, you will start to find some beauty in it.

"This empty seat," Cole points out, and his voice comes from very close to my side. "It has my name on the card. He shot at me intending to kill me and add me to this collection."

"Other foster children," Brittany explains tearfully. "Our parents were horrible people. The only good memories we have are from when our parents were away, and we would sit down to have dinner with the kids they fostered. Jeremy said that it was the only thing that made him feel like he had a family. So when our mom had a stroke, and we both came home to take care of her… Jer couldn't stop talking about wanting more people at the table. To eat with us. I didn't know he'd gone so crazy. I had to go along with his plans to try and save my mother."

"There's a place setting at this table for Scarlett, too," Zack points out from the other side of the table.

"He's going to be here soon," Brittany screams. "He's coming back soon!"

"Where is he now?" Luciana asks, lowering herself to look at the girl. "We'll go to him."

"He lives in the main house of the cemetery. He was so angry that he didn't get a body from killing Cole. He always digs up the graves, and this one was empty. He was so, so angry. He killed so many people."

To be perfectly honest, I'm not totally sure what's going on. It's a little confusing and unsettling. It's hard to breathe in this stuffy room, filled with death and disease. You always think you've experienced a lot in life, until you walk into a room with a dozen dead bodies neatly arranged around a dinner table like a scene from a religious painting.

"Let's get out of here," Cole tells me, taking my arm and trying to guide me outside. I feel too frozen to move.

"It was great work finding this place, Shields," Luciana says between coughing and covering her face with her sleeve. "Great work as usual. We're going to find Jeremy and save a lot of lives."

"Did your brother kill the woman you were impersonating?" Detective Rodriguez says, stooping beside Brittany with a tape recorder. "Dr. Annabelle Nelson, who was found dead at The Mind Spa clinic where you were working as her assistant. Her body was found maimed beyond recognition."

"Yes, he killed her. And he forced me to poison Cole in the steam room. He said he would kill our mother if I didn't. And mom's the only family we have left."

"The old woman is alive," Zack says, as he examines the corpse-looking thing in the wheelchair. "She's barely breathing. She needs medical attention."

267

There's so much happening all around me that it's hard to focus. Everyone seems to easily know their role, and what to do, and how to help. I'm just staring at the bodies with dread, feeling an ice-cold numbness and dread rushing through my veins.

"Come on," Cole says, wrapping his arm around my back. "Let's get some fresh air."

"Be careful!" Zack says. "She said the killer was returning at any moment."

"He's lonely," Brittany says as she looks out at the table. "He kills people because he's lonely. He wanted Cole to join him. He wasn't upset you killed our dad. He just wanted you to be his friend, and join his collection. I'm not mad either. Our dad was awful, so you're kind of my hero. I'm sorry my brother tried to kill you."

Cole turns back, looking at the woman uncomfortably. He is guiding me outside the mausoleum when gunshots are heard.

"Get down!" Zack and Rodriguez shout at the same time. But I am still too frozen to move. I find myself scanning the cemetery for the shooter. I want to look at his face. Is it the man from before who held the gun to my stomach?

My frozenness results in Cole covering my body with his and tackling me to the ground. I have the air knocked out of me, and my skull hits the cold stone floor of the mausoleum. The impact jostles me back to reality, and I feel suddenly more clearheaded. I can see everything clearly. I can see the ceiling of the mausoleum, and how inferior the design is to anything Cole would make.

Cole does great ceilings.

I hear Zack shooting back at Jeremy from the other side of the door. His rifle is more powerful than all of our handguns, and he moves with great precision due to all his training. The gunshots are so loud. I turn my face to the side, trying not to hear them.

"Get him to cover!" Zack shouts at me, while he is reloading.

It takes me a second to process what he means. Then I realize that my hands are sticky, and Cole isn't moving. "Oh my god," I whisper as my heart skips a beat. "He was hit? Where? Where was he hit?"

"Just move him!" Zack yells.

Tears begin sliding out of my eyes as I try to shimmy out from under Cole, at the same time that I am dragging his body. I see the large bloodstain in the back of his shirt, to indicate that he's been shot in the lower back. "Cole," I murmur, dragging him to safety. He is very heavy.

"There are multiple shooters!" Rodriguez says. "We have to take them down fast. We're kind of trapped in here, vulnerable to a grenade."

Grenade? What are these people talking about? Who would just have a grenade lying around? When I realize that the type of people who collect a dozen dead bodies would probably have grenades, I swallow down a bit of bile. The bile tastes like rotting death and tears.

Reaching out, I put pressure on Cole's new bullet wound, or where I think it might be. Luciana rushes to my side, pulling up Cole's shirt to check the damage. She curses, turning back to look at Rodriguez. "Call an ambulance!" She retrieves Cole's gun from his hand, where he is still tightly clutching it. But this causes him to stir.

"What happened?" Cole asks groggily.

"Don't try to move!" Luciana says to him. "You got shot in the lower back. You could be paralyzed from the waist down."

Cole groans he pushes himself up slightly, to look at me. "You okay, Scar?"

"I'm so sorry. You were protecting me."

Grabbing my leg, and trying to lift himself up, he turns slightly to look down at his new injury.

"Fuck!" Cole says, getting up quite suddenly. "Not again. Fuck this shit." He moves across the mausoleum to where Zack is focused on shooting at our attackers. "Hey, buddy, can I borrow this?"

"My rifle?" Zack says hesitantly, with hurt in his voice. "Why? Fine, here. Why not! You already took my girl, you might as well have my gun."

Somehow, I think he seems more reluctant to part with the gun than the girl, because his hands won't release the weapon, and Cole has to struggle to yank it away.

"Thanks," Cole says, testing the weight of it in his hands. There is something deranged about the way he is speaking and behaving. He seems almost cheerful. He seems… cracked.

Rodriguez continues shooting while this exchange is happening. He does not have an opportunity to turn to look at Cole, but he utters a warning. "Hey, brother…" he says, in a cautionary tone.

"Cole," I call out softly, seeing that there is blood dripping down his pants from his bullet wound. "What are you doing? Calm down!"

But he ignores me, and walks right out of the mausoleum holding Zack's rifle. My heart leaps into my throat, and I turn to Luciana with a look of terror on my face, which she returns. Now I know the answer to my question. I have made a really bad decision by convincing Cole to leave the desert. He is mentally unstable. He is completely unhinged. He begins screaming at the top of his lungs as he walks forward, on some kind of suicide rampage. My heart leaps into my throat as the endless barrage of gunshots begin.

"I AM SO FUCKING SICK AND TIRED OF GETTING SHOT!" Cole screams out into the cemetery as he unleashes a huge volley of bullets at our attackers. Someone hollers as though he's been hit. "AND YOUR FUCKING MAUSOLEUM IS DESIGNED SO FUCKING BADLY! HIRE A REAL ARCHITECT! A TODDLER COULD DO A BETTER JOB WITH LEGOS." Pausing to take a deep, rasping breath, he continues. "SERIOUSLY. GIVE ME A FUCKING BOX OF LEGOS AND I CAN DESIGN A BETTER MONUMENT TO THE DEAD. PLASTIC LEGOS WOULD BE MORE

RESPECTFUL THAN THIS LOPSIDED,
DROOPING, MISERABLE PIECE OF SHIT—
AND PROBABLY A SUPERIOR MATERIAL!"

"Hey!" says a voice from out in the cemetery, one of the shooters. "You jackass! I was the architect, and I'll have you know this is a perfectly modern—"

Cole releases at least a dozen bullets directly into the man's head. "No, it isn't modern. It's bad. I mean, it's awful enough you had to kill all those people, but to put them in that monstrosity? I've designed better barns for livestock. Oh, well, he's dead now. He's not going to design anything else. Problem fixed!" Cole walks back into the mausoleum and hands Zack his rifle, patting him on the back in a friendly way as blood drips down his legs.

Everyone stares at him in shock. My throat has gone very dry, and I want to stand, but my legs won't work. Did he really just do that?

"What?" he says with a shrug. "It's a pet peeve. Stupid designs like this really bug me."

"Jesus Christ," Zack says, exhaling and sinking back against the stone wall with relief. "You're fucking insane, man. How did you do that?"

Cole shrugs. "I played a lot of video games to de-stress in college. Same concept, right?"

"No," Zack says with wide eyes. "I mean, maybe if you're operating a drone from miles away. But in real life, if you try to be a hero and do stupid

272

shit like that, you end up losing a arm or a leg. Or worse. What the hell would make you walk into the line of fire like that?"

"I was inspired by this girl we both know," Cole tells Zack softly. "She calls herself fireproof. I figure that if she's willing to walk through the fire for me—the least I can do is try my best to become bulletproof for her."

My heart melts as he turns to look back at me with a boyish smile. His eyes are shining with an otherworldly sort of strength and love. It is the same look that he wore on the day I first met him, all those years ago.

"Okay, man," Zack says, checking his gun, which has been completely emptied of bullets. "You win." I'm not sure if he's talking about the gunfight, or me, but he slaps Cole on the shoulder. "We're good. I'm really sorry about being bitchy earlier. You're a total badass, man."

"He is," Rodriguez says, wiping his brow. "And very, very cool. I thought we lost you for a second there, buddy. It did look like a scene directly out of a video game."

Cole grins proudly. "Thanks!"

When Cole begins moving over to me, I struggle to pull myself to my feet on my shaky legs. I exhale as I run my hands over his chest, checking for bullet holes, with my mouth slightly ajar. I don't know what I am expecting to find, but I imagine that he will be so riddled with bullets that it feels like touching a cheese grater. Instead, his body is

273

smooth. I can't find a single hole. He doesn't seem to have any more injuries. "Cole," I whisper in disbelief. "What did you do?"

"I killed a lousy architect," he answers, pushing me back against the wall for support as he presses his lips and body against mine. His mouth is hot and he tastes vaguely of gunpowder. His body is plastered against mine as he kisses me with such fervour that I can feel the insane amount of adrenaline pumping through his body. "We should celebrate."

His kiss makes me dizzy. I don't think I've ever seen this side of Cole. It's not possible. How did he manage to do that without getting hurt? Zack should have been able to handle this. Zack has the training, and Cole just works a desk job, like me...

Brittany has been sobbing the whole time, but now she is finally able to speak. "Did you kill my brother?" she screeches. "Did you get Jeremy?"

"Oh, he got him," Rodriguez says, scratching his head as he looks at Luciana. "I think Cole just went beastmode. Like Rasputin."

"Rasputin?" Zack asks in confusion.

"Come on," Luciana says softly, moving over to us and touching our shoulders. "Let's get out of here before the cops arrive, since Cole is supposed to be dead. We'll say Zack shot him."

"I'll text you an address nearby," Rodriguez says. "There's a trusted doctor there who can take care of Cole. Again."

"What are you talking about, Roddy? I'm

perfectly fine," Cole says as he exits the mausoleum, stretching his arms up to the sky. "I actually feel great. Better than I've felt in days."

I stare after him in bewilderment, before glancing at Luciana and sharing a puzzled look. I swear, there's even a small bounce in his step that wasn't there before. Taking a deep breath, I pull myself off the wall where he pushed me, and move toward the exit of the mausoleum. But before stepping out of the room, I turn back to look at all the other people behind me, living and dead. Zack, Rodriguez, Brittany, vegetable Mrs. Brown, and a dozen decaying corpses. I shoot them all an incredulous look. Does no one else see how strange this situation is?

Cole just turned into a superhero before all of our eyes. I suppose that I'm not the only one who has that secret power. Maybe that's why we're perfect for each other.

We will both always find a way to do what needs to be done.

Smiling slightly, I step out of the mausoleum, taking a real breath of clean, fresh air. I stare at Cole's bloodstained back as he moves over to check out the bodies of the men he shot, nudging them with his toes. He looks like he is ready for round two if either of them should show the tiniest sign of life, even a twitch. He looks calm, collected, and completely in control.

He looks… happy.

This man of mine is a mystery to me.

Chapter Twenty-Eight

Sophie Shields, 2016

"You were right," Cole says as he lies on the bed in the safe house with his new injury all bandaged up. "Coming back to L.A. was a great idea."

"I'm glad you think so," I tell him softly as I do some light research on my laptop.

We wanted to go back to our house, but Luciana refused until the investigation was completely over, saying it was possible the two men were working with others. There were drugs found in the mausoleum, after all, and it turns out that Marco Polo Loco was part of a larger smuggling ring.

Cole yawns as he sprawls out on the bed.

"Everything has just been going so well since we got back here. And I really missed Miranda and Roddy! It was lonely out in the desert. I feel *so* much better now."

"Are you somehow high?" I ask him cautiously.

"Not at all. I was just so frightened before, after everything that happened, and I didn't feel like myself. It's a little funny how getting shot a third time fixed that. It must be because you were there," he says, reaching out to squeeze my leg. "Nothing ever seems as bad when you're around."

A fond smile touches my lips. "I know how you feel." Cole has been in amazingly positive spirits since he killed the people who tried to kill him. At first, I found myself wondering if he had gone insane. But then I started thinking about the way that Cole's childhood ended when he was nine years old. Since the day his parents were killed, Cole has forced himself to be an adult, work hard, and accomplish enough for ten men.

Recently, these past few days—this is the first time he's really had a break. He's been able to have fun. That might be why he likened killing those men to a video game. I think he's just letting his inner child out more, and being more relaxed. Multiple near-death experiences will do funny things to a person.

"Life only seems unbearable when you're alone," Cole tells me. "And… when you're operating at your maximum capacity for a really long time. It's just exhausting wear-and-tear, emotionally. But once you get pushed past that limit—that's when you find out that your maximum is actually way higher than you ever believed it was. We're all capable of so much more than we think we are. We are all so much stronger than we believe. Our bodies feel fragile, but they are extremely resilient little meat suits, capable of taking a beating. And our minds? Our minds are impenetrable, and no bullets can change our thoughts, our identities, our feelings—unless we let them. Your mind, especially, Scarlett, is so strong. I need to be more like you."

"I don't know about that, Cole," I tell him gently, knowing that my mind is a mess more than he could possibly imagine. "So, I've been looking into that architect you shot," I tell him as I pull up some information on my laptop. "Marco Williams Jr. has a very long rap sheet that extends back even farther than that stint in juvie with you. It looks like he applied for a job at your firm and was turned away for substandard work. He's competed with you on a bunch of projects, especially one in Venezuela, where he smuggled a lot of cocaine. He was probably growing really sick of you beating him in absolutely every respect. So, when Jeremy hired him, they probably got to shit talking you, and that's how they connected."

"I guess that's how you know you've really been successful," Cole says proudly. "When you have the power to join people together in so much hatred they become serial killers and put together a murder museum in a mausoleum!"

"Okay, you have had way too many painkillers," I tell him, touching his forehead.

"Give me your laptop," Cole says suddenly. "I have a gift for you."

"My laptop?" I say warily, pulling it closer to my body. "First Zack's rifle, now my laptop. What's gotten into you?"

"Shut up," he says, pulling it away from my grasp. He types in a website, and then some login credentials, clicks a few buttons, and passes it back to me. "There," he says. "The DNA results. You can decide whether you want to approve joining this program that will send a notification to any biological family with your contact info. I put your name in there as Sophie, just to be safe, and some vague contact info. Of course, we could always hunt them down if they don't reach out. It's up to you."

"Cole, this is the sweetest thing anyone has ever done for me," I tell him with a nervous smile. My fingers are shaking a little as I navigate through the website, reading the fine print. I am excited, but also afraid, and feeling a little crazy after the events of the previous night. Scooting back, I lean against Cole for comfort. "Press the button with me?"

"Sure," he says, kissing the top of my head. My finger hovers over the "approve" button, and Cole pushes my finger down so that I click on it.

"Ah!" I say anxiously, turning to bury my face

into his chest. "I can't wait to meet them. I hope they're really nice."

"They can't be worse than the Browns," Cole assures me. "As long as you don't have to attend any dinner parties with a dozen corpses, I'd consider it a win."

I laugh softly, and wonder to myself how I can possibly laugh at this. "Too soon," I say quietly. Then my smile disappears. "I have a present for you, too, Cole." Reaching out to grab my purse off the night table, I fish into its depths and pull out a yellowed old letter. Handling it gently with my fingertips, I present him with the same pages he left for me in that vodka bottle all those years ago.

His face displays emotion as he takes it from me and begins to read its contents. He smiles sadly a couple times, and wipes his nose. "Damn. This was such a long time ago, Scarlett. It's funny how so many things have changed, but so much has stayed the same."

"What has changed?" I ask him.

He studies me for a few seconds before responding. "We grew up." Putting the letter aside, he reaches out to slide his hand over my hips. Grasping my thigh, he pulls me closer, so that my body is pressed against his. "Speaking of which, I have another present for you."

"Oh?"

"Look what I got," he says, fishing into his pants and holding up a row of condoms. "This is a safe house after all. I thought we could have some really safe sex. Because I just got shot, and I'm really into safety right now. Girl, you know that's how I roll. Safety pins, safety belts, safety goggles, safety nets… safety… deposit boxes."

"Cole, are you writing me a love song? Because I think you shouldn't quit your day job."

"I already quit my day job," he says sadly. "So I have nothing else to do but please you all day long. You don't want to be safe with me?" he asks, with mock hurt on his face.

"No, I do," I say, giggling. "Where did you get condoms? I thought you weren't leaving the safe house until you're healed up."

"I asked Zack."

"Cole!"

"Just kidding. I asked the doctor who patched me up."

I fix him with an annoyed glare. He is grinning at me, obviously amused that I believed his joke.

I want to smack him. Taking a deep breath, I glance at the condoms warily. "The doctor said that you were healthy enough to use them?"

"Not exactly. But maybe I'll break the rules a little for you," he says playfully, tugging me down onto the bed with him.

"Hey, Cole," I ask him softly, putting my hands on his face. "Please be serious with me for a second. Are you sure you're okay? You're not just pretending to be extra cheerful for me?"

"No way," he says with a completely solemn

expression. "I am in a great mood, Scar. It was worth the trip back to civilization and the new bullet hole in my hip just to get these." He gestures to the condoms again. "Now I can make sweet, sweet love to you, all night long, and you don't have to worry about a thing."

I laugh softly at this, and wrap my arms around his neck in contentment. "Okay," I whisper, pressing my lips against his neck, "but we're going to need a lot more of those."

Chapter Twenty-Nine

Sophie Shields, 2016
A few days later...

"Cole, stop," I tell him sharply, grasping his shoulder. "Over there—do you see that?"

"I think so," he says, with narrowed eyes. "Let's get closer so we can listen." Placing a hand on my back, he nudges me closer to the corner of the room, while grabbing a fresh glass of champagne from the bar.

We are trying to act inconspicuous at the party. Cole is wearing a faux beard that conceals his features, and green contact lenses over his dark eyes. It looks very strange to me, but I can still tell that it's him under there. Things have finally begun to calm down since Jeremy Brown and Marco Polo

283

Loco were killed. Cole's injury has mended enough for him to walk around with ease. Miranda has decided to throw us a little party in her home to celebrate—a small barbeque with close family and friends.

"You're right," he says quietly, as his face lights up. "They are definitely flirting."

"Think he's finally going to muster the balls to ask her out?" I say, glancing at Detective Rodriguez.

"I hope so. His body language seems more confident today. Besides, I made a little wager that he would chicken out, so he has monetary incentive to man up."

"He's had a few glasses of champagne," I add, taking a sip from my own. "That should help."

"Poor guy," Cole says with a grin. "He's not afraid of drug dealers and pimps, but god forbid he ever has to talk to a lady at a party."

"I don't know. Luciana is scarier than drug dealers or pimps, if you ask me." My boss chooses that moment to glance over at me, and I raise my glass with an innocent smile.

She gives me a suspicious look before returning her gaze to Rodriguez. And then she yawns.

"Oh, no," Cole says with dismay. "He's boring her."

"Everything bores her. It takes a lot to excite a girl like that."

Cole nudges me. "No way. She can't be

284

harder to please than you are. I basically have to die to get your attention. I'm warning you right now, Scar, I can't keep up this level of excitement for much longer. Three bullets is enough for one year, no? You'll have to learn to be satisfied with the little things."

"What little things?" I ask him with a coy smile.

"Honey," Miranda asks from behind us, and we turn to face her. She frowns. "Scar, I received a phone call for you from the office. It's about the DNA results. The secretary vetted it to make sure it's safe. Do you want to take it?"

"Sure," I tell her softly, retrieving her cell phone. As I unmute the call and place it to my ear, I glance at Cole with worry. "Hello?"

"Hi!" says a woman's voice. "Oh my god, is this Sophie Shields?"

"It depends on who's asking," I say curiously.

"I had to call so many numbers to get to you. I hope I have the right person. Okay, this is going to sound crazy. Are you still there?"

"Yes," I say curiously.

"My name is Helen Winters, and I just received the email notification that my DNA results were ready. I—I took the DNA samples from me and my fiancé just to check up on our general health issues before trying to conceive. Well, I just saw that he has a sibling match with *you.* Did you know about this?"

"I know a little," I say, after a heavy pause.

"It's crazy because he doesn't have any siblings, but he's been having this recurring nightmare about a newborn baby girl. He believes that he killed her when he was around four years old, because his mother asked him to leave the baby at the side of the road. In the snow."

I feel like the wind has been knocked out of me. Putting a hand over my face to conceal the torrent of emotions, I move away from my friends, and out onto the grass of Miranda's lawn. I begin pacing. "In the snow," I repeat.

"Yes. Does this sound… familiar?"

I let out a little nervous laugh. All the hairs on the back of my neck are standing up, and there are cold chills prickling my skin, from head to toe. "Well, I didn't die," I say awkwardly, as if that isn't obvious. I am so nervous that I've lost the ability to use the English language. My chest hurts. I don't know if I'm happy or sad, but I find that I am holding my breath and waiting for more information.

The girl on the other end of the phone also laughs nervously. "I'm really glad you didn't. Okay, so this is going to sound even crazier. Liam—that's your brother—Liam and I are getting married *tomorrow*. We're up at a vineyard in Michigan. Do you think you could make it to the wedding? I totally understand if not, and we can totally do it another time. I just thought it would be a lovely surprise, and really mean a lot to him, if you could be here."

I turn back to look at everyone in the party, having a good time, drinking and chatting. I see Cole walking toward me, looking concerned. He is limping slightly due to the new injury to his hip, and I hate to see him in pain. I know he's been acting tough for me, but he's still tired. He needs rest.

"Why are you calling me?" I ask the girl on the phone. "Shouldn't this… Liam be the one calling?"

"I haven't told him yet. Just in case you can't make it, I don't want to upset him right now."

"I see," I say, reaching out to touch Cole's arm as he approaches. "I have been looking for my family my whole life. I had given up. Are you absolutely sure he wants to meet me?"

"He does," she says. "The problem is that he doesn't know you exist. He thinks you died when you were an infant, and he thinks it's his fault. It's been eating him up for years." She pauses. "He's been really stressed out lately, with the wedding, and family problems. I just want something good for him, and if you would like to connect…"

"Yes," I say softly, without even thinking. Inhaling deeply, I nod, although she cannot see it. I continue nodding as I stare at Cole and play with the buttons on his shirt. This could be huge for me. This could be life-altering for me. "Okay," I say with a scrunched up face. "Okay. I think I can come to Michigan. Did you say your name was Helen?"

"Yes! Yes, oh my god. I can't tell you how

much this means to me, Sophie. It could be so wonderful for Liam to meet you. I hate to tell you this over the phone, but he doesn't have the greatest relationship with his parents. He had a rough childhood, and he's very lonely. Knowing that he has a sister would mean everything to him—to us! I mean, I'm getting married to him tomorrow, so you'll be my sister too."

This girl is so sweet. So innocent, gentle, and sweet. She sounds really young and idealistic, and like she really wants the best for her fiancé. She doesn't even seem concerned that anything might go wrong. Could this really happen? Could I really have a family? I am old enough to know not to count my chickens before they are hatched. "Okay, Helen," I say, clearing my throat. "Is this your number here on the display? 646 area code?"

"Yes."

"I can send you a text message, and you can get me the details of the address and the time of the wedding."

"I'll buy you a plane ticket!" Helen says excitedly. "It says here you're in California? What airport will you be flying from? I'll send a car to pick you up, too."

"Anything around L.A. will be fine," I tell her.

"Okay. I'll… see you tomorrow!" Helen says, with enthusiasm in her voice. "And no pressure, if you need to change your mind at the last minute. I know this already *is* the last minute, with zero notice, so…"

"No," I tell her firmly. "I'll be there." When I see the flash of panic on Cole's face, I hesitate. "Well, I'll let you know if anything comes up."

"Great. I'm so excited, Sophie. Can't wait to meet you."

"Me too."

When I end the call, I look at Cole with amazement. "I think—I think I'm going to meet my brother tomorrow. My real brother."

"I'm not invited?" he asks.

I gently place my hand on his hip, indicating his recent bullet wound. But to all the partygoers in the house, and on the deck, it probably looks like I am grabbing his ass. So, I might as well go ahead and do that too, since I've had some champagne.

"You probably shouldn't travel until you're all better," I tell him softly, with my hand resting in his back pocket.

"Scar," he says with sudden worry. "I don't know how I feel about letting you go all the way to Michigan alone right now. I know I killed the bad guys, but still… I would prefer if you take Zack with you than go alone."

"Really?" I say in surprise, looking over to where Zack is talking with Mr. and Mrs. Bishop. "I don't know. I like flying alone and having time to think by myself. I don't need Zack. I'm a big girl."

"Scarlett, we've all been through a lot these past few weeks. I know you're tough as nails, but you shouldn't be alone."

"We'll discuss it. Let me just text this girl," I say, handing him my glass of champagne. I pull out my own cellphone and begin copying her number from Miranda's phone. As I do this, I hear some girlish laughter to my right, and I see Rodriguez has finally made Luciana laugh. I look up at Cole with a smile, which he returns.

"Little Ricky has some smooth moves after all," Cole says with a grin. "Want me to top you up with some more bubbly?"

"Please," I respond, and he begins to walk over to the bar. I call out after him, "But last glass for me as I have to fly to Michigan in the—"

"Be quiet," Cole says suddenly, turning around and moving back over to me. He strategically shields my body with his own, and hands me my champagne glass. Tucking my phone back in my pocket, I look at him warily, and he shakes his head to indicate that it's not good news.

The look on his face gives me a shiver.

"We're making small talk," he says quietly. "Normal little small talk chatter at a party, blah, blah, blah. Oh, haha, you're saying such interesting things."

"Cole?" I ask softly, trying to peer around his shoulder, but he grabs my waist and holds me tightly.

Then I hear it. The sound of a voice that makes my blood run cold.

It's worse than walking into a room and finding a dozen dead bodies.

And trust me, that's pretty bad.

I sharply suck in a lungful of air. An involuntary gasp; the wheeze of a slaughtered animal. I find that my hand has moved to grab Cole's arm. I am gripping him so tightly that my nails are leaving imprints in his skin.

"Small talk," he mutters softly. "Very, very small talk about very small things. We are relaxed, normal, innocent bystanders, not calling any attention to ourselves. Small talk."

I have a gun in my purse.

While Cole is blabbering on about small talk and trying to appear normal, I am visualizing the shiny metal weapon in my purse. My fingers slowly release their death grip on Cole's arm, and move to slide under the leather flap, between the sharp ridges of the zipper. I can feel the sensation of the cool metal against my fingertips, and it's almost erotic.

Oh, it feels good. My fingers drink up the metal as they plunge into the purse, scrambling for it, embracing it, spilling some of my champagne. But Cole reaches out and grasps my wrist, shaking his head slowly.

"Not now. Not in public like this."

Public. I suppose we are in public. But I think everyone at this party is an ally. Everyone cares about us. Everyone knows who we are. Then why did we decide to dress Cole up in disguise? Just in case he was seen on the way over here. Just in case a stranger came by. Just in case…

There must be some people at this party we don't trust. Caterers. Bartenders. Waitresses. I am Scarlett Hunter here, and I can't just shoot a man in front of all those people, for absolutely no reason.

No reason.

My inner temper flares, a sudden lightning storm inside my chest. I have to press firmly on my heart to make the fire and rage subside. No reason, indeed.

"Be calm," he tells me softly. "I'm right here."

How can I be calm? He is standing so close to use. I can hear his voice, his laugh. He's speaking to Miranda. Miranda's voice sounds strained.

My head hurts. My head throbs more with every word I hear him speak.

"I didn't realize there was a party happening here, Miranda. Did my invitation get lost in the mail?"

"My apologies, Benjamin. It's just a small family gathering to celebrate Cole's killer being brought to justice. Did you hear? Jeremy Brown and Marco Williams Jr. were killed a few days ago, and police found enough evidence in their homes to suggest a premeditated attack on Cole."

"Yes, yes, I heard," Benjamin says. "It's absolutely certain that they were responsible?"

Miranda pauses. "Yes. They were also responsible for a few other murders. And Jeremy's sister, Brittany, cooperated with the police and told them everything that her brother did, and made her do."

"I see. How tragic that such a bright young man was taken down by such savages."

Detective Rodriguez moves over to Benjamin then, and greets him warmly, shaking the man's hand. "Thanks for your cooperation with our investigation, Senator. I apologize again that we had to bring you into the station, but it was touch-and-go there for a while."

"I completely understand, Detective. I know that you worked very hard to solve this case, and I wanted to congratulate you on your success." Benjamin pauses. "I just hope that you are right about who is really behind the murder of Cole Hunter."

I find myself biting my lip so hard that I draw a bit of blood. I swipe my tongue across my lip to remove the acidic, watery liquid along with a bit of waxy lipstick.

Cole's face is growing contorted into a frown, which I can detect even under his disguise. I am not in disguise, other than my dark hair. I am not wearing any contact lenses, any prosthetics, anything. Placing a hand on Cole's chest, I use his body to brace myself, standing behind him and looking down to conceal my features. I see that Zack is standing across the room, glancing at me with concern.

"I believe we are correct about this case," Rodriguez says, after a pause. "One of the killers was confirmed to be associated with an international drug smuggling ring. Why would you express doubt? Do you have any information?"

"Not really," Benjamin says. "Do you mind if I have a glass of champagne, Miranda? My throat feels so parched today."

"Please feel free," she says softly.

As Benjamin pours himself a glass, the party has gone silent. Perhaps a little too silent. Everyone is focused on him. I wish they wouldn't. I wish they would keep talking and acting normal. It's so quiet that I fear he can hear me breathing. I try not to breathe.

"I just always wondered about something," Benjamin says between sips of his champagne. "All those years ago, when that poor boy's parents were killed in a house fire—it was ruled an accident, but was it really? I was just wondering if there could have been some ancient family enemy who failed to kill Cole in that fire, and decided to try again, years later. That was my theory, anyway."

I look at Cole to see his reaction, but he is no longer focused on me. His eyes are staring over my head, focused on something in the distance. The expression on his face chills me to the bone. His features have become so hard set that he resembles a statue.

"But perhaps that's silly of me," Benjamin says with a light laugh. "I must be reading too many mystery novels and watching too much CSI. I have a bit of an imagination, you know, and I like to fabricate wild theories."

"That's interesting," Rodriguez says quietly. "Maybe I should still look into that."

"You should," Benjamin says. "I mean, isn't it curious that the boy had no other family? No grandparents, no aunts or uncles or cousins, absolutely no one in the world? What happened to his whole family?"

"I really couldn't say," Rodriguez responds. "The investigation never went in that direction."

"It sounds like they were systematically wiped out, to me," Benjamin says. "Systematically. But what do I know? You're the detective. This champagne is excellent, Miranda."

Cole's muscles are all clenched so hard that his body is trembling slightly. He seems to be at the point of ripping off his beard and turning around to confronting Benjamin, but I grab his wrist to stop him. Still, he has turned halfway and exposed part of my body, namely the hand holding the mostly empty champagne glass.

"Why don't you introduce me to everyone at this party, Miranda?" Benjamin asks suddenly, as though he has seen my hand. "I don't think we've all met. I think I see some new faces, but also some very familiar faces." He pauses, and I hold the champagne glass closer to my body, trying to conceal every protruding limb. Benjamin continues. "There sure are some lovely ladies here today. And I think I recognize Ezra Bishop? An excellent lawyer, to be sure. It's a pleasure to meet you, sir."

"Likewise," says Mr. Bishop.

As Benjamin moves through the party, I begin to grow anxious. Glancing down at my outfit, I observe the clothes and shoes that I selected from my old closet at Cole's house, and wish the little black cocktail dress covered more of my body. I could still run away in these shoes. Maybe while he's distracted…

"We haven't met," Zack says loudly. "You're a senator? That's so cool! I'm actually the guy who took down Cole's killer. We had a crazy shootout at the cemetery, where I was helping Detective Rodriguez chase a lead. You should hear the story. It was insane! So we walked into the mausoleum and saw all these dead bodies. You would not *believe* how creepy it was. Putrid, decaying, rotting flesh—and that smell! I'll never forget that smell. And I'll tell you now, I've seen some awful things in Afghanistan, but that mausoleum—it was hands down the worst thing I've ever seen in my life. And let me tell you about the things I've seen in Afghanistan…"

Zack. Oh, thank god for Zack.

As Cole realizes what he is doing and begins to guide me away, I send a quick look of acknowledgment and gratitude to Miranda and the detective. We silently and swiftly make our escape while Zack distracts Benjamin, by walking around Miranda's house to my old car, which is parked in her driveway. My hand has already retrieved the keys from my purse, as I dive into the driver's seat and turn it on. As soon as Cole is seated in the passenger seat, I drive away. Benjamin's car is slightly blocking mine, so I have to drive on Miranda's lawn. I resist the urge to tear off Benjamin's bumper.

"That was too close," I say softly, once there is some distance between us and the house.

"What was he saying about my family?" Cole asks.

I shake my head, glancing over at him with concern. "I don't know."

"Do you think he knows something? Was the fire not an accident?"

Swallowing down a lump of fear, I remove my right hand from the steering wheel and place it on Cole's leg, squeezing gently. "I think Benjamin is the king of bullshit, and making people uncomfortable. I think he was just messing with everyone there."

"Really?" Cole asks dryly. "Because it felt like he was messing with *us*. It felt like he was messing with *you* and *me* specifically."

"I know. That's exactly what he sounded like during Ricky's interrogation."

"Scar. Do you think that somehow he knows—"

"No," I say firmly. "Please. Don't say that. No."

"I just can't help wondering…"

"Please," I say in a whisper.

Cole nods and squeezes my hand.

My lips are pressed together tightly in a hard

297

line, and my heart is beating so hard I can feel my pulse in my ears and my fingers. I place both of my hands on the steering wheel, and I just keep driving. Does he know? I can't bring myself to consider it. Should I have tried to get him alone at that party, and used the gun in my purse?

"Detective Rodriguez, Agent Lopez, and Zack are all there," Cole reminds me. "They will figure out what's happening and let us know."

I nod. And I just keep driving. I know that I'm still running, but it feels different this time.

Cole is with me now. I am no longer alone. He is all I need to get through this.

He is more than enough.

Chapter Thirty

Sophie Shields, 2016

"I don't feel comfortable with you going alone," Cole says again as we stand at the airport. He is still wearing his disguise to conceal his features from the cameras, along with a baseball cap and sunglasses. "Please let me come along. In fact, I am coming along anyway, whether you want me to or not."

"No," I tell him. "Traveling is hectic and you need to rest. It will only be one day. I'm coming back as soon as I can."

"Then take Zack," he tells me again. "Please, Scar. I have a really bad feeling, Scar."

"Of course, you have a bad feeling," I say, rubbing his arm. "You keep getting shot every five minutes lately. Your whole body is covered in bad feelings."

"The bullets don't bother me anymore," he says softly. "I'm not afraid, Scar. When I heal up,

I'm going to get healthier than I've ever been. I am going to get stronger than I ever was before."

"You're already the strongest man I know," I assure him. "You always have been, Cole. You come alive under pressure. You are solid, just like the houses you build—capable of surviving any disaster. And now, we've learned just how hard it is to take you down. I find it comforting."

"It is comforting—and I know you're even more resilient than I am. I'm sorry, I know I shouldn't be so overprotective and worried." He sighs. "It is such a worthwhile thrill to take a risk and survive—and accomplish something. It would have been easy to stay safe and avoid harm in Nevada. I'm sorry I was such a downer when we were holed away in the NovaTank. But you were right to make me leave. I love being around people. I love finding sneaky ways to keep doing my job. I love eating real food at restaurants instead of those disgusting MREs. Most of all, I love being with you… anywhere."

"Things are going to be different from now on," I tell him. "We're going to be unbreakable. This—me getting on a plane—this isn't goodbye. I'm never going to run away from you again, so you don't have to worry."

He nods. "I believe you, Scar."

When he wraps his arms around me, I sigh, relaxing and looking at other people in the airport. There are others who are embracing their loved ones and saying their farewells. There are siblings taking a final selfie together, and couples walking while holding hands and sluggishly pulling luggage behind themselves in obvious sadness that they have to part. Maybe they are long distance lovers. Maybe someone has to go away on a business trip for a while.

I'm one of these people again. I'm part of the world, part of humanity.

I have Cole—someone to hug as I leave, someone to wait for me. Someone to turn back and wave to, someone to miss desperately every second. Someone to text as the plane taxis down the runway. Someone to come back home to. Someone to rush to embrace as soon as I get off the plane.

Someone who feels like home.

I swear that I'll never take him for granted again. I know that I can never feel about anyone as strongly as I do about Cole. I have tried. I could search my whole lifetime, or several lifetimes, and he would still be the greatest man I could ever find.

Just how lucky am I to have had the pleasure of growing up with him?

It was worth it all. It was worth it all to have zero family, and all those dreadful experiences in foster homes, if it led me to meeting him. It doesn't really matter what I find when I fly to Michigan—I almost want to cancel the trip and stay here.

I think that Cole is the only family I will ever need.

He reaches up to touch my dark hair. "I really think you should stop dying your hair now, Scar. It raises your risk for cancer, you know."

"So does antiperspirant, but I don't want go around smelling like a wet dog."

"You can get deodorant that's free from propylene glycol," he tells me.

"But does it actually work?"

"You'll have to try it, then let me smell your armpits," he says teasingly. "I would happily prefer that you stink like garbage left out in the sun than be unhealthy. You're not allowed to get cancer and die. Ever. Those genetic tests we did said you had a higher possibility of getting breast or ovarian cancer. So maybe you shouldn't be slathering that bad stuff all over your armpits, so close to your perfect breasts."

"Oh, is there a shortage of them in the world?" I ask him playfully.

"Thanks to rising rates of breast cancer, yes."

"Well, my *new* brother is a doctor so maybe I'll ask his opinion about all these carcinogens," I say. Then I smile nervously and lower my eyes.

Cole moves closer to me, wrapping his arms around my shoulders. "You'll be fine, Scar. Hopefully, things go well with your brother— hopefully, this Liam is a good guy. Hopefully, we both gain a few new family members, so we can fly across the country for Christmas and Thanksgiving like normal people. Or they can fly to us. I don't know how to cook a turkey, but I can learn."

My eyes grow a little moistened as I imagine this. Christmas. I could have a family to spend

Christmas with? It's too much to bear. I know it shouldn't make me so emotional, but just like Cole—I was robbed of my childhood.

"I think it's all uphill from here," I say, hoping I can convince myself that it's true. "I think the worst might really be over. I don't have to hide anymore."

"That's what we've been fighting for all along, isn't it?"

"Yes."

He pulls away slightly, suddenly serious. "Whatever happens when you meet this brother of yours, Scar, I want you to remember one thing. *I* am not your fucking brother anymore."

"No?" I ask him with a mischievous smile.

Placing a finger under my chin, he lifts it until my lips are an inch away from his.

"No," he responds.

Closing the distance, I press my lips against his, seeking stability from his kiss. I seek reassurance that he is really here, tasting him one last time before I have to get on my plane. His lips are soft and warm, like Christmas morning with a roaring fireplace and cozy pajamas. There is a lingering aroma of strong coffee on his lips. My favorite flavor.

There is something different about Cole, now. Even back when he was a fragile, uncertain young boy, I loved him. But today, he feels hardened, weathered, and gnarled; he feels like pure strength. Every time I wrap my arms around him, I am amazed by the man that he has become. Maybe when the transformation was happening right before my eyes, it was so slow that I could not really detect what was happening. I was changing, too. But after a few years of separation, everything new about him is overwhelming.

The person he has grown into fills me with awe. This person takes my breath away. Being this close to him, it even makes me a little shy, although I would never admit that to him or anyone, in a million years.

But I definitely like the feeling. It makes me want… more.

He tightens his arms around me and kisses me like he means it. He kisses me until I'm dazed with bliss. He kisses me like he is never letting go, and I am definitely going to miss my flight. He kisses me like we are teenagers again, and this is the very first time. He kisses me like we are ancient souls, and have done this a thousand times before, throughout many lifetimes, spanning centuries. He kisses me like we are in a black and white movie, and he just rescued me from a creepy villain with a mustache.

Except I'm pretty sure the villain of our story, all along, was me.

Chapter Thirty-One

Sophie Shields, 2016

Anxiety has been mounting in my chest since I left the airport. Sitting in the cab as we drive through Michigan, I feel like I am having a small panic attack.

"Stop the car," I tell the cab driver. "Pull over here."

"Ma'am, it's not safe here. We're on a busy road."

"I know," I tell him. "That's exactly why I want to stop. I'll double your tip."

He shrugs as he slows down and pulls into the shoulder. "Whatever. Sure."

Stepping out of the car with only my purse, I

leave my suitcase in the back seat. I walk out onto the grassy shoulder shakily in my heels. My legs are still cramped up after the flight. Running a hand through my hair, I walk behind the car until I can feel the wind of the vehicles rushing by. I take a deep breath.

I try to process what is happening.

Seconds after I was born, I was ditched at the side of the road. It might have been a road similar to this one. But it wasn't so bad: the woman who gave birth to me was thoughtful enough to wrap me up in an old sweater first. It was a frigid February day, and I would have surely become a popsicle of placenta if not for her kindness.

I still have that sweater.

I keep it tucked away in a safe at Cole's house, since it is the only thing I own that belonged to my mother. I used to take it everywhere with me, when I was younger. Once the bloodstains were washed out by the woman who found me, it made a perfectly good layering piece for brisk autumn days.

Sometimes, I used to stand at the side of a bustling interstate, holding that tattered old sweater around my shoulders. I didn't even flinch as the cars raced by, inches away from my body. I always loved the feeling of the wind whipping my hair into my eyes and mouth, carrying the comforting flavors of asphalt and gasoline. These are the familiar scents and sensations that welcomed me into this world.

It was my favorite spot to think.

As I stand here now, I already feel soothed by the sounds of the minivans and trucks slicing through the air, like a familiar lullaby. I used to wonder about what my mother was doing on the day she discarded me. She was obviously in a big rush to get somewhere important, like the supermarket or a football game. Did she miss her favorite sweater, and regret leaving it with me? Or was she thrilled to have an excuse to dispose of the itchy, woolen gift that some distant relative dumped on her? At least she *had* relatives to give her uncool gifts. For much of my life, I would have cried with joy to receive a pair of socks from someone even pretending to care—or doing it for a tax-deductible charity receipt.

I used to be bitter about being abandoned, but I like to believe that I have matured enough to finally put it behind me. My mother gave me everything I needed to survive in this world. I mean, how fortunate was I to be born with two perfectly functional opposable thumbs? My newborn intuition to wave them around while wailing for dear life surely made me one of the youngest hitchhikers in history. However, it could have been my umbilical cord flapping in the wind that drew attention to my predicament, so I probably shouldn't overestimate the adeptness of my neonatal thumbs.

For so many years, I tried to imagine all the different circumstances that could have led to my abandonment. I tried to understand. Now, today,

I'm finally going to meet someone who was *there.* The person who actually took me from my mother's arms and left me in the snow. I have imagined a lot of interesting possibilities, such as having an extremely religious young mother (possibly a nun) who had to dump the baby or be completely shunned and disavowed. I must confess that my favorite scenario is the extraterrestrial parents who sent me away on a spaceship to avoid their planet blowing up.

I mean, there's not much you can do about a planet blowing up. You have to send the baby away, and I'd be totally understanding of that situation, more than any other.

But I never imagined having a brother there, who participated in abandoning me.

And today, I'm going to meet him.

Okay. Well, I should probably get back to doing that. I just wanted to savor this one last moment of uncertainty, before it all becomes clear. Is clarity always a good thing to have?

It doesn't matter. No matter what happens today, I know that all my pain is in the past. Here I stand, on the side of the road like all those times before, but I'm a new and improved woman.

All those dark decades of heartache are behind me.

I'm okay. I'm finally going to be okay.

Because I have Cole.

I am no longer that small, naked newborn, trembling and at the mercy of the traffic. I'm a fully grown woman, with an education and an amazing job. I have survived the unthinkable, time and time again.

There is no reason that I shouldn't be able to survive this day.

There is no reason that I should fear meeting my brother.

I am above this. I am above anything that can happen today.

I don't need this to go well.

I am already well.

With these thoughts fresh in my mind, I move back to enter the vehicle that is waiting on me, and inform the cabby that he can continue to our destination.

Chapter Thirty-Two

Sophie Shields, 2016

As I get out of the taxi cab at the winery, I rethink my wardrobe.

The bride is standing there in her stunning white gown, waiting for me, and I am wearing black from head to toe. I guess I've been to more funerals lately, than weddings. These are also just the type of clothes that Sophie Shields normally wears for a day at the office. I wasn't sure how I should dress.

Tugging my small suitcase behind me, I walk up to the girl, feeling suddenly shy and out of place. What are these people going to be like? We stand in silence for a moment, and she carefully studies my face before she speaks.

"I'm Helen," she says softly.

"Sophie," I tell her in response.

My stomach is twisting up in knots. I am not sure how I should behave when Helen reaches out to grab my hands and smiles at me.

"Thank you *so much* for coming to my wedding," she says excitedly. "Your brother is waiting at the altar. He's probably a little annoyed that I'm taking so long."

"He still doesn't know about me?" I ask.

She shakes her head. "No. I didn't feel… I didn't want to upset him today, or get his hopes up if you decided you didn't want to meet him."

"Okay," I say quietly, nodding and straightening my posture. "Let's do this."

"You can leave your luggage here for now," Helen tells me. "There's no one around for miles. The wedding is taking place in the backyard."

"It's a little strange," I say, biting my lip, "to meet my brother for the first time on his wedding day. At his wedding. I feel like I'm intruding. Should I just hang back over here while you get married, and introduce myself after?"

"No way," Helen says. "He doesn't have any family here except for you! He needs you to be here, even though he doesn't know it yet.

Pausing, I tighten my grip on my luggage. "I have never known anything about my family. My parents aren't here?"

"No. Your brother didn't want to invite them, because… well, they're not good people. They live in New York City, and we can arrange for you to meet them as soon as possible, if you want."

"I do want," I say firmly.

"Come on," Helen says lightly. "Whatever happens, there's an amazing lobster dinner after this, and an open bar where we can get wasted."

I force a smile, although I feel like throwing up. "Okay," I whisper, dropping my luggage.

Following her out into the grass, I look at the small wedding party with curiosity.

"I apologize for holding up the ceremony," Helen says as we approach, "but we were missing one guest."

"Helen, what's going on?" A dark-haired man says with a frown. Oh my god, is that him? I peer closer as he speaks. "We were supposed to start fifteen minutes ago, but Owen said that you…"

"It's okay," Helen tells him. "I'm here now, and I'm ready to get married. I just wanted to seat our final guest."

The man is looking at me. He's studying me curiously. I study him right back.

"Who is this?" Liam asks, leaving his spot at the altar and moving toward us slowly. "What's going on?"

I can't breathe. I can see anger in his face. So much anger. Is he a cruel person?

Helen speaks softly. "Liam, this is…"

"No," he says, pausing in mid-step. His face displays some kind of recognition.

My chest aches. Somehow, I know this isn't

going to go well. I already feel rejected.

It doesn't matter. I have Cole.

Liam shakes his head as he stares hard at me as though he is seeing a ghost. "This is—she is—who is this person, Helen?" His forehead is deeply creased, and his lips are pulled into a tight line.

I shouldn't have come. I know it now. I can see it on his face. I shouldn't have come. It takes a great effort to keep from turning and running. I know I should run. But instead, I grit my teeth and force myself to speak. "My name is Sophie," I say, knowing that he will never know my real name.

He is a stranger. He will always be a stranger.

Liam is getting emotional. His Adam's apple is moving and he is fidgeting a great deal. "You look like—" he begins, then he pauses and shakes his head, trying to gather his composure.

"I'm so sorry," Liam says finally, taking a deep breath. "I must seem like a blithering idiot. You just remind me of someone. You look exactly like my mother did when I was younger."

This makes me pause. I forget all about running and I take a shuddering breath as I step a little closer. "I do?" I ask softly, grateful for one piece of information about my mother. I feel suddenly thirsty for more information, before this opportunity slips away. I may never see these people again. "Really? I do?"

"Liam," Helen says gently, placing a hand on my elbow. "This is Sophie Shields. She is your little sister."

313

The backyard grows very silent then, except for the flapping of wedding decorations in the wind. Liam's face grows very pale, and he takes a hesitant step forward. His eyes have grown narrowed, and he is staring at me so hard that my face is burning. He begins approaches me unsteadily, until he is standing directly before me. A little too close to me.

I want to take a step back. More than that, I still want to turn and run. With all the gunshots I've heard lately, and all the treatment I've received from men in my life who were supposed to be family... I just want to turn and run before something can go wrong. Something is going to go wrong. I just know it.

"Clear blue eyes," Liam whispers. He lifts his hand as though he intends to touch my face, but he does not.

I flinch slightly on the inside, and I still feel a prickle on my cheek as though he has touched me. How can he recognize me? It's impossible. If he was only four years old and I was an infant the last time he saw me—I surely didn't look anything like I do now.

His fingers are shaking. "Just like in my dream. The neurologist was wrong. He said it wasn't real. But you're real."

Neurologist? Is he sick? My throat has gone very dry and it hurts to swallow. "Do you remember me?" I ask softly, peering closely into his face for signs of truth. I have never stared into the face of a family member before, and it is frightening how unfamiliar it feels. I guess I thought there would be some kind of instant bond or connection, but I feel nothing.

"Barely," he whispers. "Just barely. I was there when you were born, and I held you—for a moment." Liam shakes his head and looks up at the sky. "Oh my god, what have I done? I'm so sorry. I'm a fucking monster. I could have killed you. I could have killed you."

For some reason, in this moment, he reminds me of Cole. I guess I sort of know how to comfort a big brother who's upset. Moving forward, I tentatively try to give this stranger a hug. His shoulders begin to shake with huge sobs, and I can feel how upset he is. His emotion is contagious. Tears spill out of my eyes, but I'm not sure why.

"It's okay," I tell him, but I think I'm talking more to myself. "It's okay."

"I thought you were just a dream," Liam says into my shoulder as he returns the hug fiercely. "All these years. I thought—I thought…"

"It's okay."

"I tried to make her go back for you. My mother said there was no baby. She said—she said you weren't real. Oh, god. This is all my fault. I'm a fucking monster."

"No," I tell him. "You were just a child. You were innocent in all this."

"I knew it was wrong. I could have done something if I'd tried harder. I left you. I just left you there. You could have died!"

"You're my brother," I say, although it feels strange to say it. After calling someone else my brother for so many years, it feels like I am somehow betraying Cole when I say this. I am letting go of who we used to be, but this is what needs to be done. I need to move forward. "If it weren't for Helen, I would have lived my whole life without meeting you. All I feel—all I feel is happy. Happy to know something about where I come from, and who I am."

"Happy?" Liam demands. "After what I've done?"

"Yes," I respond quietly. "I forgive you."

He hugs me again tightly, for a long moment. I don't really know what I feel. I am so overwhelmed and scared that I think I block out my emotions so that I feel nothing at all.

My brother turns to his soon-to-be wife. "Helen. You did this? How? How did you find her? Owen? You're in on this too."

They nod. For the first time, I notice some of the other people here.

"I'm sorry," Helen says. "I know you didn't want me to do the test. But remember that night you drank too much? The surprise bachelor party? I asked Owen to…"

"You stole my DNA?" he asks in shock.

"Yes, but…"

"Owen, you helped her do this? You—you drugged me," Liam says in sudden realization. "You drugged me so you could steal my saliva.

316

What kind of a friend are you?"

"Dude, I'm sorry," Owen says, moving forward to put a hand on Liam's shoulder, but Liam grabs his wrist and twists it, roughly shoving his friend away. "Ouch!" Owen says in pain, rubbing his wrist.

That looked like judo to me. I remember Levi trying to show me a few things. I almost want to step in and try to defend poor Owen, but I think it would make a bad impression if I came to my brother's wedding and kicked his ass on the first day I met him. But I kind of want to kick his ass right now.

Liam turns to glare at Helen, and he looks like he is going to murder her. Heat and fear rises in my stomach. I nearly step between them protectively. I've seen that look on the faces of too many men. Maybe he wasn't exaggerating when he said he was a monster.

All of a sudden, Liam, my brother, turns and walks away, heading toward the house. Helen calls after him, chasing after him.

"Liam!" she calls, with concern. She walks after him a little, then seems to realize the situation is serious. She picks up her wedding dress and begins running after him. I watch the scene unfolding before me, and suddenly, I smile.

I guess we really are related.

He can run away like a scared little bitch, just as well as I can.

Chapter Thirty-Three

Sophie Shields, 2016

I am walking down the side of the road as quickly as I can in my black heels, and dragging my suitcase behind me. I just need to get away from this place, and get home. A caterer shoved a bottle of red wine at me as I was leaving the winery, which I happily accepted and stuffed in my purse for later. I am looking forward to opening that bottle up at my earliest convenience. In fact, it's tempting to open it right here as I walk down the side of the road, and continue walking while periodically chugging from a wine bottle.

Real classy.

I keep twisting my ankle slightly on the

gravely texture of the road, but I don't care. I keep on walking. I could change into my running shoes, which are in my carry-on, but my need for constant motion and speed doesn't allow me to stop to do this. I realize that I am probably going to aggravate the newly-healed blisters on my feet this way, but I can't stop walking. And I can't seem to feel the pain.

"Hey!" a voice shouts out from behind me. "Hey! Sophie!"

I pause and turn slightly to see a girl running after me. She does not have any luggage, so she is able to move a lot faster than I am. It's Helen—my almost-sister-in-law. But can you have in-laws if you don't really have a brother?

I had a brother, once. But then I married him. Does that mean I'm already my *own* sister-in-law? Wow. Mind blown.

"Sophie, damn, you walk fast in those shoes!" she says, panting as she struggles to catch up. She would probably be driving, but Liam slashed the tires on the cars so no one could easily follow him.

"You changed out of that wedding dress really quickly," I tell her in amusement.

"I didn't want to let you leave like this. And I want to fly back to New York to see if I can catch up with Liam before he does something stupid."

That's right.

I was forced to briefly socialize with Liam's friends and Helen's family after the wedding I ruined, and they were so nice that it made me feel even worse about coming here and messing up their lives. Everyone was telling me what a great guy my brother is, and how sorry they are on his behalf. They told me a little about his life, and our parents, but I couldn't really focus. That angry look on his face, like he meant to hurt Helen—even if he only thought about it for a second—I just can't feel any love for him.

A few people said that discovering what his mother did to me made him so angry that he was going to confront his parents—my parents—and possibly hurt or kill them.

I'm not surprised.

What good does that do for me now? Finding out my parents are alive just long enough to find out that they've been killed. I just don't really know what to make of the situation. So, I continue walking.

"He's not a bad person," Helen says as she walks beside me. "I've met his parents, and his father is so awful, Sophie. He abused Liam relentlessly. He still does. Your mother is just very quiet. Like she's had to deal with so much bullshit that she just shut down inside herself. She's basically catatonic. Like her body's there, but nobody's home."

This makes me pause. I turn to look at Helen, quizzically. "She has a mental illness?"

"I—I guess. I don't know. The genetic test we did said Liam had a heightened risk for Alzheimer's, so I assume that's what she has. But

320

I'm not sure. Why do you ask?"

I press my lips together tightly. "No reason." I don't want to reveal too much information about myself to a stranger, but hearing about my mother's mental health does make me wonder. Sometimes I feel completely shut down and catatonic. And then, there are those blackouts. Is it possible that my mother has similar issues? I continue walking.

"Did you call a cab to the airport?" Helen asks. "I would love to share one with you."

"No," I tell her. "I just started walking. I like walking long distances, sometimes. It clears my head."

"But it's dozens of miles!" Helen remarks. "And you're wearing heels. Here, let me call us an Uber. Oh, it's going to be a little while. We're kind of in the middle of nowhere."

"I figured that when we reach the main road, I could hail a cab or even hitchhike," I explain to her.

"Hitchhike?" Helen says in surprise. Then she smiles. "I've never done that before. Isn't it dangerous?"

I look at her curiously. She is so sweet. And surprisingly cheerful for a girl who just got left at the altar. "Aren't you upset about Liam leaving?" I ask her.

"Yes, but… I understand him," she says with a shrug. "I don't take this to mean he doesn't love me, or doesn't want to marry me. I mean, I get that he's upset about the sneaky DNA test, but… I don't regret it. It led me to finding you. And somehow, I know that it was the right thing to do."

"Thank you," I tell her earnestly. "It did mean a lot to me, to learn anything at all."

"You're not angry at me?" Helen asks. "That I made you fly all this way for nothing?"

"No, not at all. It was worthwhile to me. Even to look at his face for a second is a crazy experience for me. I just saw a blood relative for the first time in my life. If only you could know what it feels like to be a homeless orphan kid, walking around in a crowded city and looking at all these strange faces, wondering if one of these people could be your mother or father—now I finally know what a relative looks like. Even if he's a dick."

"He can be a dick," Helen says with a laugh. Then she frowns. "Hey, Sophie—did you just say *homeless*?"

I sigh, realizing that I did let that slip. "I bounced around a lot. Sometimes, homeless was better than the alternative."

"God, I'm sorry. I didn't know."

"I guess some kids get lucky. They get adopted by the right people early on, and their lives are smooth sailing, as though they were never abandoned. It's easier if they have some knowledge of their birth parents, and understanding of why they were not capable of raising them. But I guess you could say... I wasn't that lucky."

"Oh, Sophie, that's terrible. But you're so beautiful, nice, well-spoken, and well-dressed. My sister whispered to me that she recognized your clothes, and they are designer labels? You must have done really well for yourself!"

I laugh softly. "You think I'm nice? That might be the first time anyone has ever said that to me. And yes, I did fairly well for myself. I have a great job, and I have a great… boyfriend. He used to be my foster brother. *He* became really successful." I realize I am on the cusp of blabbing too much about Cole and getting carried away talking about how proud I am of him. But what would I say?

My boyfriend used to be my husband when I was Scarlett Hunter, but he recently died and left me all his millions, so I decided to go shopping for this outfit. But that was only after I walked through the desert to find him, because he wasn't really dead. Don't worry, we killed the people who tried to kill him, in this mausoleum with a bunch of dead bodies. Funny story—I have an ex-boyfriend who was also there the whole time, and it was so awkward, but he has military training and we thought we needed him. Turns out we didn't, because my current boyfriend and sort of husband plays video games.

By the way, I got married when I was fifteen— legally fifteen, but I was actually fourteen, because Scarlett wasn't even my real name or identity. My wedding sucked compared to yours. It just happened in a courtroom and I didn't even have a dress. But at least my wedding actually happened, so I guess I win.

Yes, this is why I have no female friends. What would I even say to them? How can I participate in girl-talk when almost all the things I would have to say about my life and my relationships are incredibly weird, illegal, violent, or obscene?

"That's wonderful," Helen says. "I'm so glad you have a great boyfriend. My life was such a mess before Liam came into my world. He really changed things for me. I was just this boring blind writer, locked away in the woods, afraid to go near people…"

"Wait," I say suddenly. "You're a writer? You were blind? What do you write? How are you no longer blind?"

"Liam cured me," she says with a blush. "It was this experimental treatment. I got lucky. That's how we met. And I write revenge thrillers. It's kind of fun."

"Anything I might have read?" I ask her.

"Probably not. I'm not that famous. I think my most popular book is *Blind Rage*."

"No way!" I exclaim. "You're Winter Rose?"

"Yes," she says in surprise.

"I've read all your books," I say with a genuine smile. "They're amazing."

"Oh, that makes me so happy. I can't believe you've read them!"

"Yes, my boss is also a big fan. She actually loaned me a copy of your first book, and I read it at work on my lunch break. Then I snuck into her office and stole the rest of the books and read those too. Your writing is a big hit… in my workplace."

"Where do you work?" Helen asks.

"Oh… it's just an office job where we fool around with computer stuff. Nothing too serious."

Helen squints as she looks at me, and now I can see it in her eyes—she is straining. I can now tell that she was previously blind, and that her vision is not perfect.

"You're lying," she says with a smile. "Mysterious girl in a fancy black suit. Must be a very important job."

"I do love my job," I tell her softly.

"You know what, Sophie?" Helen says, grabbing my hand. "Forget Liam. Fuck him. I think you're awesome, and you and I keep in touch, no matter what. I will be your family, okay? If you want that. I mean, I'm probably still going to marry him, and become your sister-in-law, but… that shouldn't be the only reason we get to know each other. Let's be friends. And maybe someday, we'll be sister-in-laws, maybe not. It doesn't matter."

"You don't have to marry my brother for me to consider you my sister," I tell her warmly, giving her hand a gentle squeeze. "As of this moment, I have spoken with you more than I have spoken with him—maybe more than I will *ever* speak with him. If I only considered my blood relatives to be family, then I would lead a very lonely existence. My friends are all I have in this world."

"Oh, Sophie," Helen says softly.

Just then, a car pulls up beside us, and the driver lowers his windows. "You called for an Uber?"

"Yes!" Helen says. "I completely forgot. Come on, Sophie. I want you to tell me all about your life, and this spectacular boyfriend of yours. But I hope you don't mind if it all ends up in a book someday. That's what happens when you talk to writers, you know."

A smile touches my lips as we get into the car together. "I wouldn't mind if someone wrote a book about my life. I think it could be a real page turner. But first, you need to tell me more about Liam. How long have you two known each other?"

I see Helen's smile falter for a second as she leans forward and tells the driver to take us to the airport.

"Are you worried about him?" I ask her suddenly. "I'm really sorry I ruined your wedding."

"You didn't ruin it," she tells me. "He did. I'm not worried. We've been through way worse together. This one time, I got so angry at him that I drove my car off a cliff and nearly died. I still have the brain damage to prove it."

"Wow," I say, blinking. "And I thought my relationship was bad when it comes to bodily injuries! Please, tell me everything."

Helen smiles. "Well, it's a funny story…"

326

Chapter Thirty-Four

Sophie Shields, 2016

Sitting in a hotel room all by myself, I am drinking directly from the bottle of wine they gave me at the vineyard. Helen said that her family used to own that winery, and highly recommended the bottle. She said all kinds of sophisticated things about bouquet and aroma that I didn't quite understand. I am not usually a wine drinker, but it's pretty good stuff.

The airport here is smaller than I'm used to, and there isn't a flight out for several hours. I checked into this hotel nearby, thinking it was enough time to take a nap, or get some work done. But I haven't been able to sleep, and I've mostly been moping, drinking, and texting Cole and Zack about my day. Zack is about to get on a flight of his own, back to Washington D.C. with Luciana.

Until the cab ride with Helen, I believed that coming here was a complete and utter disaster. But she was so kind to me that it lifted my spirits, and made me feel welcome and valued. I'm not just saying that because she happens to be an author I adore, and I got her to autograph the back of my Kindle.

Meeting my brother was a fiasco. I tried not to get my hopes up before meeting him, but I guess there will always be a desperate, destitute little orphan girl inside me, hoping to be magically given that family she wished for on every birthday candle, shooting star, and four leaf clover she could find. I wasn't expecting my brother to be a knight in shining armor, but I was hoping for a fairly decent human being who could stand to say more than five words to me.

The whole experience was disillusioning, to say the least. All of Liam's friends and Helen's family seemed like such lovely people. Only Liam was the rough-around-the-edges outcast, ruining the day with his damage and drama. Like me.

I guess that's what I hated most about Liam. I definitely saw myself in him. I saw myself in the way he treated Helen, who was only trying to do something kind for him. I treated Zack that way all the time. I saw myself in the way he ran away when the emotions got too difficult to bear. It was clear to see that everyone there loved him, especially his best friend Owen. There was no need to hide from those people. But I've done that too, to Cole and Miranda and Mr. Bishop. I did that again to Luciana, more recently.

I don't think that Liam deserves a happy ending. I don't think he deserves a second chance, although I'm sure he'll get one. Helen seems a little too forgiving. Maybe I don't know him well enough to judge, but I came all this way to meet a biological sibling for the first time, and he bailed on me.

That says a lot about a man.

Before coming to Michigan, I felt so hopeful about my future with Cole. I felt like we could both change and be better. Now I'm a little shaken up. What if it's just in my blood to be a horrible person? Everyone says my parents are dreadful. They must be, if they weren't even invited to their own son's wedding. Well, from what I understand, our mother was invited.

My mother, the owner of that ugly sweater. I get a shiver thinking about her, and all I've learned today. If she does have Alzheimer's or some other cognitive impairment… maybe she didn't mean to abandon her baby? But that was so long ago.

As I sit in this hotel room, drinking this bottle of wine, I think back to that small motel room, years ago, where I went to hide when I found out I was pregnant. Are my issues similar to my mother's? I thought that it was my past that made me sick, but could it be something genetic? Maybe I need help. I should have checked myself into an institution when I realized I was unable to take care of myself. There was no way I would have been in any condition to take care of a child. Am I just like my mother?

Maybe I should meet her and find out. Maybe, if I ever figure out her reasoning for getting rid of me, I could possibly even forgive her. It could feel good to let go of this lifelong anger.

I think, maybe, I've already started.

Why did I need to meet Liam so badly? I think I was looking for certain qualities in him— some sign that I would have been a better person if I had grown up with my real mother and father. A normal, well-adjusted person. It's so easy to blame everything that's wrong with me on my upbringing. What if things had been different? Even slightly. Just a little more stability. Just a little less cruelty.

The scariest thought is that I could have turned out exactly the same. Or even worse. Liam doesn't seem that much better than I am, though one might say he grew up with more privilege than I had. Even that's debatable. He was still abused. He still experienced poverty.

Maybe people are always *exactly* who they are, in spite of the circumstances they endure that could serve to make them better or worse. Maybe people always become exactly who they are meant to be, regardless of anything or anyone who might help or hinder their progress.

During our ride to the airport, Helen told me

about Liam's compassion. She told me about how he'd performed surgery on her eyes, and protected her from a crazy stalker. But overall, my impression of Helen is that she is just a really optimistic and naïve girl, who hasn't had a lot of experience with men, maybe due to her blindness. Maybe also due to her affluence, for she seems to have led a sheltered life.

I think Liam did a few good things, and it really impressed her, but she doesn't see the greater darkness lurking under his surface that I see. Maybe because she doesn't have that darkness, so she can't recognize it. I don't think that Liam deserves Helen. I could be wrong, but from what little I've seen—I think he treats her badly. He did walk out on their lovely wedding and "throw an emo fit" as Luciana would say.

Luciana would have a lot of choice words for Liam's behavior.

Smiling, I think of texting her. But I need a coffee first. I've already had too much wine. There is no coffeemaker in the room, but I saw a café downstairs.

I have been so frustrated about today's events that I haven't even been inclined to pull out my laptop and hack into Liam's life, to find out all sorts of juicy private information about him. Maybe later. Maybe I should sleep.

No. Coffee is better than sleep. Maybe I'll call Lucy and bitch about my day while I sip my coffee.

Haven't you heard? I have friends now.

Grabbing my purse and my phone, I move to the door of my room and try to take a step into the corridor. But someone is blocking my way. I see the shoes first. And the cane.

I burst out laughing.

"Okay," I say, looking up into Benjamin's face. "I get it. I'm dreaming. I fell asleep from drinking too much wine, and I'm having a nightmare that you're here—but really, you're not! Because I'm not scared of you anymore and I don't need to have nightmares anymore. Do you hear that, subconscious? You can let go now. This image is just a terrifying icon of childhood trauma, and I reject any power it has over me. I'm committed to being a happier and healthier person. Goodbye!"

Slamming the door shut, I wait for the satisfying sound. There are few sounds in existence more satisfying than the good slam of a door in someone's face. But instead, the door bounces on a wooden object. I look down in confusion. A cane.

Wait a second. Taking a step back, I pinch my arm. Ouch. Does that even work?

"Wake up, Sophie," I order myself in a nervous singsong voice as the cane pushes the door open. I scowl when he steps into the room.

Okay. Dream or not, I need to do something about this. Moving over to my bottle of wine, I take a drink to see whether it tastes like dream wine. What even is dream wine? Okay, I need to be honest with myself here: I'm not a wine kinda girl. I prefer hard liquor, or coffee. I stare at the bottle in

332

my hand very hard, hoping that it will magically transform into vodka.

It doesn't.

What the hell kind of a dream is this?

Looking up, I see that Benjamin has fully entered the room now. "Sophie Shields," he muses out loud, examining his manicure. Never trust a man with a manicure. I can't even remember the last time *I* had a manicure, if ever. "So that's how you've been hiding from me all these years. And Scarlett Hunter. I didn't even know you were right under my nose, my darling girl."

My heart stops for a second, like it has forgotten how to beat. A palpitation.

No. It's just a side effect from nearly finishing a whole bottle of wine by myself, and a mixing that with a little too much airplane coffee. It's also a side effect of freakish nightmares.

"No," I say slowly. "No. You're not real. You're not real."

"Oh, my poor little Serenity," he says, reaching into his pocket and retrieving a syringe. He turns it upside down and taps it.

Well, if I can't shut my eyes tightly and will him away, I can surely beat him into the carpet until he turns into a snake and slithers away. Actiony dreams are the best ones anyway. I turn my wine bottle upside down, ignoring that some of the wine is pouring out onto the carpet. Then I proceed to lunge forward and smash the bottom of the bottle against his head. He flinches, and I spring back, disappointed that the bottle did not break against his skull. At this point, we are both splattered with wine, resembling blood. I frown and smash the bottle against the bedside table, causing the bottom to shatter, and study my improved weapon.

Clutching the neck of the bottle, I feel like I am holding a spiked club. How do I use this? Do I continue to try to smash it against him, or stab and twist with the sharp edges? It doesn't matter. I'll figure it out.

"You wouldn't hurt me, would you?" Benjamin says as he slowly circles me. "You would never hurt me, my darling girl."

I still can't believe this is really happening. My hand holding the bottle trembles for a second, and I am furious with myself for this. I try to summon up my inner superhero, begging her to take over and handle this for me, but all her strength is just out of reach. Benjamin comes at me with the syringe, trying to plunge it into my neck. I dodge him, and slam the wine bottle into his back, twisting it. I am trying to pull the bottle out and strike again when he roars and turns around, with his eyes aflame. Before I can sidestep his maneuver, I feel the sharp prick of the needle being shoved into my side.

What the fuck is in that needle? I look down at horror, to see it sticking through the material of my blouse, into the soft area just under my ribcage. My fingers drop the wine bottle as I scramble to pull the needle out, but all the liquid has already been administered. It's empty. My hands begin to shake.

I'm not sure if it's more from fear, or actually a physiological effect of the drug.

Looking up at Benjamin, I see the glint of victory in his eyes. I want to reach for the bottle and slam those sharp edges right into his eyeballs. But involuntarily, I find myself taking a step back.

I want to talk to him, to distract him. I want to ask him if he doesn't have better things to do now that he's a senator. I want to gain the upper hand, but I am just clutching my side and cowering in fear.

Then, I proceed do the stupidest thing a girl can do in this situation. The thing that I always get pissed at girls for doing in movies. The one thing that Levi told me never to do in a fight.

I turn and run.

I manage to get the hotel room door open and run into the corridor, screaming for help before I find myself sinking to my knees. My whole body is suddenly very heavy, and it feels like I am suspended in a very viscous material. Floating.

I have a moment where I can look around at the world, and see little particles of light and energy suspended in the air. They are beautiful and prismatic in color, and I feel like I can see something that was always there, but invisible to me until this moment. Are they trying to tell me something? Are they trying to help me? I could almost reach out to touch them, these magical molecules and kaleidoscopic particles dancing all around me.

Then my face hits the floor.

The last thing I feel is someone grabbing my ankles and dragging me across the hotel corridor.

My thoughts grow dark and fuzzy, but I try to hold on.

I think about that last kiss I shared with Cole at the airport.

I wonder if I'll ever get to kiss him like that again. Probably not.

What's going to happen to me now? It hurts to think about it.

But Cole is out there, so I know I'll keep fighting. I try to find the rainbow particles in the air, but my vision is going dark, and I can no longer see them. They might have been good fairies, flapping their wings and waving their wands in an effort to free me from the sinister spell of whatever was in that syringe.

Please. I call out to them silently, praying and begging for more help. I plead with them to save me. Do fairies grant wishes? We've already established that I haven't had much luck with hopes and dreams in my lifetime. But I'll forgive all of those unanswered wishes if they can only grant me this single one:

Whatever happens now, I just need to know that I will see Cole again. We can stay locked away in the desert forever, or anywhere he wants to go. We'll stay safe.

I know I messed up.

If I get another chance to hold him, I swear I will appreciate it more.

I will kiss him so hard that the earth will shake again.

Please. Please let me see him one more time. Don't let this be the end.

Chapter Thirty-Five

Sophie Shields, 2016

When I wake up, everything is spinning. I don't know exactly where I am.

It takes me a moment to focus. I am looking at a ceiling that Cole did not design—I know that much. Still, it is a very nice ceiling.

Wait.

I've seen this ceiling before. Sitting up suddenly, I am alarmed to find that my body is cold and naked. I am not wearing a stitch of clothing. I rub my head as I try to remember how I got here. There was wine, and…

A lifelong nightmare became reality.

I rub my side where the needle pricked me.

It's a little tender and itchy. My thoughts are not yet clear, but something feels familiar about this mattress. When I move to stand up and get off the mattress, it even sounds familiar. I know the creak of this mattress.

I know the duvet cover. I know the pillowcases.

It's all pink. It's all pink and flowers. I turn to the windows, and I somehow know what I'm going to see. Pink and white curtains, perfect for the room of a nine-year-old girl. Moving toward those curtains, I push them aside to reveal bars on the inside of the windows. The glass is so darkened that I can't see outside. The windows do not open. And even if I smash the glass, I can't fit through those bars.

I couldn't fit through when I was twelve. I certainly can't fit through now.

Moving to the bedroom door, I wonder if I should bother to try the handle. Every step I take makes me colder in my nakedness. Out of sheer habit, and knowing it will be futile, I turn and twist and yank at the bedroom doorknob. Nothing happens.

I know this door. I know this doorknob. I have spent many, many hours crying and screaming to be let out of this door. Banging on it until my hands were raw. Scratching at it until my nails bled. Kicking at it until I broke the door, and my leg, and then having it immediately replaced with a stronger door. There's an old fashioned keyhole in the door.

I take a few deep, ragged breaths.

Against my better judgment, I lower myself so that I can peek through the keyhole.

There is an eye staring back at me.

I gasp and move to the side so that the person cannot see me. I sit on the floor, naked and shaking, and deeply disturbed. Then it occurs to me that the eye looked exactly like mine. Pale and blue. Was it just a mirror? Crawling back to the keyhole, I peer through again, but there is nothing. No eye. No mirror. I can see nothing.

This is unsettling. Am I losing my mind?

Rubbing my forehead, I look around the room, searching for anything that can be used as a weapon. I know more now than I did then. Everything is a weapon. My body is shaking so hard.

I consider moving the dresser in front of the door, but then how will I receive food? Rubbing my hands together, I consider going under the blanket to get warm, but I don't want that vile blanket to touch my skin. Still, warmth is important—as much as food or water. If I'm going to fight my way out of this room, I will have to get warm.

And I know I'm going to get out. I've done it before. I will always get out. I will always survive.

I will get back to Cole.

The mere thought of him makes tears prick my eyes. Things were just starting to go really well. Things were perfect. I should have listened to him. I should have taken Zack with me.

I am sure Cole will find me. And if he doesn't, Lucy will find me. Or Zack. Or Detective Rodriguez.

I am not just a pathetic nine year old girl anymore, like when I first met Benjamin.

I am not alone in this world. I have an amazing boyfriend, a caring ex-boyfriend, and a brilliant boss who works for the CIA, and was able to find me in the middle of the desert. I even have a real, biological brother who seemed like an asshole, but is probably not as much of an asshole as I believe he is. I was communicating with them all before I was taken, and they should notice I am missing fairly quickly.

Surely Luciana can find me here, in…

Am I in Benjamin's old house? I'm not sure. This room looks identical to the one I used to live in. But is it the same room in the same location, or a perfect replica? I can't tell with the windows all blacked out like that. Either way, someone went through a lot of trouble to set up this whole charade.

And it's creepy as fuck.

Definitely the scariest haunted house I've ever been to.

But how can every detail be so perfect? Guys don't pay attention to such details, do they? There is no way this room sat unchanged like this for all those years, is there?

Finally growing truly uncomfortable with how fucking frozen I am, I move to the dresser and begin opening drawers, looking for an article of clothing.

They are all empty. I move to another piece of furniture, an armoire, and another, until I have opened every drawer in this goddamned room.

There is only one place left to look. The closet. I don't really know why I am avoiding it so much, but I feel an overwhelming sense of dread as I approach it. My face twists up with fear as if I am bracing myself for a saber tooth tiger to leap out of that closet and rip me to shreds.

Swallowing down a bit of saliva, I find that my throat is very dry as I reach for the hand of the doorknob. My cold hands are shaking violently. As soon as my hand touches the metal, I pull it way, feeling cowardly and spineless.

"No," I tell myself. "No, no. No. No."

But I can't stand here forever, naked and shivering, with someone possibly watching me through the peephole. This is too damned disturbing. Gathering all my courage, I reach for the doorknob again and twist it, pulling the door open.

The closet is filled with cute pink clothes and princessy dresses, all items that would fit a very young girl. My face contorts in disgust. I reach up and sort through them, searching for something, anything to wear. I pull the items of clothing apart, looking at them miserably, feeling appalled and sickened by their extremely small size. Are these my old clothes? I don't remember. They seem smaller than I imagine I was, even at age nine.

My eyes are narrowed and concentrated in focus as I try to think of how I can combine these tiny pieces of fabric to make adult clothes. I keep flipping through the clothes with frustration until I pull aside one dress and see an item that makes every drop of blood in my body turn to ice.

I stand, frozen in shock for a long time. I'm not sure how long.

Then I reach up to touch my neck, where the skin feels like ice.

I have been holding my breath as I stare at the item, and now I must finally force myself to breathe. My lungs are cold. My throat is cold. My tongue is cold, and my lips feel like they might be turning blue. My whole body is shaking now, as I fight away memories and feelings I can't bear to have.

There is a pain in my chest. A dull, deep ache. Moving both hands to touch that naked area between my breasts, I feel around to check if I have been stabbed, but there is no projectile I can rip out. Still, the pain is growing, as though the object stabbing me in the chest is being shoved in deeper by the second.

I begin to claw at the skin with my nails. I tear at my breastbone, digging, trying to make the pain stop. I try to sink my fingernails in deep between my ribs in an attempt to perform surgery to remove whatever jagged object is causing this pain. As my nails pierce my skin and slice into my flesh, rivulets of blood begin to slowly drip down my stomach. Still, I can't reach the offending object that is giving me such agony, maybe even trying to kill me.

Then it occurs to me—

I am trying to rip out my own heart.

Tears are sliding down my face incessantly now, and my body is growing very weak. My mind is shutting down. The item I'm staring at is a perfectly normal item you might find in any closet. In fact, there are dozens of others in this very closet.

But this particular one is twisted up into a horrifyingly recognizable shape.

It's mostly straightened, but the few curves it does have give it the shape of a screaming swan.

A screaming, dying swan.

I remember it well. I remember every curve and angle of that coat hanger, as though it were part of an distant dream. A recurring dream. A bloodcurdling dream. When I reach out to touch the coat hanger, I see that there are blood stains on it. Little flakes of deep red blood, so darkened they are almost black, come away on my fingertips.

I stare. I stare in absolute horror.

The emotions are sharpened knives and toxic chemicals, slashing and fusing together inside me.

The feelings are sinking and rising and swirling, like a mushroom cloud.

The grief is a deafening explosion mounting in my chest.

I cannot sustain this.

Tilting my head back, a mournful wail escapes my chest, like the scream of a banshee.

And it's not enough.

Falling to my knees, I scream and I scream. I

smash my fists into everything I can reach until they are bloody and bruised. Then I smash them some more until I am sure that I have broken my hands, smashed them clean into bone dust. I scream until it hurts my throat, my voice, my head.

I scream until it infiltrates all these walls. If I am to die here and now, I am sure that this scream will continue to be heard here for centuries.

I scream until I wake the dead, and make them feel what I feel.

I scream until I summon the dead, and feel their phantom hands all over my body.

I scream until I have emptied everything in me.

And now, I am no longer me.

The End

Coming soon...
The Shatterproof
Heart

Sophie is trapped in a hellhole by her worst enemy, and is forced to face her deepest darkest secrets. She hopes to be rescued while she desperately tries to rescue herself.

As her mind breaks and bends and transitions between her different identities, she is forced to come to terms with herself. Can Sophie win a battle of wits with her captor to survive and escape, or will she have to find another method of saving herself?

One thing is for sure: Cole will do anything it takes to get her back.

Thanks for reading!
Join Loretta's mailing list to be
notified of new books.
You will receive a FREE book
for signing up!

*Subscribe to Loretta's mailing list to be
informed of new releases.*

www.LorettaLost.com

Acknowledgments

For my father. Someday, when I have kids of my own, I hope I have a man in my life who inspires me to write stories about wonderful, devoted fathers. Someday, I really hope that I'm less obsessed with writing about fathers who are murderers and rapists.

But that day is not today.

Thanks for that.

I thought I got it out of my system over twenty books ago, when I first published *Drowning Mermaids* as Nadia Scrieva. But it just occurred to me that Benjamin is another manifestation of you. How deep is my anger? How deep is my hatred? I guess we will check in and see, another twenty books down the road.

USA Today bestselling author Loretta Lost writes to experience all the love and excitement that can often be lacking from real life. She finds it therapeutic to explore her issues through the eyes of a different person. She hopes to have a family someday, but until then her characters will do nicely.

Loretta has recently discovered Instagram, and she is now obsessed. Follow @loretta.lost for cute photos of her cat reading books. He refuses to cooperate unless they are really good books.

You can also subscribe to Loretta's mailing list for updates: www.LorettaLost.com

Connect with the author:

Facebook: facebook.com/LorettaLost
Instagram: @Loretta.Lost
Twitter: @LorettaLost
Website: www.LorettaLost.com
Email: Loretta.Lost@hotmail.com

Made in the USA
Middletown, DE
23 February 2017